Bicycle Dreaming

Praise for *If It is Sweet*

'...beautifully spare and evocative, with turns that are riveting, surprising, and revealing of the mysteries of the human psyche.' —Manjushree Thapa, *Outlook Magazine*

'What counts more than the narrative is the language—tender, poetic, informed by our mutilingual milieu. The stories retrieve to fiction, if not to history, marginalised lives around us. But they aren't shown as objects of condescending pity, but as real beings with their own joys and longings.' —K. Satchidanandan, *Tehelka*

'...this is absolutely rigorous and distinctive work, and there is a sound and a sense in these stories that make Indian fiction a bigger place.' —Chandrahas Choudhury, *Mint Lounge*

'Here is a natural stylist, with an easy, accessible turn of phrase...Hers is a determined, stealthy eye, born of fierce concentration, often conjuring up a rustic quiet.' —Rajni George, *India Today*

'A short-story collection of rare eloquence and maturity...*If It Is Sweet* mines the lives of ordinary people in the great metropolises of India...What is surprising is the intensity and freshness of the author's prose, her gift for the dramatic compression of opposite emotions, and the striking sense of drama she brings to her characters' interior lives.' —Cameron Woodhead's Pick of the Week, *The Age* (Australia)

Praise for *Not Only the Things That Have Happened*

'*Not Only the Things That Have Happened* is a kind of literary diptych, like those artworks that consist of a pair of painted surfaces joined in the middle by a hinge, so that they face in two very slightly different directions...The result is a novel that is complex, yet so elegantly written that it manages to read lightly and pleasurably, without ever showing its inner workings. And that is what makes it so special.' —Anvar Alikhan, *India Today*

'Leaps nimbly between times and styles and its characters' points of view. The sheer quality of Koshy's prose is probably the best reason to read her...Koshy manages to touch upon the politics of adoption, language, exile, identity. Such a novel could easily have fallen into the trap of being dull and worthy. That it doesn't is something of a triumph; this is a fantastic book.' —Aishwarya Subramanian, *Hindustan Times*

'Koshy is a deft literary seamstress, intricately weaving a tapestry of voices and offering us a rich, layered glimpse into the workings of memory, community and family.' —Janice Pariat, *The Sunday Guardian*

Bicycle Dreaming

Mridula Koshy

SPEAKING TIGER

SPEAKING TIGER PUBLISHING PVT. LTD
4381/4, Ansari Road, Daryaganj,
New Delhi–110002, India

Published in India by Speaking Tiger in paperback 2016

ISBN: 978-93-85755-16-3
eISBN: 978-93-8755-17-0

10 9 8 7 6 5 4 3 2 1

Typeset in Adobe Caslon Pro by SÜRYA, New Delhi
Printed at Gopsons Papers Ltd

To the children of Deepalaya Community Library and Reading Project: for all the reading and thinking we have done together.

Contents

Prologue

Landfill was the wrong word for it. This was no modest depression at the edge of town, filled with garbage and covered over with soil, green grass over the top of that. This reared, mountain-high, compacted black—nearly indistinguishable from the less compacted grey soot of the horizon. It was mirage-like, but not in the distance; it was right here in the city.

Soon enough, the nose was assaulted. The stench was not the lesser stench of Delhi's naalas, those creeks and rainwater runoffs smothered with garbage and rooted over by translucent-skinned pigs. This was the septic scent of faecal matter dredged from the sludge at the bottom of the naalas, and transported in tankers to the landfill. The tankers released the sludge as they travelled the winding road up the garbage mountain. When they were done, the road was pasted in slime and left to dry. Now there was a high shine to the road's black surface, but the tinsel effect when the sun struck and broke elsewhere on the mountain's sides was not from the sludge; it was from the thousands upon thousands, from the hundreds of thousands upon hundreds of thousands, from some incomprehensible number of hundreds of thousands of halved and discarded razor blades aglitter underfoot in the soft dust.

There were no pigs. There were dogs. They were not rabid. There was even a litter, eyes shut, tumbling by feel as they did in the womb, in dust that was so soft, it was nearly as soft as the fluid in which they recently swam. This dust hung in the air, lighter than the air, filtering the last light from the setting sun. It was time for herds of cows to give over picking through rotting garbage; it was time for them to head down the slippery mountain and find rest elsewhere in the city.

Two children descended the mountain. Were they the last stragglers? Earlier in the day there had been scores of children. And men and women. They had worked the mountain, pushing their legs in shin deep, anchoring themselves at impossible angles in its yielding sides so that, hands free, they could dig from it buried glass and metal and plastic.

The two were midway in their descent. They appeared to have had no luck today; they trailed deflated bags. On the other side of the mountain there were three different couples, loading their respective carts with bag upon bag of garbage they would haul away to recycling factories. The children laughed when asked the reason for their empty bags.

They looked away when asked their names. The girl continued to chatter. She boasted of making two thousand rupees yesterday. They'd found iron. Broken down machinery. At twenty rupees a kilo.

Did they haul a hundred kilos of iron off this mountain?

The girl's skin was clear, and her eyes clearer still. The boy's skin, though, was pitted all over. The black that settled over the whole of it was the black of the mountainside; the brown and yellow patchwork underneath spoke of long acquaintance with hunger. It was impossible to see his eyes. He kept them fastened on the ground but neither was he timid. He shrugged, shoved his free hand deep into the pockets of his two-sizes-too-large pants and spat to the side. But he answered the question amiably.

Yes, of course. There was no way other than by carrying. What was a hundred kilos? They only carried it two kilometres. His home was two kilometres away, in a bustee. The thekedar, the contractor, kept a storage shed there. It was on the other side of the mountain. Today though, they had no need to rush to cover the two kilometres before the thekedar took in his weighing scales and closed shop for the day. They were headed in the opposite direction, into the city.

Why?

The boy made a scoffing sound and repeated the question to himself as if disbelievingly. Why? Because we have money. And there are many good things to buy.

What will you buy?

Nothing. He just talks about buying things. He doesn't actually buy anything. He is saving his money.

All this tumbled from the girl, and though the boy never stopped making his scoffing sound, it now had a quality of being pleased with what the girl was saying. Something like a smile flickered across his face. Did he like the idea of himself as thrifty even as he scoffed at her need to explain him?

What about her? Did she not want to buy something for herself?

Not really, she said. But we will see a movie.

There was a loud snort from the boy and she dissolved into helpless laughter. Were they laughing at the credulity with which their story of Rs 2000 had been swallowed? They couldn't be making a tenth of that in one day, could they?

The girl explained the laughter. He doesn't like movies, but we see them because I like movies.

Yes, he agreed, she likes all things that are not real. Again, the flicker of a smile, and as quickly his long lashes swept across his eyes and he returned to looking down. Perhaps what seemed to be hostility was actually shyness.

He said the bag wasn't empty. There were books in the bag they were dragging. He said this dump used to be good till the incinerator plant was built down the road and they started dumping the ashes from it here. No, the sludge did not do the damage that ashes did. The sludge was confined to the road. Malba, that fine dust left over from the constant reconstruction of the city, fogged the heap, but it did not do the damage the ashes did. Books could survive malba, but not ashes.

Would he sell the books for pulp?

The boy looked up, and even in the waning light, his anger was clear to see.

I can read, he said. I will use them for my studies.

Do you attend a school near here?

They did not answer though the girl straightened her back and stood erect, possibly in a sly pantomime of the school neither could possibly have attended that day. Their hands were black with the dirt and ashes they had been digging in, their clothes filthy. And even the clear-skinned girl's nose ran a trail which she now carefully wiped with the inside hem of her green dress.

She put her hand out and he took his hand out of his pocket to allow her to hold it. They returned to the path they were descending.

The words he flung back up the mountain were spoken loudly, they might have been angry, or perhaps not. They were not without the indifference and possibly indolence that seemed to be his way of being in the world:

What do you care what our names are?

And he turned and looked over his shoulder and up at you, and you studied his face for the brief moment he held it open to you. But it was increasingly difficult in that grey light to know what was meant by an expression, or a few words, or their inflection. By the time the two children had rounded the road ahead, disappeared into another fold in the mountain, and emerged again, they were mere silhouettes against the night sky. What had been invisible in the day now came into sight: the small fires everywhere fed by gas escaping from deep within the heap leapt and subsided and leapt again. Now it was night and the next day was far away.

1
Birthday Morning

Noor woke with her feet pedalling the bicycle she had ridden in her sleep. For some time she was happy just to lie still remembering the dream. What colour had the bicycle been? She switched through colours in her mind, riding a blue one, even a yellow. But this was an exercise in delay. She knew which colour she would want her cycle to be—green—if she only owned a cycle, a green cycle.

She nudged her mother.

'Noor,' her mother scolded, 'it's not morning yet.'

This was true. A crow had cawed a minute earlier. But it would easily be many more long minutes before all the neighbourhood crows, then the sparrows, and finally the squirrels with their 'chip-chip-chip' joined in the ruckus to announce morning. The curtain hanging in the doorway of their single room lifted every so often and Noor could see out for an instant—grey—then the breeze shifted and the curtain dropped again. Soon the bright hot high summer sun would be up.

Noor sucked noisily on her teeth and held her breath. Oh when would they wake—her father on one side of her, her mother on the other side, and her brother asleep on the charpai outside the curtained front door? Didn't they know what day this was? July 14. And thank goodness it was a Saturday.

The crows were cawing by now—all of them; she blew the breath from her mouth with a whoosh. Her father reached a whack in her direction.

'Baba,' she said, 'you will be late for work. Listen to the crows.'

'You mean late for your birthday.' And he sat up in bed and looked at her grinning face. Slowly he passed a hand over his face, and stopping when he got to his chin, he took a hold of his beard and pulled.

She lay back and watched him, loving the way he waggled his fingers at her, trying not to show the love, pretending instead to be hurt when he addressed her mother.

'Listen to this child of yours making sure we don't fail to wake early on her birthday.'

Her mother turned in her sleep toward Noor and scooped her close. Noor squirmed.

'Not true. I was just making sure Baba got an early start. I heard him say yesterday that these days he is never the first one in the colony gate. And isn't it Baba who says the first one deserves to take the prize, and the second one might as well have never tried?'

*

It was true that Noor had lain awake, listening to her parents speaking to each other the night before. The talk was of a new man. He had, it seemed, shown up from nowhere to ride the same route her father rode. Someone, her father had said, must have paid cash somewhere, greasing the way for this upstart to acquire a vendor's license. Yes, an upstart he was, making certain to show up every morning before Noor's father arrived, both of them competing to call out to the householders of Panchsheel Colony to come sell them their kabadi.

Noor's father was a kabadiwala. He rode his bicycle from his home as early as seven-thirty on some mornings. Panchsheel Colony was just across the way from his home in Chirag Dilli. It never took him more than five minutes to cross Outer Ring Road. Often he stopped at the colony gate to chat with the guards. If he timed it just right he was there when the chaiwala came by with steaming cups of chai for the guards.

'And what about me? You don't think I have three rupees to pay for that weak stuff you call chai?' And Noor's father would pull from his kurta pocket a knotted handkerchief full of clinking coins. A fold of bills—fives, tens and twenties—was kept in the same pocket. He replaced the handkerchief and pulled a five from the fold and demanded change for it from the chaiwala.

Change was important in Mohammad Saidullah's line of work. When he finished weighing the goods—stacks of old newspaper, used up school notebooks, not a blank page left and the covers fallen apart, glass bottles empty of ketchup and liquor, metal tins sharp-edged at the rim—and named what he was willing to pay to haul away these discards, the householders all claimed they had no change. If he quoted Rs 18—a fair price for a good-sized load that would earn him at least five rupees more when resold to the recycling factory—they would pocket his twenty and shake their heads 'no'. They didn't have two rupees in change for him.

'Sorry, no change today. Adjust it against the next time you buy from us.' Next time would not roll around for at least another two weeks. And they would make certain to forget what they owed him by then.

Her father would often remark to Noor that if he had even a small part of her education, he would have forced the householders to sign a piece of paper promising to pay the amount owed to him.

It never pleased Noor to hear him talk about her education. She didn't know if this was because she was uncomfortable with the idea of her father getting cheated, or if it was because she wasn't a particularly brilliant student. She knew if he asked the householders to write down what they owed him they would simply refuse or, for a joke, they might write rubbish and her father wouldn't know the difference. She squirmed at that thought.

But, in fact, her father wasn't cheated. He always kept enough change on hand to pay the exact amount agreed upon. Never a rupee more that could be refused him in change.

His problem at work these days was the new man. Noor made a face thinking of this devil who was giving her father a hard time, getting to the colony before her father got there, getting to his customers before her father got to them. Her father would have to beat the man at his own game. This was what Noor's mother had advised him. But Noor's brother Talib—from behind her closed eyes, Noor had strained to hear his muttering—had groused, 'It's money that will win this game. Another bribe is what they want from Abba. And if Abba thinks I am handing over another paisa to prop up this losing enterprise, he can forget it.'

*

'Why such a face on your birthday, Noor?'

Her mother added, 'The wind will change direction and before you know it your face will become fixed in that expression.'

Ameena Saidullah was practised in imparting the bits of wisdom she had acquired from her mother. And she didn't mind at all her daughter's pert reply.

'There is no wind blowing, just you blowing your words.'

She appreciated her daughter's wit. This girl of hers was thirteen years old today, the age she was when her parents began entertaining marriage proposals for their daughter. No, there had been little time for Ameena to banter with her mother. Marriage and departure from her home to her husband's home had come within two years of turning thirteen.

Ameena rose from the bed. With her back to her husband and daughter, she pulled the clothes she had slept in around her, adjusting the chunni around her head, and retying the drawstring of her salwar loosened to allow her stomach room to breathe while she slept.

Looking away from his wife's adjustments and still speaking in his earlier teasing voice, Mohammad Saidullah addressed her, 'Wife, now what do you think this daughter of yours wants to eat on her birthday morning? Maybe some of last night's roti and bharta? Tell us Noor—will some dry roti do for you?' He pulled harder at his chin. Noor flung herself head first into his middle.

'Baba!' she shouted.

But her mother was already reaching for one of the high-up tins kept neatly lined in a row along the wall that served as their kitchen.

Noor's brother stuck his head in through the curtain at the front door.

'I want halwa,' he announced.

Noor saw out the door to the corridor. Along one side, the corridor was an open-air affair, affording her a glimpse of trees, crows and sky. But along the other side, the corridor was a series of open doors leading to the homes of other families who lived in their building. And not wanting anyone to glimpse the newly thirteen-year-old girl still in bed, and dressed in a holey undershirt of her father's, she pulled the bedsheet over her head.

'Talib Bhaiya, close the curtain,' she pleaded.

'Halwa,' he repeated his demand.

'Go on with you,' his mother scolded Talib gently. But her hand hovering among the tins settled on the third one. It was the sooji tin; she knew which kind of halwa Talib preferred.

Noor spoke quickly: 'I am fine with halwa.'

But her father's face was darkening.

'Let the child choose. It is her birthday.'

Noor pleaded for peace: 'Baba, I really want sooji ka halwa.'

And her mother spoke with a smile in her voice, 'Shall I make pooris with that?'

'Yes, Ammi. You know how much I like poori with halwa.'

Noor was grateful to her mother for helping settle what could have been yet another fight between her father and her brother. On her birthday morning! She jumped out of bed and hoping her mother would notice, she began folding the three sheets she and her parents wrapped themselves in during the night. These sheets were protection from mosquitoes, and Noor was satisfied to see two red spots on her sheet—mosquitoes so swollen when she swatted them in her sleep they had left splats of blood to mark where they met their end. She scraped the hardened blood from the sheet with her nails and announced triumphantly, 'Got two of them last night.' Then taking the heavy bedcover she shook it, shaking it in the direction of her brother's face. His head still poked from between the two curtains and she could see his fists outlined in the curtain edges he had pulled close around him.

'Talib Bhaiya, do you want your towel?'

'And my toothbrush.'

She handed him his mug. He kept his own these days. In it was his toothbrush and transparent red-coloured toothpaste she guessed was expensive, and the kind of razor Baba curled his lips at but she thought quite the thing. (She'd tried it out one afternoon, shaving her arms—no cuts. Not the result she'd gotten when trying out Baba's heavy steel razor.) Talib Bhaiya's towel on the other hand was just one of the many threadbare ones they all shared. He let go the curtain and stepped into the room, took the towel from her and shouldering the mug as if it were a rifle, he marched a circle around her. He came to a halt and saluted her.

'Thirteen, are you? Still a long way to go if you plan on catching up to twenty-one.'

She giggled at this joke from her past. She had believed when she was young that it would be possible to someday catch up with her much older brother. Talib bent down and kissed her on both cheeks.

Now he was an actor in a movie and not a soldier. Patting her head, he reeled off dialogue in his movie-father voice. 'Live a long life, my child. Live well. Surely you will spread your light in this world, Noor, my child.' He stepped back from her and exaggeratedly pulled at his chin.

Mohammad Saidullah lunged toward the impersonator. Noor's voice squeaked from her, 'Run Talib Bhaiya. Run.' He was already gone, having shot through the curtain, and crashed into sleepy neighbours lined up along the corridor. The line broke apart, cursing him, and re-formed its way to the two shared bathrooms at the end of the corridor.

Noor braided her hair quickly, tucked her scarf around her head and ran out the doorway with four empty cooking oil containers in her hands. She was thirteen years old today. From this day on, no one need tell her what to do and when. She would fold sheets, make the bed, bring water from the downstairs tap and help her mother cook breakfast without anyone having to call her to do it. The perfume of ghee, sooji and sugar followed her and so did the greetings taken up one after the other down the length of the line:

'Happy birthday, Noor.'

'Happy birthday.'

2
Best Friends

That evening Talib Bhaiya shot in and out the door just in time for four o'clock cake. Even Baba returned early from the wholesale market where he sold his day's haul from Panchsheel Colony. He too left in a hurry, his face as clouded after cake as before. If Ammi had reason to leave on an errand that took priority over Noor's birthday, she could not have. Ammi never went anywhere in the evening, at least not alone. That's the only reason she is still here, Noor thought. Noor would have continued thinking her mournful thoughts and sucking on the bits of candied fruit she had picked out of her cake slice, if Ammi had let her. But at six-thirty, Ammi sent her to fetch water from the downstairs tap.

Noor groped her way down the dark flight. Someone had pried the lightbulb from its socket so long ago, it must have been in some lifetime before her own. She paused to savour the satisfaction of the idea of her own lifetime. She didn't mind the soft deflating suck of the paper cup underfoot. Another step and something slippery, likely a polythene bag, nearly sent her on a slide down the last two steps. The important thing was she had perfectly good rubber chappals to protect her feet from nearly everything. The really important thing was to not step on dog shit, which would no doubt ooze over the edges of her chappals. Her toes curled at the thought. And she cursed under her breath, 'Damn these dogs. And damn the gossipy hags in this building who think one cleaning a day is enough on these stairs.'

She paused to shake Talib Bhaiya from her head. Repeating his overheard obscenities, she was instantly uncomfortable. There was more, words that didn't bear repeating.

Later, standing at the tap with all four containers filled, Noor was wondering who to ask for help with watching the two containers she would leave behind when she headed up to her second floor home with the two containers she could just barely carry—one atop her head, held there with one hand, and one jammed onto her yet non-existent hip and held there with the other. If only Ammi had sent her to the tap a few minutes earlier when there was yet a line of people to help her.

'Happy birthday, Noor,' came the voice behind her and she was in sudden darkness. Two warm hands, clapped there quickly, covered her eyes.

But she knew who it was. 'Haseena,' she shouted in her excitement, 'it's you. Let me see you.'

The hands were removed and Noor was spun around. She set her containers to the ground and leapt to grab her friend. The two girls embraced and, that being not enough to convey their happiness, they jumped up and down, their hands on each other's shoulders. The thin dog by Haseena's feet jumped and barked. At this, Noor stopped. She didn't want the dog to put its paws on her as it was now doing to Haseena.

'When did you get back? I was so afraid you wouldn't come back. You remembered it's my birthday.'

Noor was out of breath from all the jumping. She gave up trying to choke out months of stored up words. But she could not stop touching Haseena, now touching her cheek, now returning her hand to rest on Haseena's shoulder. All the while she looked at Haseena's face, her eyes wide from the effort to confirm every detail there was as it used to be.

It had been three months since Haseena vanished from Noor's life. One morning she had simply not been at Jyotimala Charitable Trust Senior Secondary School. Noor had made her trepidatious way to Haseena's home, just a few unfamiliar lanes over from Noor's own home. She was told that Haseena had gone to the village. 'The village', Noor knew, was not the same one in Noor's life. Noor's village was the one in which her mother had grown up and where Noor's grandparents and uncles lived even now. The village in Noor's life was only a bus ride away and a visit there was accomplished in all of one afternoon; it did not involve disappearing for months at a time.

'Haseena? Why I just got back from leaving her there a day ago,' Haseena's father made reply to Noor.

'Then she won't be back at school tomorrow also?'

'Well, Jyotimala School will have to manage without Haseena in it.'

'They'll cut her name, Uncle.'

'Why, why will they cut her name? Do I send her to a government school that they will cut her name? They may call themselves a charity but that principal doesn't hesitate to take money from a poor man, does she? And I don't pay Rs 350 every month so they can cut her name when they feel like it.'

'But Uncle she will fall behind.'

'That may be, but she has other responsibilities; she must care for her grandmother.'

Noor knew any number of other children who had left school to care for any number of younger brothers and sisters. There had been nothing to question in that arrangement. But now she seethed inside: how could Haseena care for her grandmother? Children aren't supposed to take care of grown ups.

*

Haseena looked with affection at Noor. 'Yes, I'm back. And I'm staying. My grandmother's illness grew worse. I was no use to her.'

'What do you mean no use?' Noor interrupted. 'I saw your father in the market just a few days back. I asked him if you were still taking care of your grandmother. He said yes, and when I asked him when that would be over, he hurried away. Oh, I was so afraid I would never see you again.'

'After my father left me with my grandmother, her illness only grew worse. I tried to call my father from the STD booth in our village. But even that was three kilometres down the hill and I was afraid to leave grandmother alone. So I only did that a few times. And my father said not to keep calling. If somebody could have come to help maybe…But in the end I didn't even know how to take her to the hospital. I thought I should wait at the road for the shared taxi but I also thought I shouldn't leave her side.'

Noor shook her head, not following any of Haseena's story. 'But how did you come back then?'

'She died. After that there was no need to remain there. My father came to bring me back.'

'And your grandmother?'

'Aren't you listening? I just said she died.'

'Oh.' Noor looked down. 'I was listening,' she pleaded, 'it was just confusing because you must have been so…'

But Noor did not want to finish the sentence. Haseena must have been sad. Haseena must have cried. But maybe it wasn't polite for Noor to ask her for those details.

'Maybe I should have left her to get the taxi to take her to the hospital. But the shared taxi stops for only a second by the road and everyone inside hurries you to get in. I didn't know how I could carry her to the taxi, and I also didn't know how to tell the taxi to leave the road and come with me to our home. It's not by the side of the road, you know. You have to go a little up the mountain and through the fields. You should see how we plant our fields along the side of the mountain. But the path is narrow between the fields, only enough space for a person to walk alone so…Cars don't come through there.'

'So she died?'

'Even though Abba had said to not keep calling, I called him. I was getting worried about Ruku and Aseef. If Ruku was even going to school, and if she was, then who was taking care of Aseef? And about Blackie. I was worried about who would feed Blackie while I was gone.'

Haseena and Noor turned toward the dog lying legs splayed and belly lowered into the puddle behind the communal tap.

Noor didn't know what she should say to Haseena. There was the fact that she hadn't done anything about feeding Haseena's ugly dog. It wasn't a pet, at least not in any way that resembled a pet; it wasn't fluffy and white like the pet dogs on TV. You couldn't even really say it was black though Haseena had named it Blackie. It was more of a pink mess, skin scratched up, speckled with blood and loose. But it did behave like a pet, following Haseena everywhere. As for whether Ruku had been in school these last few months, Noor really couldn't say. She had missed Haseena terribly. But only now did it occur to Noor that she might have given a thought to Haseena's sister and baby brother. And then Noor really didn't know what to say to Haseena about her grandmother.

There had to be a village somewhere that was home to Noor's other grandparents—her father's parents. But she knew nothing about that. What she knew was the warning in her mother's eye and silence on her father's part when Noor attempted to ask him about his parents. They might even be dead, she thought. She tried to feel a tear in her eye, but nothing came.

Noor gave Haseena a small smile. 'I am glad you have come back.'

'I wanted to be sure to return home by your birthday. I hurried my father. See. Here. For you.'

Haseena thrust something into Noor's hand.

Noor was relieved. She would not need to say anything to Haseena about her grandmother. She looked at what she held in her hand. There was paper and string. It took her a second to realize what she was holding.

'A present.'

First she tugged at the string but it wouldn't snap. And when she tried to undo the bow she realized she had pulled it into a hard knot. She gnawed with her teeth. A moment, and there was only the paper to get past. Inside was a set of bangles stacked into a cylinder. She had known from the shape of the package what to expect. But inside the cylinder, another package. A quick look at the bangles—how they glittered, pink and green and cream and gold. But no time now to slip them on. She thrust them into Haseena's hand. And tore into the little crumple of paper left in her hand. Inside was something orange and black. She turned it over in her palm and then held it between thumb and forefinger. Was it a bead? No, it was a seed.

'A seed?'

'It will bring you a good destiny. You must hide it somewhere in your house for now and take it with you when you leave. Because of this seed you will find a good husband and make a good home with him. There you will have your own family. My grandmother had three saved from when she was a girl. I am keeping one for me and one for Ruku, and this one is for you.'

Noor nodded her head. She was disappointed. But she did not want to show it. And she did not want to say, I don't need this seed. I have a home already and I don't need a new home.

She squeezed Haseena's arm. 'Thank you, this is the best present ever. Your coming, and the seed, and the bangles are so beautiful. This is the only present I got today, you know.'

'You never asked your father for a bicycle?'

'How can I ask? Maybe some other time when things are better with Baba's work. There's a new man, you know.'

Haseena looked at her blankly. Then shaking her head she offered, 'You could still ask him. Your father lets you do anything you want. Not like mine. And if he doesn't have the money for it now, he will at least begin saving for later. And anyway what's the point of buying a cycle if you can't even ride one? At least this way there will be time for him to teach you on his cycle.'

'The green bicycle. I dreamt I was riding it last night.'

'The green bicycle. Of course you dreamt about it last night,' Haseena spoke forcefully. 'You know what I think? I think you don't even want a bicycle. You are too scared to actually want one, to actually ride one.'

Noor felt uncomfortable. She had been congratulating herself for not asking for what her father could not afford. But here was Haseena saying something else, something that stung. And why did it sting? Was there something true in what Haseena had to say?

'But I,' Noor began and then she stopped.

'It's true, isn't it? You're afraid. Otherwise you wouldn't need a green bicycle from your dreams to ride one. You could ask your father or even your brother to teach you to ride your father's cycle.'

'You don't know anything. My brother has no time to teach me. And my father is very tired these days. And he's busy. And worried. You are the one who doesn't listen. Didn't you hear me say there's a new man in the colony where Baba goes to get kabadi? And this man has a better bicycle.'

This part was completely untrue of course. At least, Noor didn't know if the new man had a better bicycle, or not. For all she knew he had an even more dilapidated one than her father's. But now she was stuck in the middle of something thick and oozy and there was no way to go back. So she waded in deeper.

'Matter of fact it's the reason I want a new bicycle. I am going to go into business with my father. Why else would I want to learn to ride a bicycle?'

'Oh, Noor.' Haseena rolled her eyes in exasperation. 'Just ask your father to show you how. What are you going to do with your new bicycle when you get it if you don't know how to ride one?'

'How do you know I haven't asked him to teach me? In fact I already talked to him a little about it. And he was happy to hear what I said. He said he will teach me. He said he will teach me after this school year. I will learn and I will join him in his work. He was so happy to hear me say I want to help him in his work.'

'Will you be a kabadiwali, then?' Haseena giggled.

Noor giggled too. She knew Haseena knew she was not going to join her father in his work, and that she hadn't even talked to her father about learning to ride from him, much less talked to him about wanting a bicycle of her own. She was grateful to Haseena for not calling her a liar.

'Why not? If a man can ride a bicycle and call loudly "Kabadi, kabadiwala", then a woman can do the same. Or better. I will be a kabadiwali. And I will call to my customers. "Kabadi, kabadiwaleeee".'

'Delhi's first kabadiwali.' And they giggled together.

'Actually I got a new dress from Ammi. But there's no chance to wear it. Not even on Monday to school. We have a new Principal Ma'am, who is so strict. I don't want her to scold me or to say I am showing off.'

'What! You can't wear birthday clothes to school on your birthday? Then where are you supposed to wear them?'

'I know. Isn't it awful? But I will wear it next Friday, after school when Baba takes me to the mosque to say a birthday prayer. And Ammi made me so many good things to eat. And she even bought cake from the sweet shop—six slices and only four of us. So there's still some at home. Come home with me. Ammi will want to see you. She asks all the time—has that Haseena come?'

This set them both giggling again. They knew full well the tone in which Noor's mother would say 'that Haseena.' Noor's mother liked to say the two of them together spelled trouble. But 'that Haseena, take her by herself and you couldn't ask for a prettier or more well-behaved child. Now if it would only rub off on you, Noor.'

'Come,' Noor pleaded again. 'Help me with the water cans. I was just wondering who I would ask to watch these two while I took the other two up. But now you can carry for me.'

'Oh, just like that: I must carry for you.'

'Well,' Noor replied with asperity, 'if Talib Bhaiya would only help like he is supposed to. Or if I did have a cycle, I could put all four cans on the cycle and....'

'And what? Ride it up your stairs?'

Again they laughed together. And catching each other's eyes, laughed harder still.

Noor mimicked riding up the stairs to the second floor. A canister of water swinging from each handlebar, one canister strapped to the rear rack and one balanced atop her head. Then she tumbled the imaginary canister from her head, tumbled herself from her imaginary cycle and tumbled the imaginary cycle from the stairs. Haseena laughed so hard passersby turned to look who the girl was who was making this much noise in public. Haseena, who was not one to bear this sort of scrutiny, covered her mouth with her hands and turned away from Noor to escape the cause of her laughter.

Noor was pleased. She laughed louder still to show Haseena that she couldn't be bothered to hide from the disapproval of strangers.

'You're just the same Noor,' Haseena gasped.

And at that moment Noor was thinking much the same thing. *And you are the same Haseena from three months ago.*

Blackie made as if to jump on Noor. This time she said, 'Shoo, Blackie.' He slunk a few feet away and plopped himself on the pavement and with a sigh began scratching at his skin.

A few minutes later, the two girls, short of breath and red of face, burst through the curtain and into Noor's one-room home.

Startled by the noise, Ameena looked up from dinner preparations. 'Why it's that Haseena. Back from the village, are you?' And she set the girls to eating the last slices of cake.

3
Special Food

Friday evening, after school Noor dressed in her new clothes. The green top was stitched in the fashionable anarkali style—fitted to high above her waist, and flared from there into a gracefully swirling skirt.

She twirled in front of the mirror hung by the door. The sleeves—elegantly long, gathered at the wrist in a row of chooris, and tight-fitting—made her sigh with pleasure. She raised her arms above her head and checked to see how her face looked framed between such elegant arms. The light was hazy and this made her thin face pleasant to her. If she drew closer she would see the fine hair on her cheeks and upper lip. But she did not draw closer and from this distance she saw what anyone looking at her might see—eyes that shone and brown hair braided tight to her scalp. And at this distance she could not see what else there was on her face for anyone to see—strain in her wide-set eyes, a furrow deepening between brows that were anyway so thick and straight as to overhang everything on her face, a mouth that was wide from the use it had been put to smiling, to laughing out loud. At this distance, she could see just her face and a bit of her shoulders, but not the upraised arms or the swirling skirt. She checked quickly to make certain that she was alone and pulling the ends of her skirt as high as her shoulders, she twirled again.

'Five metres, it took me.'

Her mother was standing in the door. Not quite in and not quite out. Noor jumped with a start and threw her skirt back around her. Then smoothing the garment she went up to her mother. 'Ammi, let me help you with that.'

Her mother answered her with great tiredness, 'You're a grown girl. Standing in front of a mirror isn't going to get anything done around here.' Her eyes swept past Noor and took in the school uniform Noor had thrown in a heap on the floor, the bags—her school bag and Talib Bhaiya's work bag—piled on the bed. The churidar pyjama—the second part of her birthday outfit—was stretched across the bed, its extra-long legs, which on wearing would bunch in chooris at her ankles, were stretched to the edge of the bed and over to the floor. Next to the churidar lay the little stack of bangles—Haseena's gift to her. Noor bit her lip anxiously as she took in everything her mother was seeing. And now her mother's voice sounded even more tired.

'You are thirteen years old, Noor. What if your brother or father or heaven forbid, someone else, were to walk in? Please put your churidar pyjama on before you offer to help me with anything. And remember, these are your birthday clothes and your clothes for Id. There is no money for a new outfit next month so you will have to make this one do.'

Noor grabbed the garment from the bed and ran to the cupboard, pulling shut the curtain hung from its door diagonally across to the wall. Behind this screen, she quickly changed out of the new kurta and into her faded home clothes. Without being told, she put the bangles away and set to washing and chopping the vegetables her mother had bought in the market.

Her mother sat close to the floor by the single-burner stove, on a low wooden stool, shelling peas into a steel plate; the pile of pods discarded on the floor was already quite high. 'Come sit here,' she gestured to Noor. But Noor shook her head. She preferred to stand at the cement counter and chop onions in the small square of space left free between the atta bin and the plastic basin in which their dishes were neatly stacked.

'Ah, just like your brother,' her mother commented. Noor threw her mother a quick look from under her lids. No, her mother wasn't complaining; at least there wasn't the grief she sometimes read on her mother's face when the topic of her brother came up.

'You will understand someday when you wake up to see your children completely different from you,' her mother waved the limp pea pod in her hand at Noor. 'It's in the nature of every generation to want to be different from the previous one. But who would have thought it would take the form of eating what no one's ever heard of. For as long as there have been people, we have been eating food. The food our mothers fed us. And you children eat…' And here her mother halted, searching for what she wanted to say.

Noor supplied the missing word, the word loathed and loved in her family—'noodles.'

'Yes, that noodles. Pepsi, even I like. There is no harm in drinking something that comes out as quickly as it goes in. Your Amreekan fry, I know how to make at home. Even if you think it is something special in the Magdunaals place, I can see the only difference is they put less salt and give it to you in a nice red box. But how do you know what kind of poisons there are in this powder you want to eat with your noodles? There could be ground glass in there, you would just swallow it up. There now, this should be enough.'

Ameena scooped the peas into the pot of water bubbling on the stove and tore into the packet she had kept hidden under the stove.

'Go call your brother. Quick now before your father gets home.'

Noor's stomach rumbled and her mouth flooded with saliva. She could smell the salt taste the dry noodles gave off as her mother broke them into the pot. Reluctantly she turned from the stove and walked out of the room to search for Talib Bhaiya, but not before the scent gathered even greater force as her mother snipped the foil packet and stirred into the pot the masala that came with the noodles.

Talib was neither next door at his friend Ashish's, nor two floors down at his even better friend Shehzad's. Now Noor felt the urgency of her job. The cricket field was two lanes over, nearly all the way to Triveni market. She would have to run if she meant to get her brother home before her father's return from work. And though her clothes were bound to be dirtied by the mud her chappals, flapping at her heels, splattered, and though her mother was always admonishing her that 'Girls must walk, not gallop like horses, Noor,' Noor took off, sprinting past the public water taps—four of them poking out from the rusted white of a tiled wall.

She turned the corner where the jalebi man was already setting up—his big tawa of oil awaited the fire he was now stoking—Noor could see the coals catching, beginning to glow. Nearly five o'clock. Oh no. Oh no, the voice in her head panted. Her stomach stitched itself tight shut and she heard her father's advice to her, 'Noor, send your breath all the way to your stomach and god willing, the pain will leave.' No time for that now, she remonstrated with Baba's voice in her head.

Crossing the naala, she paused a bare second on the bridge and leaning over the corrugated tin side, she flung the bag of garbage her mother had shoved into her hand at the last second as she ran out their door. The bag landed with a 'glub', the sound already in Noor's past. But as she raced she saw in her mind the jagged mirror of the creek's surface accepting the bag, dragging it to the fetid dark of its bottom. Noor shuddered. She had nightmares about slipping into the creek, of the creek swallowing her—'glub'—as it had her garbage bag, and before that the hundreds of thousands of bags belonging to her neighbours. Another half kilometre and she rounded the three-walled cement kooradan where the last of the day's garbage haul from the rich colonies nearby was being sorted by a group of young boys. They hollered after her, 'Where's the fire?' Nearby cows, briefly alarmed, twitched their hides and returned their noses to the garbage bags at their feet.

She stood at the edge of the maidan and between huffs of breath she searched the field; four, maybe five games were underway. She jerked her head from side to side, searching the dusty brown field dotted with dozens of players—which one was her brother?

'Talib Bhaiya. Talib Bhaiyaaa.'

A second later her head jerked from the smart rap he'd just given it.

'How many times have I told you not to come screaming here for me?'

'Ammi sent me to get you.'

'Well, tell her I'm playing right now. No, tell her I had to stay back at work. Tell her I called at Ashish's to say I had to remain at work and that he passed the message on to you. God knows when we will get a phone at home so I can call you directly.'

'Well, we have Baba's mobile. And I checked at Ashish's earlier and Ammi knows that there was no message and she won't believe me if I tell her something different now. Anyway Bhaiya, Ammi bought noodles specially for you. Come and eat before Baba gets home.'

'Chowmein?

'No, it's packet noodles.'

'Tell her I ate already.'

'You know she buys noodles only when she has money left over from the rest of her shopping.'

'Am I supposed to feel bad about that? I didn't ask her to buy anything specially for me. I eat noodles every day at work. And even chicken. All kinds of other things. Hot dogs. Things she knows nothing about. Who told her to scrape up five rupees to buy me food?'

'Bhaiya.'

He chucked her under the chin. Shouldering the bat, he turned away from her.

'You eat it, Noor.'

'It's only for you, Bhaiya.'

He had walked quite a distance from her when he turned back.

'She shouldn't be doing that.'

Noor shrugged.

'Go home, Noor.' He turned away again.

'Bhaiya, she already saw your workbag. She knows you are back from work.'

But her brother kept walking.

Amit was by her side in the next instant. 'What's the matter Noor? Is your mother upset with Talib?'

Noor turned stiffly and began to walk away. Amit was a boy older than Talib. He might even be a man, of this Noor was not certain one way or the other. His cheeks were smooth like a boy's and his shoulders bony. But he was easily taller than any other boy and older at least in that he had been a fixture on the playground—a big boy—since when Noor was a very little girl. By now he might easily be a man.

Amit was the neighbourhood pervert and harmless since no one was ever fool enough to take him up on his offers to go to his home, to drink tea, eat sweets, see his newest toys. Everyone old enough to know simply knew to stay away from him. And it was the job of everyone old enough to know this to tell everyone else as they grew old enough to be subjected to Amit's invitations. And somewhere along the way as she grew old enough to be warned, someone had warned Noor. And sure enough he was issuing one of his invitations, 'I have a new badminton racquet, with special graphite handles. Do you want to come and see? It's from Saudi Arabia. My father lives there, you know. I told him the last time he came home, I want a badminton racquet.'

She waved to him, more a wave of dismissal than of goodbye. This was not the first time he had asked her. And to be honest since no one had ever taken him up on his offers she wondered, not for the first time, if they were all being unfair to him—maybe he really did just want to make friends. As it stood, he was always alone, at the outskirt of the maidan, always approaching a girl to tell her about some new toy he could show her. Her brow furrowed.

There was something wrong with him. For certain. Why else did he turn her stomach?

She determined in her mind to talk to Haseena about Amit the very next chance she got to be alone with her friend. Haseena was the one to consult on tricky questions. She always knew the answer to why people behaved in the way they did—why, for example, Maths Sir threw pencils. 'He knows these things that are so big and he is supposed to tell us about them. But he already doesn't believe we will understand these things—things like the degrees inside triangles. In fact he thinks we don't even deserve to understand things like triangles. But it's his job to teach us. So sometimes he wants us to understand, so that he can prove that he is able to do a good job. Other times he doesn't want us to understand, so that he can believe Maths is too big or too hard for us, and that he is too good for us. Don't you see?'

Yes, when Haseena explained it, Noor could see what she was talking about. Maths Sir was caught in a bind and that's why he threw pencils. But actually, Noor could see all this, holding it together in her mind's eye, only for a split second, the way she sometimes knew Maths for a split second—everything falling into place, everything shining and bright, all the edges of all the numbers so clear that she saw beyond the numbers, beyond the lessons that had been taught and saw even the lessons waiting to be taught. But before she could grasp it so as to hold on to it, all of it vanished, like Haseena's words and the understanding they held.

Noor left the maidan and walked back home, slowly, so slowly, with a hope in her heart that she nursed and despised herself for nursing. She hoped her father would be home, that he would shout at her mother, then her brother, then he would throw out the stupid noodles, with their stupid Chinese taste, throw the pot out with a clang, set the dogs howling out in the street, scoop her up and carry her to the market and buy her favourite—seekh kebab wrapped in roomali roti. And that cost much more than five rupees. She scowled fiercely as she imagined her father's great anger, the dishes flung and the door banged. She set the dogs howling again. And she imagined herself back into her anarkali and took an imagined twirl in front of her father, thanking him for the kebab roll, and for her new green dress and for being her good and kind father.

But Noor remembered soon enough that her father was her father—neither a hero, nor a villain from a film. Yes, a kind man, who never shouted as Akshay Bhaiya's father did. Never threw anything, not even a pencil. No, her father was nothing like Maths Sir.

Standing at her doorway on the other side of the curtain, she tried to hear if her father was home yet.

'Is that you, Noor?' her mother called out. 'You've come alone, have you?'

Noor pushed the curtain aside and slid in the doorway. 'Ammi,' she began to think up an explanation. 'Akshay Bhaiya said Bhaiya has to help him with something to do with Maths and…'

'It's all right, Noor. I thought I could call him home with a treat and then he could eat the evening meal with us. If he wants to eat elsewhere I can't stop him. And neither can your father. But your father is right about one thing. If he won't eat here, he won't live here very long, either.'

Seen through tears, her mother sparkled in front of Noor. Wolfing her way through the bowl her mother handed her—'Hurry now,' and a little later, 'but don't you choke'—Noor remembered her earlier resolve to turn gracious and responsible at thirteen.

'Ammi,' she began, 'it's like you went into my dreams and saw exactly what I wanted. My favourite colour green, and the skirt took five whole metres?'

4
The Small Comfort of Drawing the Dream

Two months into being thirteen and Noor had forgotten that she ever had a birthday. It was hard to remember that she had equated thirteen with any sort of transformation. Being thirteen felt like nothing at all.

In fact, when she stopped to think about it once, during morning assembly, wedged between Shailaja with the smelly hair (something powdery and pink her mother put in her hair) and Josy with the krr krr hands (skin like a lizard's, her hands when they touched yours rasped you all the way to your brain), Noor could no longer remember what it felt like to be twelve. Nor eleven, nor ten, nor nine.

Which of course prompted the thought: but then there's no way of knowing if there is anything different about being thirteen.

She tried to bring up a memory from when she was twelve. The morning assembly was already past singing and praying and announcements. Children were already on to 'Stand at Ease' and 'Attention.' She found it hard to move her body from one position to another, to keep up with the present and simultaneously travel back into the past. She gave up in frustration and looked around to see what she was to do in the present. She saw Haseena trying to catch her eye. It's okay, she winked at Haseena. But Haseena only blinked rapidly, signalling something. Simultaneously there came to her mind a memory of shouting at her mother. Was she six then? She was shouting, 'Wait till Baba comes home. I'm going to tell him what a horrible woman you are.'

A hand clapped her on one shoulder. Now she understood Haseena's frantic blinking, which was giving way to wincing. The hand on her shoulder belonged to Maths Sir. Also known as

Bengali Sir. Pencil and chalk thrower. Also thrower of chalkboard dusters, of trash cans and, rumour had it, once, of a child out a window. The rumour did not clarify the height of this window from the ground.

Noor was made to step forward and stand facing the portrait of the school patron. The practice was to have children atone for their misbehaviour in front of him.

Apparently years ago, he had given this building to Jyotimala School and then promptly died so that teachers were forever alternating between garlanding him and forgetting to garland him. Noor looked up at the portrait and Bengali Sir batted the back of her head so she looked down again to mime her shame, but not before she noted that the garland hanging over the portrait was a mouldering brown. Probably no visitors from his family were expected in the near future.

Because of his generosity, poor children like her did not have to go to a government school with its bad education. This, the teachers never tired of telling her and her classmates. Her father had told Noor that this was all nonsense. She didn't go to a government school because he worked hard to pay for her to go to Jyotimala and if he only had the money he would send her to a private school and not some NGO school where god knows what kind of English they taught her since he certainly had no way of knowing himself.

Indeed, if he had the money she would go to a school with a proper playground and not one with a dirt compound. This proper playground would have football in it.

'For girls?'

'Yes, why not. I have seen girls playing in that Panchsheel colony. Football and what all other things. Why shouldn't you play?

'But first your school should do something about that water problem it has. It is a shame to take fees from us and then run a school in which every other week the motor pump breaks and children come home having soiled their clothes. Forget teaching you English. Just water in the bathrooms so children can go when they need to go.'

'Baba, that's only babies who can't hold themselves,' Noor pleaded.

'Of course, of course, its only babies,' he soothed her. 'But yes, some other parents who have babies have been talking and I have been listening. And if we decide to complain, we will complain. If they have to sink the well deeper, let them sink it deeper. If they have to get a better motor to draw the water, let them get it. Running a school for some four hundred children without water. What nonsense.'

Noor could picture her father at the head of a group of parents. He wouldn't hang his head like all the other parents did when they came into the Jyotimala School office.

'Daydreaming were you? Let's wake you up then.' And with that she was spun so she was no longer facing the grey man in his grey turban inside the grey frame. Now she faced the assembly of four hundred children—their tightly smashed together lines from LKG to Class XII overspread the small interior courtyard of the school and climbed up the stairs and re-formed all along the upstairs hallways from where children peered down into the courtyard. The courtyard was held in a painful silence but the sound of snickering could be heard from those inhabiting the relative safety of the upstairs perch.

Bengali Sir stepped back and signalled with fingers held up—Ten.

She squatted. She rose and squatted again, then rose again. Two. She saw Haseena looking at her. But she couldn't make any sense of who Haseena was. The contents of her head, her thoughts, were churning; they had slipped their current, a normally placid one, and were spilling the bounds of their shore—a shore constructed of small ideas about home and school and the rightness of being Noor.

Gibberish, and not words, was what ran through her mind. *What? I hate. I hate. What? Was it Attention I missed doing? Stand at Ease?* Three. Her knees ached at Four.

At Six she stumbled. Hand to her head, Bengali Sir pushed her down, and down she went. She was weeping when she finished.

Though at least half of her wept from anger at giving Bengali Sir what he wanted—herself reduced to weeping—the other half wept from fear. Why, and of what, she could not say. Ten chicken squats were nothing, she knew. Boys like Santosh never wept, not even when they were asked to do fifty chicken squats. Regardless of the number, they would boast afterward that they had not felt a pinprick of pain. Did they also not feel any of this fear that rose competing with anger and humiliation to clutch at her throat?

She returned to her place in line—between Shailaja and Josy. She met Josy's eyes before she turned to look at the back of Shailaja's head. She could claw Josy's eyes out for the pity that shone in them. And for good measure, Shailaja's eyes, as well. She still didn't know what she'd done to make Bengali Sir angry.

In class, Anita Ma'am entered wearing a lime green and brown striped saree. The girls in class quickly exchanged looks—elegant, they agreed. And Anita Ma'am was usually not elegant. Most of the girls were engaged for the rest of class with wondering about the reason for this unexpected change. But Noor had her thoughts to think. They were ordered now and contained in words, but still far from placid.

During break, she tried to ask Haseena what she'd done wrong at morning assembly. But Haseena was busy discussing whether or not a teacher's mood could be predicted by her choice of saree. Haseena spoke quite passionately, 'Watch out when Principal Ma'am wears red. Someone is sure to get slapped.' At which point, unable to bear being ignored by her best friend, filled with disbelief that her best friend was thinking about sarees, and about colours of sarees, and about teachers and their sarees and their moods when-when-when, when here she was, she, Noor, Haseena's best friend, suffering because of a teacher and his mood, and he didn't wear sarees, and there was no predicting his moods, and now full of horror at what she was doing, Noor pinched Haseena's arm. She pinched Haseena on her upper arm, and didn't let go, not even when everyone started shouting, not till someone, maybe Muskaan, pried her off the weeping Haseena.

'Oooh,' chorused any number of girls who gathered at the spot quickly. Haseena twisted her neck turning it toward her arm and twisted her arm turning it toward her neck, trying to see what it was that hurt at the back of her arm. Two drops of blood welled up to meet Haseena's eyes. They stood shining red against her pale skin. 'Oooh,' said the girls.

'How could you?' cried Haseena.

How could I? Noor wondered. She ran back to the safety of the classroom.

When the bell rang, Haseena slid in next to her and placed the tiffin box Noor had abandoned in the compound on the desk in front of Noor. But she sat as far from Noor as their two-person bench would permit her to.

Shilpa Ma'am came in wearing a dark blue saree hitched high above her ankles, ridden this high by the enormity of the belly she carried in front of her. In the back, the saree was higher still. The girls in class winced in unison. Bad enough the belly and the pregnancy contained within. But it was what was happening behind Shilpa Ma'am that left them gasping.

Noor did not participate in the girls' exchange of glances and the agreement affected that (a) there was nothing to fear from Shilpa Ma'am and (b) when they grew up and became women they would never be caught—and never mind the notion of themselves pregnant—with their sarees even a centimetre off the ground. They would wear their sarees trailing in the dust, the pleats in front folding and breaking at the feet, the hem at the back streaming from the pointy tips of the high-high heels they would wear everywhere, while catching buses to work, while at work in fancy shops and offices and even while washing dishes at home.

The class rose in one accord to sing: 'Good afternoon, Shilpa, Ma'am.'

Noor thought gratefully that Haseena too had held herself apart from the classroom-wide consultation over Shilpa Ma'am's poor dress sense. Very cautiously she moved her feet closer to Haseena's. Haseena's feet stayed right where they were, on the ground in front of her. Noor moved her feet an inch closer. Haseena did not move. Now there was a fire running through Noor's legs. They were at such an odd angle to her body. They pulled away from her in their effort to move toward Haseena. Very, very slowly Noor moved her bottom to follow her legs and feet toward Haseena. Another inch. And another. And her thigh just touched Haseena's. At which Haseena jumped up with a yelp. Her face was as red as if she had been burnt.

Shilpa Ma'am stopped talking about 'How the Camel Got its Hump.'

'Yes, Haseena?'

'Nothing. Nothing, Ma'am. Sorry, Ma'am.'

For a sickening moment Noor thought Haseena might tell Shilpa Ma'am. Tell what? Again her thoughts churned and she lost her words and when she regained them she was sure she was listening to Haseena saying, 'Shilpa Ma'am, Noor wants to ride a bicycle and become a kabadiwali.'

Noor listened for laughter from the class. There was none. And she could hear in her head what Haseena had actually said:

'Ma'am, can I go to the bathroom, Ma'am?'

'Yes, yes, of course Haseena. Hurry back. I have a surprise for the whole class.'

Haseena slipped out of her half of the bench as carefully as if to suggest she could not bear for even a vibration she generated to reach Noor. Noor kept her head down, the better to stare glumly at the dusty toes of her shoes. When she looked up Haseena was gone and Shilpa Ma'am was reaching into her canvas bag. She brought out a stack of thin notebooks. These she placed on the table in front of her.

'What do you think class—what have I here?'

'Copybooks, Ma'am,' the class chorused.

'Yes, but what do you think we can do with these copybooks, class?'

At this everyone looked hard at the stack in front of Shilpa Ma'am. The notebooks were the thinnest and cheapest kind. The kind their parents for the most part knew not to buy, not if they expected their sons and daughters to accomplish anything in class. 'How do you expect me to study with a copybook that falls apart when I touch it?' a studious child might ask an erring parent. And the parent would understand: how to study when one's cheap notebook spelled one's poverty out to one's classmates. Never mind that the classmates were all in actual fact just as poverty-stricken. What mattered was that parents imagine an end to the poverty and thus encourage similar imagination in their children.

No, the notebooks on Shilpa Ma'am's table encouraged no such imagining. The class could imagine only that inside the covers, which would crease at first touch, the pages would be grey; so grey, pencil lead would disappear into the page, only to reappear on the studious child's hand as a smear of grey.

The class shuffled in silence. With all of that empty space beside her on the bench, Noor not only joined in the shuffling, she felt compelled to do an extra amount of it.

Shilpa Ma'am looked at the class in exasperation, then in despair. She was not one of those who bridged exasperation and despair with anger. She was kind. Remembering this, a couple of hands waved half-heartedly.

'Homework, Ma'am. Homework copybook?'

Shilpa Ma'am gave a short laugh and said. 'Come on now. We have some smart students in this class. Speak up.'

Poonam's hand shot up. Immediately, Ajith's followed. While Poonam held hers steadily, even serenely, Ajith's began doing a jerky dance in the air. Those two, Noor thought. Poonam was always first in class. Ajith sometimes unseated her in some subjects—Maths or Drawing—but he was never able to take the overall rank from her. He had been second in class for as long as anyone could remember.

The only reason any of this even remotely concerned Noor was because she, and not Poonam, was Ajith's rival for first—in Drawing. Sometimes she was first, and sometimes he was.

'Poonam?' Shilpa Ma'am beamed at the most studious of her students.

'Homework, Ma'am.' Poonam stood to deliver her answer. Her hands clasped behind her back and her legs apart in the Stand at Ease position proclaimed, as did the sharp pleats in her skirt and even the ribbon woven intricately in her shining braids, this was a future head girl in the making. 'If we have one more copybook, we can do more homework in our free time, Ma'am.'

'Didn't someone already say that answer? Didn't we just conclude this was the wrong answer?' Shilpa Ma'am shook her head, visibly disappointed. Poonam was not used to teachers looking at her with disappointment. Mouth open, she stood till Shilpa Ma'am nodded at her to take her seat.

'Anyone else?' She looked toward Ajith who had already lowered his hand. Clearly he had thought as Poonam had that notebooks could only be for homework. And he and she had both thought: if that answer had already been shot down it was for no other reason than poor phrasing or poor delivery. And buried under that thought was the belief borne by experience that the wrong answer in the right mouth is often enough the right answer, just as the right answer in the wrong mouth…

Noor caught Ajith sneaking a look around the room. He was looking to see if anyone else had an answer to the question. Or, Noor thought, he was looking to see if anyone had noticed his hand go up, then down. An involuntary giggle escaped from her when she saw how discomfited he looked: of course, everyone had seen.

'Yes, Noor? Something funny to tell us about how we can use our new notebooks?'

Not again, Noor thought in panic. Because now Shilpa Ma'am stood at Noor's side. A kindly look insisted that Noor rise and answer. How was it that two different teachers had twice in one day snuck up on her without her noticing it?

She stood up reluctantly. She looked at her toes, and then with a sigh upward at the ceiling. Odd bits and pieces of information flashed through her head: Agartala is the capital of somewhere, and a circle is what a cow draws on the ground when it pulls at the rope by which it is pegged to the ground. Same is true if it is tied to a tree. Same is true when she herself digs her heel into the soft dust and pivots all the way around. Maths Sir said the rope was the radius. And a rainbow has only seven colours. But what about all the other colours?

'Well Noor, what do you think you would like to do with your notebook?'

'Draw a cow making a circle?'

The class laughed.

'A rainbow?' Noor suggested next.

Shilpa Ma'am looked puzzled by Noor's answer, then nervous, as a fresh wave of laughter overtook the class. But since she was also not in the category of teachers who bridge consternation and discomfiture with anger, her face brightened and she said, 'Well yes, children. I suppose you might want to draw in your diaries. Whether it is in pictures or words, your diary is where you can express your innermost thoughts and feelings. Your every longing. Children, you can dream in your diary notebook.'

Shilpa Ma'am turned again to Noor. 'Does your family keep a cow, Noor?'

The class laughed again. Noor wondered why Shilpa Ma'am thought her family would keep a cow. Where would they keep a cow in their one room on the second floor of the Prakash Lumber Building? *Ma'am thinks we are some type of village people only.* Noor felt sad at this realization. Shilpa Ma'am was easily her favourite teacher. But she was also clearly not that smart. Noor wanted to tell her teacher that yes, there are people who keep cows, but they are mostly rich enough to afford feed for their cows.

Meanwhile someone was volunteering, 'Noor's father is a kabadiwala, Ma'am.'

Noor whipped her head around to see who dared speak of her father. From elsewhere in the class, someone else called out, 'Kabadi, kabadiwala.'

It was an accurate imitation of her father's call that he sang from his bicycle, not only loud, but nasal, so it broke free from the thicket of other calls: the flat and unaffected 'Come buy apples. Come buy papayas. Come buy mangos' and the hideously affected 'Cookerwala. Get your pressure cooker, stove, gas burner fixed.' The cookerwala was a man who rolled his 'R's with a love for the sound he was making. And, 'Sabji, sabjiwala.' This last, the call of the vegetable vendor, who announced 'cauliflower, peas, potatoes, tomatoes, jackfruit' and many, many more vegetables in a voice full of grief at the passing of seasons.

'Class. Quiet. Quiet please.' The laughter gave way. But Noor continued to direct fierce scowls from one side of the room to the other at her classmates, daring anyone to meet her eyes.

'You must be very proud of the good work your father does?'

Noor looked at her teacher in surprise. No one had ever invited her to take pride in her father. Her father came home at the end of the day, his kurta sweat-stained, his pyjama greasy with the stains left by the cycle chain, his face tired but his eyes eager to find hers so he could share the joke he had brought home with him that day. She wanted to say, 'Yes, I am proud of my father' but was confused about what good work her father did.

She launched courageously forward. Whatever Shilpa Ma'am may understand or not understand about good work, Noor was not going to stand by and let the classroom laughter go unchecked. 'My father is a kabadiwala. This is not a laughing matter.'

Of course the class viewed this as an invitation to laugh again. But they made a show of stifling it with their hands.

'Noor, your father does a very needed service in our community. You must be proud. Very proud.' Noor's teacher wrung her hand and then in a state of confusion added, 'We are speaking of our longings. Noor, you must be longing to become a nurse. Or maybe you will become a policewoman. You know we have women police now. Only some years back even our police commissioner was a woman.'

'Kabadiwaliii,' someone half-snickered and half-wailed from the back of the room. The 'waliii' was long drawn in an attempt to emphasize the joke. In this joke, Noor wasn't simply the daughter of a kabadiwala, but was herself a kabadiwaliii.

Lifting Noor's chin up gently, her teacher said. 'Now kabadiwalas are important. But you've never seen a kabadiwali, have you? That's because women do not do that sort of work. No, Noor will become something truly important. Maybe something to do with computers. You like to draw, don't you now? There are people who draw on computers—pictures of buildings, plans for machines, all sorts of things.'

Noor shook her head against that or maybe it was against some other idea. Against. She knew she was against something. But she was blinking hard against tears and couldn't sort out much and was grateful to sink to her seat clutching the notebook Shilpa Ma'am handed her.

She opened her book and bent her heated face to it while the rest of the notebooks were handed out. Little circles of rippled paper appeared on the page in front of her. Ignoring these spots where the paper was already disintegrating Noor drew a line with her green colour pencil. Two green circles followed and then pedals, all of it joined by more green lines and then curves—handlebars and mudguards. Her tears dried on the page and on her face. The cycle on the page seemed ready to ride right off the page. She wrote MY INNERMOST LONGING on the top of the page. She thought about it. Yes, she was good at drawing. She could possibly draw machines as Shilpa Ma'am had suggested.

She would have to study her father's cycle to see how the fender should be drawn. The fender and chain she had drawn were a bit messy. But no, she wouldn't become a person who drew on a computer. She would become someone who rode a cycle. She would become a kabadiwali, why not?

Noor turned in her seat and glared at the bent heads all around her. She wanted to shout. 'I will become a kabadiwali. Why not? Who's going to stop me?'

Shilpa Ma'am continued instructing the class: 'Your diary is for you to write in. We will have ten minutes of daily writing time. At the end of the ten minutes I will collect your diaries. But they are yours. I will not look at them or read them. A diary is a place where you can write anything that comes to mind because no one else will ever read it.'

Her head down, Noor concentrated on perching a girl atop the cycle she had drawn. She didn't need to switch colour pencils. The girl on the green bicycle wore a green kurta—anarkali style—cut from five metres of cloth. The skirt part of the kurta billowed behind the girl. From her angry green mouth the girl in the drawing called out to the world.

'Kabadiii. Kabadiwalaaa.'

She ran a line through the words and wrote again. No, a kabadiwali would have a call of her own.

'Kabadiii. Kabadiwaliii.'

Noor underlined the long string of 'i's. Now the world would have a kabadiwali, not a kabadiwala, a girl who rode her cycle and proudly called to advertise her presence in the neighbourhood, to advertise her trade.

She looked at her picture. She wasn't happy with it. Maybe it was the part where the chain went around the wheel. But she couldn't really fix those without taking the diary home and drawing them with Baba's cycle nearby. And Baba parked his cycle below the stairs. And it was dark there. So how then?

Never mind. For now what mattered was she knew the answer

to Shilpa Ma'am's question. Under MY INNERMOST LONGING she wrote the word kabadiwali. She knew now what she would grow up to do for the rest of her life. She would grow up and become a kabadiwali. Because, Noor told herself, I am proud of Baba.

Noor didn't notice that Haseena was back in the classroom whispering to Shilpa Ma'am. She didn't notice Shilpa Ma'am start to gesture toward Noor to come forward. She didn't see Haseena shake her head 'no.' She didn't hear Ma'am call Poonam to come forward and didn't see Poonam and Haseena leave the classroom, hands clasped together.

Noor looked up from her picture only when Shilpa Ma'am clapped her hands to signal an end to writing time.

Looking quickly over to the others she noticed they had all been scribbling—words. No one else it seemed had drawn a picture. She slapped a hand over the page. Oh no, now what had she done?

'It can be poetry if you like. Or a story. A letter to yourself or anyone. Like I said earlier this is your notebook to do with as you please. There will be no marks given and none taken away.'

Noor wanted to ask, 'Can it be a drawing?'

As if in answer to that, Shilpa Ma'am said, 'Remember I will not even open your notebook. It is not just any notebook. It is your diary. And a diary is a notebook for you to read—only you. It is a conversation you can have with yourself.'

Poonam called from the door, 'May I enter, Ma'am?'

'Yes, yes, Poonam. You may enter.' Then returning her attention to the room, she added, 'And just in time. It seems you are, all of you, growing.'

The class was used to Shilpa Ma'am's quick bird-like hops from one thing to the next. To snatches of songs thrown in with bits of English lesson. To interjections. They would have ignored this bit about growing if Shilpa Ma'am's normally bright voice hadn't also suddenly become so serious. When they checked, her face seemed sad. Some of the students parroted as they often did other lessons—'You are, all of you, growing.'

Then Noor remembered Haseena had yet to return from the bathroom. And with that thought there opened a dizzying vacancy in her chest, a sickening thump followed and she restarted her breathing. Had she pinched Haseena, pinched her hard, so hard she had drawn blood, so hard Haseena was not speaking to her?

5

Growing Up

As soon as the bell rang signalling the end of class, Noor dashed from her seat to the bathroom. 'Haseena,' she called. The first stall was empty, of course. It was the stall avoided unless a friend could be persuaded to stand with back turned in front of it; the iron door was so eaten away by rust, it looked like lace and the girl squatting on the ground behind it could expect no privacy.

The other stall door opened with a violent bang. A senior girl pushed past Noor to the single sink. There she washed her hands and then splashed water at her face and eyes. Finally, bending over, she washed her neck and, reaching into her blouse, wiped her underarms. Her eyes, in the mirror, were closed. She wore the look of concentration Noor felt on her own face when she probed for a bit of meat stuck in between her teeth. Quickly before the girl opened her eyes, Noor fled. The second bell was ringing the start of a new period. Noor knew Bengali Sir would do worse than make her squat in the 'chicken' if he caught her wandering the corridor. Still, she ran and taking the steps two at a time she reached the second-floor bathroom just as the bell stopped its ringing. No Haseena there either.

The stairway and corridor were quiet now. Classes were underway in the classrooms she walked past. She tiptoed to her classroom and peered in the door. Bengali Sir was in the room, his back to the doorway. She withdrew and stood with her back to the wall outside. She could hear Bengali Sir ask about her and Haseena's absence.

She heard Poonam reply, 'Sir, please Sir. Shilpa Ma'am said Haseena could go to the sickroom, Sir. I took her myself, Sir.'

'And Noor? Is Noor also in the sickroom?'

Luckily Bengali Sir did not wait for an answer. 'Class, today we will study irrational numbers. But before we do that, let's review. Who can tell me what a rational number is?'

Noor peeled herself from the wall. Her back was wet. Had she perspired this much running up then down the stairs? Or was it fear of Bengali Sir that made her sweat? Her heart hammering, she peered in the door again. Bengali Sir was still facing the class. She tried desperately to signal to Poonam—What? Why? Poonam wrinkled her nose at Noor. Some others stared curiously. Noor was afraid of Bengali Sir, but she was more afraid now for Haseena. What had happened to Haseena? Why was she in the sickroom? Did it have something to do with Noor pinching her? Was it possible to pinch someone hard enough for them to end up in the sickroom? Could Noor perhaps have pinched Haseena hard enough not just to break skin but bone as well?

She couldn't stand there peering in any longer. Any minute now Bengali Sir would turn and seeing her outside the classroom, clamp down on her.

There was the time Bengali Sir had come late to class. The entire class, having concluded he was absent, was playing French Cricket. Girls vs Boys. Girls were fielding. Lalita had just bowled. A crumpled ball of paper was flying through the air. VK was standing on the teacher's desk, knees bent, Maths textbook at the ready to bat. Various students were on their desks. Others fielded in the crowded aisles, trying not to trip over lunch boxes and bags, waiting for textbook to make contact with crumpled ball. VK was known for lifting the ball and sending it on a tricky course. Pinky and Shardha were the only ones seated at their shared desk; heads down, they concentrated on the latest *Amar Chitra Katha* comics circulating in the classroom. They were immune to the noise created by thirty-three of their classmates shouting for the ball to fly their way. In the next moment all was instantly hushed and the two readers looked up to see VK lying huddled against the blackboard wall where he had been felled by one blow from Bengali Sir.

Bengali Sir had made the class stand with their hands in the air for the rest of the period. But VK had been dragged up by the ear and made to stand not on the ground but on his desk, and not just for the rest of the period but also through the lunch period that followed.

We kept him company, Noor remembered. No one had left class for the compound that day. The goonda boys in class had grumbled some about going on strike. But an action of that magnitude could be undertaken only by senior students—like the eleventh class students, who the previous year had greeted the low scores awarded them in the final exams by throwing a number of chairs out of their classroom window and by marching in the corridors afterward, shouting the opening lines from the song, *Masti ki Paathshala*: 'Lose control, lose control, one more time, lose lose lose control.'

*

Noor came to with a start. She was alone in the corridor. And while it was impossible for her to enter the classroom, nor was it possible for her to remain where she was much longer. She went back up the stairs. This time she was headed to the sickroom.

Outside the sick room she paused at the door to listen if a teacher was with Haseena. She could hear voices. And yes, one of the voices was Haseena's.

'No, it doesn't hurt. I mean hardly.'

Noor's heart hammered painfully in her chest. Haseena was still insisting, 'I mean I feel something. But I'm okay.'

'Outside my bathroom window is where I throw mine. You have to ask your mother where you can throw yours.'

'Don't worry about throwing. Worry about the pain. It will be hurting soon. You will see. The first time mine didn't hurt either. Now I roll on the floor when the pain starts.'

'You can ask your mother to let you stay home. Mine says I can stay home when it hurts.'

'Enough now, what are you going on about her mother for? Why do you think we were asked to come talk to her?'

Noor eased the door open. Of course it creaked. She squeezed her eyes shut and held herself still as if the creaking were in her body and not in the door; as if by holding herself tight and small she could still the noise.

The creaking stopped. And when she could no longer hold it, she let her breath out and opened her eyes. Four pairs of eyes were watching her. Thankfully, none belonged to a teacher. She registered Haseena's face and then sorted out the faces of the others—big girls from Class XI and Class XII. What were they doing with Haseena?

'Haseena, are you hurt?' she blurted out.

Haseena shook her head mutely. Noor wanted to go over to Haseena and take her face in her hands, to look right into Haseena's eyes and tell her 'I am sorry.' But this was impossible with the three senior girls present. Noor's hands hung uselessly by her side.

One of the big girls asked her, 'What are you doing out of class? Did Shilpa Ma'am send you?'

'No. Shilpa Ma'am's class period is over. The bell just rang. Now it's Maths period with Bengali Sir.'

'Well of course we heard the bell. It was Shilpa Ma'am who asked us to come talk to your friend. You are from Haseena's class aren't you? You are *his* little sister, aren't you? Talib's, who passed out of school a few years back? I didn't know he had such a little sister. Is Bengali Sir asking for Haseena to come back? You can tell him Haseena is not well and Shilpa Ma'am has given her permission to stay in the sickroom for the rest of the day.'

Noor backed away then. Another of the big girls smiled at her. 'Tell Talib we said hello. Tell him Uma; he'll know.' The big girls smiled something secret to one another. Noor was used to secret smiles. When she was much littler, Talib used to pull her out of class during lunch break and make her carry notes to this girl or that girl. She knew what that was about. Stupidity, somewhat related to the stupidity of different food, transparent red toothpaste, and oh so many other things she couldn't bear to think of at the moment. She was at the door and about to leave the room and she wanted so much to lift her hands and make them do something—something that would comfort Haseena, something that would tell Haseena how sorry she was that she had broken Haseena's arm. But her hands wouldn't obey her. They flung up in the air and then grabbing the door by its latch they flung her out the door and back into the corridor.

She slunk into the bathroom at the end of the corridor and stayed there in the smelly dark till it was time to return between bells to class.

In class, Poonam explained with a toss of her head, 'She's having her period. You know. She is becoming a woman. What arm? Her arm is perfectly fine. Arms have nothing to do with periods.'

Her whisper did what it was supposed to do, carried to the girls whose desks were next to hers. Soon Poonam was surrounded.

'Ohh.' Josy opened her mouth wide, and then clapped a hand over it.

'Mine came at home,' someone volunteered.

Period? Noor couldn't fathom how a period came to somebody. And how was Haseena having a period when she was in the sickroom skipping one and two and now three periods.

Jaffrey Sir skipped into class, dropped the rolled up map he was carrying under his arm, bent to re-roll it. Poonam took the opportunity to meet Noor's eyes over the mayhem of the dozen students that were scrambling on the ground pretending to help roll up the map that they made certain to unroll every time it was close to being rolled up.

'Children, children,' Jaffrey Sir pleaded.

Poonam hissed to Noor, 'Didn't you hear Shilpa Ma'am say we're growing up? Don't you know what that means?'

'Of course I know.'

Noor didn't know what Poonam meant by 'growing up.' She understood only that it had nothing to do with the birthday kind of growing up. After all she had just had one as recently as a few weeks in the past and no one had mentioned anything about a period for growing up. Although there had been plenty of teasing about how Noor looked taller and Noor had in fact waited till she was alone in the room to get out the tape measure and mark herself on the wall and measure—no taller than the last time she checked.

She did understand that Haseena who was somehow having her period in the sickroom or to whom her period had somehow come, and who as a result knew about growing up was unlikely to explain any of it to Noor. Haseena, who wouldn't meet Noor's eyes, was possibly no longer Noor's best friend.

6

Too Much Thinking

Noor was right about the end of her friendship with Haseena. Long after her mother explained to Noor that the periods that had come to Haseena had nothing to do with the many periods the school day was divided into, and that she, Noor, would have her periods soon, as well, and as a result grow up—long after Noor understood that pinching Haseena had not precipitated the crisis resulting in her stay in the sickroom—Haseena was still not speaking to Noor.

Of course neither was Noor speaking to Haseena. It was an impossible situation. They still shared the same two-person bench and desk at school. But now Haseena had drawn a line down the middle of her bench and desk, scoring the soft wood with her ballpoint pen to do it. Afterward Noor saw Haseena struggle to get the pen to write and nearly reached into her pencil box to hand Haseena her extra pen. But already Haseena had turned to Poonam, who was handing her a pen from across the aisle.

In her diary, Noor wrote Haseena a very short letter:

October 15, 2012

Dear Haseena,
I am sorry I pinched you.
Your loving friend,
Noor

Then she wrote to her father:

October 15, 2012

Dear Baba,
How are you? I hope you are fine. Today I want to ask you to buy me a green cycle. I will grow up and become a

kabadiwala like you. But you will not call me kabadiwala because I am not a boy. I am a girl. I will be India's first kabadiwali.
Your loving daughter,
Noor Saidullah

Noor took out the four-coloured pen her aunt from Pune had given to her on her eleventh birthday. It was a pen that two years later still looked new. Selecting the black point, she drew the wheels first. Then switching to the green, she connected the wheels with a flourish of lines and then sat back contemplating her dream cycle with satisfaction. In the old days of her friendship with Haseena she would have given Haseena a quick kick to draw her attention to the drawing.

With some remorse she realized—I am a kicker *as well as* a pincher.

She returned to her drawing. To conserve the green ink which was running low she wrote in blue below it:

My Friend The Green Bicycle.

It didn't look right in blue. Then she underlined what she had written.

<u>My Friend The Green Bicycle.</u>

Writing time was not over yet. She spent the next few minutes fiddling with her pen, switching colours till she had the idea that she might write to her aunt.

Dear Shabbi Mausi,

Shilpa Ma'am promptly announced the end of writing time.

*

Walking home she trailed behind Haseena. Haseena walked alone, but purposefully, as if the way home from school was not meant to be dawdled over, was not a distance strung over the perfect amount of time in which to trade ghost stories. As if she didn't know Noor was right behind her. For a bit Noor matched her steps to Haseena's and assumed the haughty air she imagined Haseena wore as she strode ahead. But very quickly she caught up to Haseena and before she could stop herself, her shoes spiked the back of Haseena's ankles where they emerged from her dust-covered shoes. Haseena spun around.

'What?'

Noor had nothing to say.

'You.' Haseena quivered from head to foot. The word spluttered from her again. 'You.'

Noor saw Haseena's eyes were filled with tears. And she realized that the tears were not recent. Her face was streaked and her nose a mess of wet. So she hadn't been walking with the haughty expression on her face Noor had imagined. Noor was filled with satisfaction. She stuck her nose even higher in the air. Now it was her turn to ask, and she did it coolly.

'What?'

She flicked the word from her. It was hard meeting Haseena's eyes for longer than a second. So she looked down at her hands. Too late, she realized her haughty expression was quite ruined by this action. She compensated by flicking some dirt from her fingernails.

Haseena spun around. The next moment she was gone, sprinting from Noor. But not before she flung over her shoulder: 'Careless.'

Noor thought, ha, that's the best she can manage, 'Careless?' She said the word out loud, testing it, and then, 'So what? It was an accident, wasn't it?' But she wasn't convinced. She felt like crying herself. She didn't. 'Am I so bad?' she asked, voicing what had been rising in her for days. She sat down not far from the cows chewing outside the kooradan. She gave herself a few minutes to get used to the smell of garbage rising all around her. She opened her rough copy notebook and tearing a sheet from it she wrote out the letter to her aunt she had been working on in her mind ever since Shilpa Ma'am interrupted her writing it in class.

October 15, 2012

Dear Shabbi Mausi,

How are you, Shabbi Mausi? I hope you are well. We are also all well.

Here Noor paused. But she wasn't truly well, was she? She was a pincher and a kicker and most recently a spiker of heels. She chewed at the end of her pencil and then wrote some more:

Thank you again for the pen you gave me on your last visit for my eleventh birthday. You never came after that visit for my twelfth birthday or for my thirteenth birthday. My thirteenth birthday was on July 16, 2012. I enjoyed my birthday very much. Only I was sad you did not come. I only wanted to see you and talk to you. I did not mind if you did not bring me a present. The present you gave me last time is very special and I take care of it. People all say about me that I am a very careful person. The green ink is the only colour I have used too much so it is finishing. Sometimes I have to shake the pen to make the green colour come out.

Noor was embarrassed when she read over what she had written. It sounded like she was asking Shabbi Mausi for another present. Yes, possibly it sounded that way. This was not what she had imagined writing. She crossed the letter out and began again.

October 15, 2012

Dear Shabbi Mausi,

You told me you know how to ride a bicycle. I want to ask you to advise me how I can ride a bicycle.

Satisfied that she had gotten the bicycle into the letter right away, she readied herself to bringing the letter to a close. Should she sign it Sincerely or Lovingly?

*

The previous week Shilpa Ma'am had asked them to write letters to the chief minister of Delhi. Of course these were just practice letters but thrilling nevertheless. They had addressed the chief minister as Honourable Madam Chief Minister and Noor had signed off at the end of her letter with:

Sincerely
Noor Saidullah,
Student of Class VIII
Jyotimala School

Shilpa Ma'am had asked everyone to include in their letter one positive and one negative aspect of their neighbourhood. The students brainstormed a list of positives and Shilpa Ma'am wrote the list on the blackboard.

i. School

Poonam said, 'Ma'am we are proud of our school.'

Shilpa Ma'am promptly added a tick mark.

i. School ✓

Students scrambled to be heard, each speaking out of turn.

'Ma'am, Ma'am we love our school.'

'Shilpa Ma'am, please put how we painted our school during break.'

'Ma'am, put we love our teachers.'

'Ma'am, my favourite is Drawing Class.'

'Mine is English.'

Laughing, Shilpa Ma'am added a dozen rapid tick marks next to the first one.

i. School ✓✓✓✓✓✓✓✓✓✓✓✓✓

'Children, think. We must have many other positives we can share with our chief minister. Is there anything in your neighbourhood that is fun for you and your family, or maybe something that makes life easier for your parents?'

'Ma'am, cinema hall.'

'Yes, Yes. Movies.'

The classroom was filled not only with the voices of students speaking out of turn but also with the noise of students coming to their feet in their excitement. Some students were jumping up and down in an effort to have their raised arms noticed.

Santosh rolled up his sleeves to better demonstrate his admiration for a favourite actor.

'He has so many muscles, Ma'am. Like this. Hrithik Roshan, when he flexes his muscles, he rips his sleeves, like this.'

Before Santosh could pull at his sleeves to rip them, Shilpa Ma'am hurried to ask, 'And how does Hrithik Roshan having muscles, or even having enough muscles to rip his shirt sleeves—I'm sure that's not something his mother likes him to do—how does all that help your neighbourhood, Santosh?'

'Ma'am, it's fun, Ma'am.'

'Yes, movies are fun. But I want us to talk about what our government is doing in our neighbourhood to make this a better place to live. Poonam?'

'Ma'am, we have elections. Since India is a democracy, we choose our leaders through a process of elections.'

'Yes, that's right. And what do elections do for us?'

'Ma'am, it lets our parents vote for the lotus or the hand.'

Ajith spoke scornfully. 'My parents don't vote for the lotus or the hand.'

Shilpa Ma'am looked warningly at him. She took a deep breath and began again,

'Okay, let me ask you something. Whether your parents vote for the lotus or the hand or some other party, what is it that your parents want from the party they vote for?'

'Ma'am, please Ma'am, we want onions to be cheap.'

The class laughed. Someone punched the boy who spoke for cheap onions on the arm.

'So shall we put that on the list of positives? Is food easily available in your neighbourhood and is the price fair?'

Shilpa Ma'am pointed to Ajith. He looked confused for a moment, then shook his head. No. Her hand moved quickly, pointing from Ajith to Santosh to Jitender to Shahzad to Rajveer. But at the tail end of a series of 'no's', Manoj, never one to contribute a single word in class, given he was new, given he came from somewhere in the south, given he spoke no Hindi and his classroom English was as limited as that of everyone else, now spoke haltingly:

'Teacher, my father sell. But he cannot sell cheap. First he buy from Azadpur mandi. It is no cheap for him.'

'Why do you think it is expensive for him to buy from the wholesale market in Azadpur?'

Very shyly Manoj offered, 'Petrol?'

Shilpa Ma'am explained to the class that when the price of petrol and diesel went up, the cost of transporting food from faraway fields went up, as well.

The class remained silent as they digested this bit of understanding. Some students nodded in recognition of what they had just learned. Why, they had known it all along. Didn't their uncles grow bananas high in the hills of the villages from which their parents had migrated long ago? Didn't they haul those bananas to the roadside where they waited impatiently for trucks to come haul them away to the city? And trucks—yes, they ran on diesel.

Shilpa Ma'am is strange. Contemplating this thought gave Noor pleasure.

When Noor had next looked up at the blackboard the list of positives was much longer.

i. School ✓✓✓✓✓✓✓✓✓✓
ii. Cinema ✓✓✓✓✓
iii. Election
iv. Market (but food is expensive)
v. Mosque
vi. Temple

vii. Kooradan (but it is smelly)
viii. Naala drain (but it is very smelly) ✓✓✓✓✓
ix. Water taps

The rest of the period was devoted to a discussion of water rationing: neighbours who cheated and drew more than their fair share from the communal tap; the inconvenience of having to draw from the communal tap; and what about how some people—the rich—had endless water in their homes; wasn't water free for everyone to have; no, but the convenience of the communal tap, but how horrible it tasted from the tap, oh but the sweetest water could be had near the kooradan where the main leaked, yes, that was sweet water, but far away unless you wanted to share the cost of a redi to transport water home, not so free then was this sweet water, back in the village water was sweet and free, but then it could only be gotten by walking a long distance to the talab, what about that? And wasn't the government good to send a tanker twice a day for extra water for those who wanted more water?

Noor had not raised her hand during any of this discussion. She had wanted to—to somehow get the word bicycle on the list. Her aunt in Pune rode a bicycle that was given to her by the government. But Noor couldn't figure out how to connect that to water. Her aunt used her cycle to gather firewood far from where she lived.

Noor had been surprised when her aunt told her about it. 'You mean you burn a fire in your house?' Only after getting this question out did she grasp the import of what her aunt was telling her: 'You mean you know how to ride a bicycle?'

Her aunt had nodded in answer to both questions. 'You are lucky you have a gas cylinder. But your uncle says as long as there is wood to gather why rely on the cylinder. "It is expensive," he says. But he doesn't realize how far I have to go to get firewood. To the edge of the city. If I am late going, there are no proper lights. And before I had the cycle, walking in the dark, Ameena…'

This last bit she threw at her sister, Noor's mother.

'Thank goodness you have a cycle,' Noor's mother replied softly.

But not so softly Noor hadn't heard. Noor had been eleven when her aunt paid them a visit and was only just then beginning to hatch her bicycle dream. She had stared open-mouthed at her mother's support for the idea of riding a bicycle.

'Your uncle,' and Noor's aunt returned to speaking to Noor, 'insists food tastes better from a wood fire. But we have one room to live in, same as you, maybe a little smaller. I cook inside and the walls are black and I cough all day. Make sure you marry a man who grew up eating food cooked on a cylinder.'

'Did Baba grow up eating roti cooked on a cylinder stove?'

'Shush now,' her mother had said.

*

Sitting on the ground by the smelly kooradan, chewing on her pencil till her tongue developed minute cuts, Noor formulated her plan afresh.

She would rewrite the letter to the chief minister. She would tell Madam Chief Minister that her father was a kabadiwala who hauled away the discards in the area. He did the work easily and well on his cycle.

But, Madam Chief Minister, she continued in her mind, the kooradan and the naala in our area are filling up with garbage. Noor thought of her neighbourhood's waste—vegetable peels and tin drums of chemicals used in the treatment of wood—discarded in the naala for lack of any other place to haul it away. The richer neighbourhoods employed people from her neighbourhood to haul their garbage away to the cement kooradan which filled up daily as fast as it was emptied of the previous day's haul. Some people in the area raised pigs that rooted in the naala and kooradan. Their neighbours next door, Ashish's family, used to keep pigs but they stopped after one of their pigs died getting at garbage tied up in plastic bags. A bag stuck in its throat and it died choking. Noor's mother had been happy when she heard the news.

If only everyone in their area was to receive a bicycle from the government the waste from each family could be carried far away by a member of the family—a son or even a daughter could do the carrying away. Just as her father carried away old newspapers, cans and bottles. Just as her aunt carried firewood home from faraway places.

For a happy moment Noor pictured the faraway places her bicycle might take her. Perhaps on the edge of the city there was a forest like the one at the edge of her aunt's city. And there they could leave their garbage. Instead of her mother handing her plastic bags of garbage to throw in the naala, in this new era of the bicycle her mother would say, 'Noor, would you ride this over to the forest on your new cycle?'

Noor paused again at the vision of the forest filling with girls riding their bicycles, sailing bags of garbage through the air, landing them in growing heaps under trees. *It would soon look like the naala. And what if there are women who, like her aunt, come there to collect firewood?*

Too much thinking, Noor admonished herself. After all, what matters is our naala will become clean. After all, our naala is nearer to us than wherever the forest might be. And soon the water in the naala will be so clean we will swim in it. And ride our bicycles just for fun alongside it.

7
Birds

At home that evening, her mother wanted to know why with all her chores done was Noor still moping around indoors.

Noor shook her head—a mute denial. Of what? Yes, all her chores were done—onions, ginger and chilli chopped, water brought home in two trips, carrying two heavy canisters each time, garbage taken out to the naala; and she was done with her homework and her bath and laying out her school uniform for the next day. She looked around for more to do.

'Noor, how much more polish do you need to apply to those shoes? They are plenty shiny. Stop dipping your brush into that tin. Leave some for your brother. He needs new shoes is what he needs and here you go taking all the polish.

'Why don't you go out and play? You know, I haven't seen you go out to play in days. What's the matter with you? Don't you feel well?'

She made as if to bustle over and put a hand to Noor's forehead to check for a fever. But she squatted back down instead by the stove, stirring the lone piece of mutton around and around in the dal with one hand, holding her other hand up as if to take the temperature of the air between them. Noor would have liked her mother to actually come over to her. Maybe find her feverish and lay her down and lay down beside her. As if, Noor thought, holding her hand in the air will tell Ammi anything about the blazing temperature I might be running.

'I'm fine,' Noor muttered.

'Then why this endless sulking?'

'Ammi, how many times are you going to ask me the same question? I'm not deaf, you know. And I am not sulking.'

Ameena Saidullah recoiled from the sharp tone of her daughter's voice. She stirred the pot a little harder. Noor hung her head. Neither mother nor daughter knew how to proceed. It was not like Noor to answer back to her mother. She had resolved long ago that she would never answer back to her parents, much less shout back at them in the way Talib Bhaiya did. She had not only seen her mother's eyes fill with tears as Talib Bhaiya slammed his way out the door but she had heard her father sob in the dark to her mother, 'What does he want that we haven't tried to give him?

'It's not reasonable for him to want what isn't possible. It isn't possible. Better clothes. Other food. How much better do clothes have to be—what we eat and wear isn't good enough for him?'

Noor's head hung lower, but she didn't want to retract what she'd said or how she'd said it. Retracting, apologizing—involved admitting to being angry at her mother. And really she had no good reason for being angry at her mother. So instead, she swung her miserable eyes up to meet her mother's and spat out, 'Well, you already asked me that ten-fifteen times, at least. What's the matter, Noor? Why are you sulking, Noor? Why is it sulking if I just want to be left alone? Is it my fault there is nowhere else to go in this house besides this one room? I'm actually perfectly fine—in a really good mood, in fact.'

Ammi surprised Noor by smiling. 'You're right. It's annoying to answer the same question over and over.' She went back to her cooking.

'Pincher, kicker, spiker, shouter.'

'What is it, Noor?'

'Nothing. I didn't say anything.'

Ammi put a katori of puffed rice in Noor's hands. 'Sit out on the balcony and eat.'

'I'm not hungry.'

'Go let the pigeons out for a bit. You can feed it to them if you don't want to eat it yourself. But go. You need to see the world is out there, absorb your eyes and mind in something else, something other than whatever fight it is you and that Haseena have gotten into.'

Silently Noor took the katori of puffed rice and went to sit on Talib Bhaiya's charpai in the corridor. How did Ammi know? Did Haseena talk to her father and Haseena's father then talk to Baba, and then did Baba talk to Ammi?

When they were little, Noor's fights with her friends were sometimes brought to resolution by her mother's interventions. Back then Noor had been a whirler of arms. She hadn't been able to help it. When she was her happiest, her arms seemed on their own accord to swing themselves round and round, whirling themselves as she whirled like, like…Noor couldn't think now of anything that whirled like her arms. Not tree branches in a windstorm. They swayed extra hard, but they didn't whirl. When they were cut, kites spun faster and faster till they crashed to the earth. She shrank a little thinking of the crash, and shrank some more thinking of the many friends her arms had inadvertently crashed into—sometimes it was their shoulders or stomachs but most often it was their heads, even faces.

'But I didn't want to hit her, Ammi. We were just playing a game.'

'Well, was it a whirling-arms-till-you-hit-each-other game?'

'Nnnnnno. We were playing house-house. I was the ammi. And she didn't want to be the baby. So I let her be the ammi's friend who is also an ammi, a different one, but she lives nearby.'

'Well, if she wasn't playing a whirling-arms-till-you-hit-someone game, it's not fair that she got hit.'

'But but but I didn't want to hit her. I was just going round and round, showing her how happy I was.'

'Well, you can say to her, "I didn't want to hit you. It was an accident." And then you have to say, "I am sorry." Even when you don't want to hurt someone, if you hurt them you have to say, "Please forgive me."'

*

How easy it was back then. Her mother would walk her to the friend's house. They would knock on the door. The friend's mother would look up from the same kind of stove her mother used, and immediately removing what was cooking on it would put a pot of water to boil for tea. Sometimes there would even be a small plate of biscuits. Then this other mother would call to Noor's friend: 'Poonam, it is Noor who has come to see you.'

As if tea and biscuits and an announcement was the order of things when Noor came to call Poonam to play on those other friendlier visits?

Huh, Poonam?

She had trouble believing this now but yes, she and Poonam had once been best friends. Everything changed when Haseena came into the picture somewhere back in the past when they were in Class I or II. With Haseena there had never been the need to go through the tea and sometimes biscuits routine that ended with two girls brought together face to face or more likely face and eyes to ground.

'I didn't do it on purpose, you know.'

'It's okay. It doesn't hurt anymore.'

'Ooh did it hurt?'

'It's okay. We can play if you want.'

'Was there blood?'

And Ammi breaking in: 'That's enough Noor. See Poonam is calling you to play.'

How crazy to think that Poonam used to be her friend. She was a goody-goody even back then. Always wanting to play house-house and hijab and make-up. Stupid girl. She wasn't even Muslim. I bet she wasn't even hurt all those times I knocked into her by mistake. By mistake! She knew it was by mistake. But she had to go crying to her mother. And then Ammi was told. Not that she ever scolded Noor. She just helped her to become friends again.

And all that had ended when Haseena and she had become friends. Haseena didn't cry when Noor ran into her, not even when Noor's flailing arms caught Haseena upside the head and her lip was cut and bled.

'So why is she making such a fuss—all these years later?'

Noor kicked at the cluster of pigeons coming closer to her feet. They lifted scant inches off the ground and approached once more, casually pecking at the ground, guttragoong-ing, and blinking their red eyes everywhere but at the katori of puffed rice they drew toward.

'Guttra-goong-goong. Guttra-goong.'

She had a good mind to kick them. Cunning beasts. They thought she didn't know what they were after.

They guttra-good in alarm as she sent them flapping. She threw some rice after them. 'Here, this is what you wanted. Now take it.' But they stayed still in the dark under the charpai.

Now that she was a thirteen-year-old and mature enough to think through such things, she knew what she hadn't known in the past: if Haseena never needed to be reconciled to Noor with the flailing arms it was in all likelihood because there was no mother in Haseena's home for her to go crying to.

Well then, that was settled. No more need for Noor to think about Haseena. That's right. Haseena wasn't a tough girl, certainly not in the way Noor thought of herself. She was just as much of a baby as Poonam. Just that there was no mother at home.

But this thought brought no comfort to Noor. She peered under the charpai and flung the last of the puffed rice into the dark housed there. Faintly she could make out their white plumage, grey in the dark. But as for the tiny white grains she scattered, they were swallowed instantly by the dark.

She was lucky, she knew, to have a mother. One who sent her out to think her thoughts, and with a katori of puffed rice to munch on or throw away as she pleased.

'Noor?' her mother called from inside. 'Spread your brother's sheet and quilt for him. Dinner is ready. Let him take a quick nap as soon as he eats. He has to be at work later tonight.'

With a sigh Noor returned indoors. Just when she was thinking good thoughts about Ammi, there came Ammi's voice to tell her to work-work-work. What else was a daughter good for, but work? It's probably why Ammi and Baba had her—so they could get the work done by her. When did Talib Bhaiya ever make Noor's bed for her, or do anything at all around the house?

Noor collected her brother's bedding from inside their home and spread it on the charpai.

Now what else had Ammi just asked her to do? Oh probably just to make sure to give Talib Bhaiya his pillow. She returned from inside with a pillow she threw desultorily in the direction of the head of the bed she had just made. It landed with a thud.

From under the charpai came the faint rustling and cooing of a fainter alarm.

Talib Bhaiya ruffled her hair affectionately as he went past her. He seemed in a good mood, ate his food with no complaints. And why should he complain? Noor thought sourly. Ammi's given him the only piece of mutton and enough dal that he can drink it up if he chooses.

Ameena had indeed fished the single piece of mutton from the dish of dal, justifying it in her mind by arguing the poor boy had to work at night while they slept. She looked with apprehension in Noor's direction. Knowing that Noor hated to chew through this kind of stringy mutton, which was all they could afford these days, Ameena had kept aside just a tiny bit of meat, broken from the single piece, for Noor. But she also knew her daughter was still upset and on the lookout for a fight to get the upset out. The size of the piece offered Talib could well become the reason for such a fight.

But Ameena was wrong about Noor's need to fight. Her need to maintain peace in her house was much the bigger need. So she simply continued her silent grousing: If Baba were here…But no, Baba was yet to come home. And their meal eaten from the communal plate was still an hour in the future. Talib Bhaiya must eat quickly and catch the little sleep available to him in the corridor crowded with the evening traffic of bathroom-going neighbours. The company van was to pick him up for the long drive somewhere outside the city where he made coffee and tea and ran errands for the call centre operators all night long. Noor had heard Bhaiya tell a friend that he would soon join an English coaching institute so that he could talk to foreigners on the phone himself—in English.

It was the foreigners that impressed Noor. They must be something to talk to! Probably they were beautiful and brushed their teeth like Talib Bhaiya did with transparent red toothpaste. Noor giggled at the thought.

*

Late that night she lay in bed practising her English.

'Trees are the kindest things I know, they do no harm, they simply grow.'

She repeated the lines to herself a few more times. Noor relished the heavy weight in her chest as she pictured Haseena in a faraway village shaded by a tree, larger, she was certain, and shadier and probably kinder even than any growing in the city. Oh, she said to herself, I am the one who needs somebody to be kind to me.

The only other bit of the poem she remembered tickled her memory now: 'And leaves to burn on Halloween.'

She had learned this poem, which she could no longer remember fully, two years ago in Class VI. That was the year Farheen Ma'am joined Jyotimala School. Principal Ma'am had told Class VI they were lucky to have this teacher fresh from teaching college where she was only yesterday learning the latest things about teaching CBSE. Noor asked Bhaiya why this was lucky and he laughed. 'It means, Noor, your Principal Ma'am is making fun of your new teacher for not knowing much about how to teach.'

Then he added, 'But sometimes new teachers can be good. She might actually know what she is supposed to teach you in Class VI. There is a list of things that the government says you have to learn in Class VI. It's supposed to be the same list no matter what kind of school you go to. But most of the teachers I had didn't have any idea what they were supposed to teach. Even when it was right there in the textbook. This one might actually know. And if you learn what you are supposed to learn in Class VI, by the time you take the CBSE exam in the tenth, you will know enough to pass.'

Noor and the rest of Class VI knew they were lucky to have a teacher who promised them toffee in return for keeping quiet whenever Principal Ma'am was due to visit the class.

Then came the day Farheen Ma'am taught them the kindest tree poem. She had gotten quite flustered about the word Halloween and said it was the name of a season in America, similar to the season of falling leaves in Delhi. But Noor had known she was wrong. Ma'am's agitated voice had given her away and later when Noor had checked with Talib Bhaiya, he had said scornfully, 'So much for her knowing CBSE. Her CBSE is government school CBSE. The real CBSE is in private schools. If I had the money, you would be going to one of those schools and not with children of vegetable sellers. Halloween is not a season, it is a festival for children to wear fancy dress. Probably she got the line about leaves all wrong. This festival has nothing to do with leaves.'

Noor had wanted to tell Bhaiya that the line about leaves was written in the textbook, so Ma'am couldn't be wrong about that. But Talib Bhaiya worked in a call centre where people spoke to people in America, so he would know about their festivals, wouldn't he?

'Too much thinking,' she admonished herself again, now in Ammi's voice, now in Haseena's.

Oh that Haseena again. Not her friend anymore. So what if she had come back from her grandmother's village in time for Noor's birthday. She might as well move back there. That's how much use Noor had for Haseena.

The jumbled thoughts of Haseena and the poem gave way to sleep filled with dreams of Haseena's dead grandmother chasing

Noor around a giant tree. The poem came to her completely intact in her dream. The poem and Haseena's grandmother did battle in Noor's dream and she thrashed about, nagged by the sense even in sleep that she was forgetting something, by the sense that she needed to wake and address the forgotten something. But she did not wake.

She did not hear her mother pad to Talib's bedside and wake him. She did not hear her mother sigh or her father groan in his sleep as Talib Bhaiya's company van honked from the alley below. She did not hear the cat pad over from the animal-loving Ashish Bhaiya's home next door to jump up on the charpai and curl up in the warmth left over from Talib's recent sleep.

No one heard the light thud of the cat jumping off the charpai, abandoning the warmth there in favour of the warmth it sensed below. No one heard the cat reach an exploratory paw into the dark below the charpai, or hiss a preparatory hiss. After which the only sound was time ticking silently by as the cat tore blinking red and gold eyes and grey and brown and white wings from the bodies of Talib's thirteen pigeons. Silence reigned. Pigeons don't coo when it is pitch dark; they don't guttragoong, much less scream, not even when they are being ripped apart.

Blood everywhere and the cat skidded as it went about its greedy work.

8

Portents and Blame

Noor accepted the blame. But not nearly fast enough to prevent it being shoved on her. She heaped prodigious amounts of it on herself, but not nearly enough to bow under the weight of it, so others did their heaping and she did her bowing. And through it all she had the satisfaction of finally hearing out loud what she had held in silence till then. The noise and thrill of being found monstrous by an entire building full of concerned animal-loving neighbours was a relief after her own silently chanted 'pincher, kicker, spiker, shouter' and the even softer 'careless' Haseena had flung over her shoulder.

They came knocking the next day. The early risers, stumbling in toward the bathroom at the end of the corridor, could not see in the dark, and so they stepped on the broken bodies. People reported with relish—thirteen dead.

Later in the morning the cat was observed licking its paws on the sun-splashed ledge that ran the length of the corridor. But then this was the customary time of day for the cat to sunbathe. Talib's friend, the cat's owner—Ashish—claimed this as fact. It couldn't have been his cat. Noor hung her head—it wasn't the cat's fault. Even if she had never seen the cat on that ledge before, even if the cat were there to revel in its crime, it was only doing what was in its nature. It was Noor's fault. She was the one who had failed to secure the thirteen pigeons in their coop the night before. Failed to do it even after her mother had called her to—and Noor could hear her mother's instructions quite clearly now:

'Noor?' her mother had called to her from inside. 'Spread your brother's quilt and sheet for him. Dinner is ready. Let him sleep as soon as he eats. He has to be at work later tonight.

'And Noor don't forget to lock the pigeons up. Your brother

flew them earlier this evening. He isn't going to want them out for any reason now. Not with that cat about.'

'Yes, Ammi,' she had replied, never paying attention to what she was agreeing to.

At 7 a.m. the gory mess was still spread about. Morning light shone bright, allowing those in line for the bathroom to skirt the area around the charpai. Ammi sat by the stove, her head in her hands. She refused to light the stove, refused Baba tea when he asked for it. Noor was frightened. Should she step out with the pail and cloth, to clean the floor before her brother returned from work? But how to touch those mangled bodies?

Baba headed out the door to forestall Talib, and met him rushing up the stairs. Talib had already been told the news. Neighbour children had lain in wait for him eager to see what would happen to the expression on his face when he heard. He had heard them out with unchanging eyes and only on reaching the stairs did he react—he took the steps in twos and threes. At the front door, he reached around his father to slap his sister. Noor danced from his reach. In the past such an encounter would have been accompanied by squealing and pleading on her part. But she was silent now. And so was Talib. Silently, he batted at her while his father held him off, then breaking free he turned to the dead birds. He counted—piecing together torn wings and limp bodies, scraping up clumps of feathers to confirm what everyone had already guessed—yes, all of them, all thirteen, gone.

'Not one left,' he kept repeating disbelievingly. Neighbours tut-tutted.

'Was the latch not properly secured?' they asked solicitously. Though of course, by now everyone knew the facts of the case—Talib had reared these birds, starting with his first pair when he was a boy of eight or nine. Among his pigeons were lal and kala chapka, white kagdi and kasni kasak, some pigeons sleek and grey and trained to fight, others pure white and fan-tailed, trained to dance. All of them trained to fly together, trained to come when Talib called.

He searched in the mess for his favourite—his only Neelam kaathwa—he had raised with a bottle dropper and mutton fat when its mother refused to feed it, pecking it and pushing it from her nest.

The neighbours knew the birds had been left out overnight. That it was Noor who had failed to count them off and lock them up—this after she had let them out to play with them, let them out from the safety of their home, the coop Talib built for them and had secured them in earlier. No, it was not the failure of a loose latch, it was the failure of the girl, a careless child. Though old enough to have some sense of responsibility, she was seen running around the neighbourhood, head uncovered and wild, when she should be home helping her hardworking mother, or at the least applying herself to her studies.

The tut-tutting was endless. It included in its scope her unlegendary marks at school, her altogether unamazing record as a talentless child (she could not sing or dance or cook or mend a ripped seam), and even her unremarkable looks that everyone agreed could be summed up with 'too thin, too dry, altogether ordinary.' Noor relished all of it—her eyes hard, her fists bunched where she had tucked them under her armpits—she scowled fiercely at the ground. Now everyone knew what she had known all along. She, pincher, kicker, spiker, shouter, whirler of arms, and most recently—pigeon killer, was a careless girl. Care Less. Without a care for others. Wasn't that what Haseena had accused her of yesterday?

Noor banished herself to the darkness under the stairs. But soon enough it was time for her to head to school. Someone must just have cleaned the mess because when she tiptoed upstairs, the corridor outside the front door was shining wet and the smell of disinfectant hung heavy in the air. Baba was long gone. Ammi put her finger to her lips. Talib never looked up. Noor went to the corner, pulled the curtain around her. When she stepped out in her uniform, Ammi was waiting with her lunchbox and a rolled up roti for her breakfast. Noor left as silently as she had entered, skirting at the last the bucket and cloth by Talib's feet.

When she reached the spot near the kooradan where she had stopped the previous day to write to her aunt, she pulled the letter from her bag and ripping it to pieces she threw it from her. The bits of paper clumped together, then came apart and hardly travelling a foot from her, landed all around her. Of this she was sure: she did not deserve a bicycle. She surveyed the mess all around her. Yes, she would give up her bicycle dream. Maybe she should go to Haseena and tell her that she would be happy to live without a bicycle if it meant Haseena could be happy. 'I'd give up anything for you,' she rehearsed her apology to Haseena. Noor knew how stupid she sounded and how unrelated to Haseena's happiness or her brother's unhappiness her green bicycle was. And the truth, she admitted to herself, was that her bicycle dream was just a dream. Giving up the dream was not the same as giving up an actual cycle.

She wondered if she should pick up the pieces of paper. Maybe they could be pieced together and she could recopy the letter on a fresh page of her notebook. She bent down to a scrap of white that had swirled back to stick to her socks.

*

A second before it was upon her, she felt it. Its weight pressed down on her bent head. It was as if the air above her compressed and then expanded, as if the sky momentarily descended then snapped back to its rightful place. And before the weight was lifted, for a second she was lifted, plucked from the ground and brought to her toes. 'Aaaaaaaa,' she screamed and her hands went up to stave off the danger of a falling sky.

She was returned to the ground where she landed on buckled knees. She kept her head down, fearful of seeing what it was that meant her harm. Back on her feet, she dared look; from under her arms she looked up at the sky. There it was winging from her; its wings so heavy they had nearly flattened her to the ground like so much torn up, scattered paper.

A cheel, dark grey and brown. She couldn't see its curved falcon-beak or curled claws but could imagine what they looked like—punishing. The bird turned as if to return. Before she could scream again, it turned yet again and, leisurely flying those distant currents that circled above her, it climbed higher and higher till it was a distant speck.

She realized she was small. And the speck in the sky, huge. The weight of it pressing on her head was new and painful knowledge. She fled down the road, no cover anywhere in sight. The wild idea entered her that she would never find another person again, no matter what distance she ran. The world, she realized, had come to an end. She was alone.

She ran in the open till she drew up to other girls and boys walking in groups. Around her, there was noise and chatter, the sudden cropping up of market stalls, a line of autorickshaws waiting patiently for customers and ahead the school gate, swung wide open. The weight of the cheel's body pressing her to the earth, the claws that pulled her momentarily from the earth, very nearly obliterated these sights and sounds, then gave way to them. She was safe.

Yet she continued to feel fear. In class she was afraid. Even with the ceiling above her, she could feel a whirring overhead and her head sank into her shoulders in response. She wanted to crawl under the desk. She did not hear her teacher enter and later leave. She left the page of her diary blank during writing time.

By lunch period she was able to articulate the question in her mind: was it a sign? What did it mean? Close by the school building to which she clung while others ran out in the open ground, she tripped over Ajith. His lunch, like hers, was uneaten. He was hunched over his book and rocking back and forth as he recited to himself.

'Jawaharlal Nehru Stadium is the third largest multipurpose

stadium in India. It is named after the first prime minister of India. The first largest stadium in India is Salt Lake Stadium in Kolkata, West Bengal. Salt Lake Stadium is the second largest stadium in the world. The first largest stadium in the world is May Day Stadium in Pyongyang.'

Noor squatted down next to him.

'Don't sit here. Can't you see I am studying?'

'You don't have to say "first largest".'

'What?'

'First largest.'

'Why not?'

'Largest means the largest in the world. The same as first largest.'

'Well, that's what it says in the textbook.'

'No, it doesn't.'

'Here. See. Now go away.'

And he began again: 'First largest, May Day, Pyongyang. Second largest, Salt Lake Stadium. Also known as Yuba Bharati Krirangan.'

'What's the third largest?'

'In India or the world?'

'I don't care. Either.'

'Well, you have to care, if you want an answer.'

'I think a cheel tried to carry me away today. It grabbed me by my hair. It slapped my head with its wing.'

'You're crazy.'

'It might have been a sign.'

'Of what?'

'It might have been trying to tell me something.'

'Were you trying to get at its nest? They will come for you if you even look in the direction of their nest. So, were you?'

'I don't know. Maybe accidentally.'

'Did you have food in your hand? They'll swoop down to snatch food.'

'No, I had a letter. I had just torn it up. That's all. I was throwing it around me. Maybe it thought the paper was food.'

'No, cheels are smart. They don't get confused about things like bits of paper. They can see more than any other creature. Otherwise just think—they'd be swooping down on garbage all day. Probably you were looking at its nest.'

She was silent, wondering where in the cement block of the kooradan could the cheel have housed a nest. The nearest tree was far away on the outer boundary of the open maidan where Talib Bhaiya played cricket.

'There was no nest nearby. But I did something bad. And maybe the cheel knew.'

'Oh that's very possible. So what did you do?'

She felt caught in his curious gaze. She had stumbled across him then sat next to him because she had always seen him as someone far removed from her. His second rank in class, his endless studying, even his tiny figure, she was possibly taller than him, had all made him someone so inconsequential that for a moment she had felt she could tell him anything and simply walk away unburdened. But minutes into the conversation he was looking at her with curiosity; he was forming an opinion of her. How could she proceed when minute by minute they were both becoming real to each other and unexpectedly his opinion of her mattered to her?

Ajith broke in, 'Don't tell me then. Go away so I can study.'

The curiosity was gone from his eyes and she felt deflated. A little desperately she asked, 'Why do you have to study? We don't have any exam today.'

'What kind of a stupid question is that? First of all I prepare ahead for exams. I need to get top marks in all my exams and go to university, maybe even one that is in a foreign country and then I want a good job, like an engineer. I bet you've never heard of naval engineering. Soon there will be no airplanes. Well, maybe a few still. But jet fuel is going to get more and more expensive. You know like what we talked about petroleum in class. All the things we have in our homes and shops, all that comes from this or that country and has to be flown here and there. How do you think they are going to be transported in the future? There will have to be new inventions for new ways to travel. Not like what we see in the movies—rocket ships and outer space, but like the way we travelled in the past—sail boats, but with new inventions to make them faster. You probably don't know anything about hybrid? No. Well, it's complicated. But that's what I need to become—a naval engineer.'

'Oh.'

'Besides when I am not first in class my father gets angry. Not only at me. But at my mother, my brother, everyone.'

'Does he beat you?'

'He beats everyone.'

'Why does he do that?'

'It makes him happy.'

'It makes him happy?'

'Yes, he ties us first.'

'Ties you?'

'To a tree.'

'To a tree?'

'I'm joking.'

'What?'

'Just joking.'

'That's a really stupid joke.'

She felt terribly angry at him, and also terribly surprised. She had thought his head was full of first largest and second largest stadium, but actually…And what, she wondered, is hybrid? Why would he know about this hybrid thing? He was a show-off; that's what he was. And what a stupid joke! And this was the most confusing part. Did his father beat him, or not? Probably he did. The Hindus, very few of them in Noor's building, but the few there were, did a lot of beating. It was because they did a lot of drinking. But she couldn't ask Ajith about that. Girls didn't talk about things like drinking. And it was important to do only those things she was supposed to do and avoid those things she wasn't. She shuddered. This must be what the cheel wanted her to know. Yes, she was certain now that the cheel was letting her know she had stepped out of line one too many times.

'What is hybrid?'

He mimicked her, 'What is hybrid?'

'You're very bad.'

'You're very bad.'

'Stop that.'

'Stop that.'

'I don't know why I ever talked to you in the first place.'

'Okay. Tell me what bad thing you did and I will tell you what hybrid is.'

So she told him about forgetting to put the pigeons back in their box, about letting her mother's instructions go in one ear and out the other, about how everyone cared about something or the other, like Talib Bhaiya cared about his pigeons and his job, but she cared about nothing, at least not enough to work hard and pay attention.

'So maybe Haseena is right about me. It is because of my carelessness that bad things keep happening.'

She expected him to respond with her good points, like didn't she sometimes come first in class in Drawing. And she knew many jokes—good ones.

Instead he said, 'Yes, but you do care about something. You cared when everyone made fun of your father. Remember? Kabadiwalaaaa.'

She couldn't tell if he was mocking her. He looked as inscrutable as ever. She should shake him just to see some expression on his face; he was so tiny it wouldn't be difficult. She reminded herself of her resolve to stick to only those behaviours she knew were allowed.

'Yes,' she said loftily. 'I do care about my father. In fact I am thinking of being a kabadiwali. I will become just like my father and do work that is good for the environment.'

'Aw, just leave it be,' he muttered.

She was pleased to note he looked pained. But then he added, 'Look Noor, there is no such thing as a kabadiwali. And what's more you don't even want to become one. You just feel like you have to say that because of what was said in class that day. As for being careless, probably you are careless. Probably the cheel has nothing to do with that. But you already know you are careless. So when a cheel comes knocking on your head, it's the first thing that comes to your head. So yes, in a way the cheel is telling you something.'

He stuck his hand into his lunch box and pulled out a roti; he took a big bite of his roti. Then he stuck his hand in again. She wanted to slam his lunch box lid shut on his hand. But she stayed sitting next to him instead. And after a while she got out her lunch box and they ate together.

9
Girls vs Boys

Chasing after the cricket ball that had fallen into Bhawna's open school bag, Santosh found instead a mysterious object. He waved it around in the air. 'What kind of art project is this?'

Bhawna turned in her seat to look. She screamed. Others screamed with her. Shailaja and Lata and Puneeta and the twins, Bano and Gano. To everyone's surprise, the ever icy Poonam started crying. No one was sure where to look—toward Poonam who was hiccupping noisily in between sobs or toward Santosh and the object in his wildly waving arms.

Bhawna bravely launched herself in the air and made a grab for the object—large and white and now held high above her reach by Santosh, who was both confused by the girls' reaction and enjoying it. Some boys shouted at Santosh to put it back.

'But what is it? It's not an art project?'

Ajith walked over to Santosh and spoke softly to him. VK saw his chance and grabbed the object from Santosh. Now Bhawna began crying. Ajith stepped forward and said loud enough for all to hear. 'This is something that has to do with what happens to girls. Show some respect. Give it back.'

Sheepishly VK handed it to the weeping Bhawna. The girls crowded around to give her cover; she bent down to return the object to her bag.

Well ahead of the bell signalling an end to break, everyone was back in their seats, the girls in their half of the class and boys in theirs. Entering the silent classroom, Aarti Ma'am felt she should be silent, as well. Then reminding herself she was the teacher, she asked the class to put their art projects on the table so she could check their progress. For the last few weeks she had had the class working on mirror-work cards to give to their parents on Diwali.

No one, not even the goonda boys dared snicker at her repeated use of 'art project' throughout class that afternoon.

For the rest of the day the girls held their heads high and the boys hung theirs. Only the goonda boys dared try and speak with the girls. Approaching Poonam, the de facto leader of the girls, Habib and George asked if the girls couldn't just 'forget about it. It was a mistake. Only Santosh would be fool enough to do something like that. He doesn't have sisters, you know.'

Poonam fetched up her most cutting look and replied frostily, 'We don't know what you are talking about.'

'Come on, Poonam. You don't have to be all hoity.'

Josy sprang forward. 'Hoity. Who are you calling hoity? We girls are not hoity. It's you. You're all goondas.'

Poonam turned away. She may have broken down in the moment of crisis, crying publicly the way she did, but next to Josy's hysteria Poonam's queenly demeanour did much to earn her the respect of her classmates. Bhawna pulled at Josy's hand, 'Shhh, Josy. They are not worth talking to.' She said this in what she hoped was something near to Poonam's coolness of tone.

Josy allowed herself to be led away. She couldn't keep the smile from her face; she loved the drama. Some of the girls shook their heads disapprovingly. That Josy was a recognized floozy. Always talking to boys, sometimes laughing with them. And often enough fighting with them, even using her hands, and getting into pushing matches with them. It made the girls uncomfortable thinking about it. They'd just have to be firm with her—no more talking to the boys, not even to fight.

*

Noor had completely missed seeing the object waved overhead because she had been rewriting the letter to her aunt in Pune. When she looked up to see what the screeching and carrying on was about, it was to notice Ajith, a centre of calm in the mayhem. She shook her head in bafflement. What was that light shining around Ajith? She looked around to understand what was happening. It seemed a fight was going on, and there was Ajith toe to toe with that bad boy Santosh. She looked hard then. Yes, there was a light. He was glowing. Radiant. And toe to toe.

And oh god, short. So short.

Indeed he was worse than short. Next to Santosh, who was tall and had recently grown quite a few hairs on the upper lip, Ajith looked like a mouse.

By now Santosh had lost the thing he was waving in the air to VK. And Ajith, who had begun by addressing Santosh, turned to VK, the Class Prince, who was taller even than Santosh. VK held the object behind his back and seemed for a second to want to refute Ajith's words; then he brought the object forward and hesitantly held it out to Bhawna. The air was sucked out of the room for the one electric second it took for the object to change hands. There was collective horror: *Imagine his hand and hers on it at the same time.* Then the girls converged around Bhawna, and Noor lost sight of the object.

Though she had never seen one up close, Noor recognized the 'art project.' Like everyone else in class she had seen ads for Kotex and Stay Free and Whisper and Freedom and all those other ones meant for light days and heavy days, and with wings and without wings, referred to on TV, but nowhere else, as 'sanitary napkins.' In Hindi it was simply 'pad.' Before she knew about periods, these ads had made her wonder at her family's reaction to them. When they played, everyone in her family bustled around extra loudly, or they were conversely extra silent and stony-faced as they stared at the television. She may have wondered but she also knew to not ask—neither about their reaction, nor about the thing itself. Later when her mother taught her about periods and pads she understood the reason for alternating between noise and silence. Now when an ad played she too was confused—whether to make noise to drown out the television or to pretend in strained silence that she did not notice the ad. Sometimes she did the one and at other times the other. Neither reaction worked to address the discomfort she felt.

For the next many days after the incident with the 'art project,' girls and boys kept apart. It was, as it turned out, rare for the teachers to need them to work together. In addition to seating them separately in the two sides of class the teachers seemed already to have been practising various other means of keeping them apart. Now the children noted that when teachers needed corrected homework notebooks to be distributed they picked a boy to distribute to the boy's half of the class and a girl to the girl's half. When the bell rang for library period, they formed a boys' line and a girls' line to exit their classroom. They reassembled in the library, the boys in one half of the room and the girls in the other. When they lined up to drink water from the water cooler, the boys formed a line to the left of the cooler and the girls to the right. Of the five taps that ran the front of the cooler, two on the left belonged to the boys. The girls cupped their hands and drank from the two to the extreme right. No one approached the middle tap. There was always an empty space in front of it. Why was this? There had been no fight between the boys and girls. Not prior to the incident with the object. So why was this? No one knew, but it had always been so—the space between boys and girls. And after the incident it was a convenient space. After all, they had to put their anger somewhere, and there it was—the space waiting to be filled.

When Library Ma'am got ready to distribute books for the class to take home, she had with her two stacks. She called on Mohan to take charge of one stack and Shailaja to distribute the books from the other stack. The books for the boys had pictures of sports or cars on the cover and the girls' books were as requested by girls—princess books. There were Amar Chitra Kathas in both stacks—Karna and Chandra Shekhar Azad for the boys, Shakuntala and Malavika for the girls. On Friday the boys went off to play cricket with other boys from other classes who were also let out for

PT period. The school had no proper playground, but there was the empty lot next door where the boys set up their wickets. Girls sat in the small stretch of open ground in front of the school and chatted. Friday was also the day they had Practical Education. Again the boys and girls formed different lines and this time they went to separate rooms—girls to learn tailoring and boys to learn cellphone repair.

*

By Friday of the following week the fight had a sulky quality to it; Noor was tired from the effort it took to sustain the 'Girls vs Boys fight.' The fight obliged her to eat her lunch alone; she snuck looks at Ajith seated at their usual spot, not ten feet from where she now sat leaning against the school building. He ate and studied and ate and studied without looking over at her. When the bell rang he went inside and she trailed in with the rest of the girls who seemed bent on making nearly every entrance into and exit from class as a group.

She counted back in the past; it was four months since her fight with Haseena. But where were her other friends? Wasn't she friends with any of the other girls then? Wasn't she friends with Shailaja? Oh yes, of course she was. And Pooja too. So why had she been eating lunch exclusively with Ajith? And how many weeks had gone by since she began this practice?

She had a vague memory of a time in-between the two—Haseena and Ajith—when she had perhaps tried to eat lunch with some of her other friends. But Haseena was always there in the midst of the girls, making her feel stupid. For what? All she had done was pinch Haseena. And to be fair to herself, hadn't she pinched Haseena in the past, as well. Why was Haseena making such a fuss about it this time?

Girls vs Boys meant then she had no one to eat with. Her longing to sit at lunch with Ajith was an outsize ache; she ached to share not only her lunch but also her thoughts and ideas as she had been doing since the day the cheel launched itself at her.

But no, 'Girls vs Boys' was a relief. Now she had an excuse to not sit with him. And she needed to be more grateful for this. Because the part of her that longed to sit with Ajith had a counterpart—a part that wanted nothing more than to put distance between herself and Ajith. There was the awful business of the radiance she had glimpsed around him. She knew what the radiance was, of course. It was in all those films, and in the Amar Chitra Katha comic books. Girls were always looking at boys—Radha at Krishna and Shakuntala at Dushyanta—and the boys always had some sort of light coming out of them. As if they were gods. When really, they were only boys.

It was love that did this. Horrible love. Love that made her talk to him in her head all day. And how long had she been doing that—from well before the beginning of 'Girls vs Boys.' Oh how ashamed she was to think of how long she had been feeling it—this horrible love. Love that shamed her when she saw radiance and shamed her again when she saw not radiance, saw only '*Short. But he is so short.*'

And what if other people could see any of this? Had they already seen it?

She made herself look at him seated ahead of her, seated in fact in the front row of class. She looked hard at the back of his head in the hopes she could cure herself of radiance, of love. Next to *short* she listed other flaws—he reads all the time, he is dark, his hair is too thick, it makes a puff on each side of his face, covering his ears and covering his eyes, he wears glasses, he keeps pushing the glasses off his nose, there is flaky white skin on his nose, he has a habit of staring at nothing, he is bad at games, he says stupid things in class, he raises his hand all the time, he probably wants to marry Poonam.

Yes, she succeeded in making the radiance disappear. Oh, but this just made her feel worse. How could she go looking for faults? And really, some of the faults were not even faults. Like his hair and the way it kept flopping over so she wanted to be the one to push it off his face, and those glasses that needed to be propped up on his nose. And instead of '*Short. But he is so short*' she saw again—radiance. A radiance that made her…well, queasy.

And she was certain he knew. This thought left her extra queasy. Yes, all told it was a good thing—Girls vs Boys. At least this way she could avoid talking to him.

She wondered if Haseena knew. Haseena had always known everything in the past. But then they had not talked in some months and their old friendship was so faded in her memory that even the sadness of its ending no longer rose unbidden in her. She wondered then if Haseena too had forgotten—forgotten their talks and games, and the beyond good feeling of playing those games.

When Shilpa Ma'am handed them their notebooks for writing time, Noor couldn't bring herself to write about or draw her cycle. The letter to her aunt remained half written. She read it over and it made no sense to her. How could she have ever wanted a cycle? Such a silly thing to want. Now she was one of those mad girls, someone like Josy, who spent her lunch period talking to a boy. She was worse than Josy because she talked to him outside of lunch period, at home, in her head—confiding in him things like her feelings about her brother and her father and her mother.

Oh no! She was actually talking to him about her family. It was the number one rule her mother had taught her—'Never ever talk about our problems in the home to anyone outside the home.' But no, she didn't actually tell him about Talib Bhaiya's fights and her father's sadness or about her mother putting off their landlord for one more month with promises to pay the rent the next month, about her mother and father talking late into the night about work drying up and money drying up with it.

No, the conversations with Ajith were all still in her head. *And may they remain that way,* she offered up in prayer. When she had met Ajith at lunch it was strictly to rattle off facts and figures—isosceles triangles: two sides the same length two sides the same length two sides the same length, and the formula for benzene—C6H6 C6H6 C6H6. And when they strayed from study material, it was so Ajith could talk to her about his plans and ambitions.

He talks too much. She added this to the list of his faults. She winced. The list was growing. For certain the radiance would too.

*

After school, Noor trailed Haseena on the walk home, past the maidan and kooradan, and then they were nearly at the public water taps where Haseena would turn left toward her home and Noor right toward hers. She felt desperate. The thought of two days with no one to consult nearly choked her. She needed to stop Haseena. Maybe she should throw a clod of dirt toward Haseena and when she turned to see where it had come from they might strike up a conversation. How stupid! Typical of the pincher and kicker that she was—to want to throw a clod of dirt. Screwing up her courage Noor called, 'Haseena.'

Haseena stopped, and then as if unbelievingly she shook her head—a little shake that made her earrings and her plaits and the bows at the end of her plaits shake. She took a step and another. Noor was looking for a clod of dirt when Haseena turned.

'Did you just say my name?'

'Yes.'

'What is it?'

'Nothing. I just wanted to…nothing important. I just wondered what you thought…isn't it horrible what the boys did?'

Haseena shook her head. 'No, they didn't do anything wrong. Maybe Santosh really didn't know what it was when he held it up in the air. Or maybe he did. But it doesn't matter. It was only Santosh. Everyone knows Santosh is like that—an idiot. And why does Poonam have to go make such a thing out of it? Now we are all forced to go along. She's only doing it because, you know, she got stuck. She cried and she's afraid everyone is going to say, "Oh Poonam, you cried. You can't be head girl. You're only a Bhawna."

You know she wants to be head girl someday. Someday is like four years away. But she's preparing already. It's stupid. And because she cried she is making us all fight with the boys.'

This made perfect sense to Noor. How had she not thought of it herself? Now she understood what she had most missed about Haseena. Haseena was smart in a way that Noor wasn't. Haseena could explain Noor's life to her in a way Noor might never have come to understand by herself. She needed to talk to Haseena—about so much—about Talib Bhaiya, who had announced last week he was leaving home, about her father who had announced last week that he would cut Talib's head off before he let him leave, and about.... No, impossible. Not about Ajith. She stalled.

'But Haseena, aren't you and Poonam friends?'

'Yes,' Haseena spoke sharply. And looking directly at Noor, she added, 'She doesn't hit me.'

'I didn't hit you. I pinched you.'

Haseena turned, her plaits slapping her cheeks. Noor shouted before Haseena could run, 'Stop. I'm sorry. It was so stupid. I should have said sorry right away. Then when I saw you, you were in the sickroom and all those other girls were with you and I thought I had made you sick. All the more reason I should have said sorry. But you know me. You know how stupid I can be. Then you didn't come back to school for some days. I thought—I don't know what I thought. I only found out about that, the thing, about you starting your periods, I only found it out later. I had to ask my mother because I didn't understand. It still hasn't happened to me, you know. My periods.' With a sigh of relief Noor turned her voice off.

'That's it then?' Haseena smiled her question.

'Yes, that's it. And I am so sorry Haseena.'

'All right then.'

'All right?'

'Yes, all right.'

'You're not angry anymore?'

'No, Noor. I haven't been angry for a long time now.'

'You haven't? But you are always looking away and busy talking to Poonam. And the line you drew with your pen, on the bench between us. And you never look at me anymore.'

'Noor, you are the one who is always busy. Drawing your cycle. And writing about your cycle. And cycle cycle cycle.'

'So you *were* upset at me.'

'No, not really. I was upset at other things. Things you don't know about.'

'Things I don't know about?'

'I have to go now. But it's okay. We are friends. And listen, my father is calling. I have to get home.'

Noor stared at Haseena's retreating back. *Things I don't know about.* It was true Noor could hear Haseena's father's voice calling for her. And she knew Haseena always went straight home from school to get preparations for the evening meal underway. But were those tears in Haseena's eyes when she turned away? Tears made no sense, not when Noor knew she herself had the biggest smile her face had worn since forever.

'Haseena,' she called once again.

Haseena turned and waved. 'I have to go. We'll meet like we used to. This evening, at the water taps.'

'And I'll bring a treat for Blackie. You'll bring him, won't you?'

Haseena waved again from the turn toward her lane, but shook her head. 'No, not Blackie. But I'll come.' And then she disappeared into her lane.

10

God Listens to Children

Noor turned and faced the Prakash building. Shielding her eyes from the bright winter sun, she looked up at the second floor corridor. Her eyes followed the corridor to her front door. The curtain hung there was drawn aside, twisted and looped over the long nail on the upper right corner of the doorway. Ammi was home. Next to the doorway, the charpai stood on its side against the wall. So Bhaiya wasn't home. Maybe she could tiptoe in, leave her bag and tiptoe out before Ammi pulled her into helping with housework. And Friday was washing day. Ugh.

Noor crept in silently and stopped short. The room was dark but her mother was visible in the light from the single window. Her hair covered, her long white gown drawn around her, Ammi bent to the floor then stood again. Her thin legs and round belly were sharply drawn black shapes in the light streaming through the cloth of her gown. Drops of water glistened on Ammi's fingers and face. Something tightened in Noor's throat. She waited till her mother completed her prayers and then drawing up to her, Noor whispered, 'Can I help you with anything, Ammi?' Her mother was so pure, so good. If Noor could have, she would have squeezed her tight. But Noor was as tall as Ammi and the days of squeezing Ammi's legs and even her middle were in the past. It was awkward putting her arms out to Ammi to find that it was Ammi's shoulders that came within them.

So Noor bent to pick up Ammi's prayer mat. And in that position she wrapped her arms around Ammi's knees. Noor's embrace pulled at Ammi's gown where it stuck to her wet legs. Inexplicable sadness seized Noor as she caught a glimpse of Ammi's bare goose-bumpy legs. Ammi laughed at the tangle of Noor's arms and her own gown and bent herself to work the gown free.

Looking up, Noor saw there were dark smudges under Ammi's eyes. Worse ones than usual. And her mouth that always smiled—the result of teeth that protruded a little—her mouth that was laughing just a second before was too quickly shut thin and tight.

'Noor, you haven't been offering namaz regularly. Today, you have come at the right time. Fix your mind on your brother and pray that he will listen to your father's words. Come child, god listens to children.'

Obediently, Noor went about her preparations. But her mind strayed and during the recital of prayers she thought of her mother and her brother, of Haseena and Ajith, then again of Ajith and Girls vs Boys, and shaking her head she tried to bring her mind back to prayer. As she finished, she thought hard as Ammi had asked her to about her brother and her father. If god willed it, Talib would remain in their home, not only to come in to sleep but also to play cards with her, to help Baba sort kabadi, to purchase vegetables in the market for Ammi to cook.

If god willed it, Talib Bhaiya would hand his pay to Baba. And Bhaiya would understand that this was the right way. And Baba would take Bhaiya's money and his own earnings and put the two together for the needs of the family. Noor was certain now that Baba was right in this matter and every other matter concerning the family. Up to now hadn't they been the best family ever? She couldn't think of any other family—not Ashish Bhaiya's next door and not Haseena's on the other side of the water taps—to which she would have rather belonged.

If god willed it Talib Bhaiya would forgive her his lost pigeons. He might buy two pigeons and re-stock the coop once more. Without saying a word about it, she would check every night to make certain the coop was locked tight. And when he went to clean the coop, she would appear by his side to scrub the wood boards and to fetch and carry water and dirty and fresh newspaper. She would never say a word; she would do everything. By her actions he would know how sorry she was. If god willed it the two pigeons would lay eggs. And then there would be many baby pigeons.

But it's already beginning to be winter. They won't lay eggs in winter.

Noor squeezed her eyes shut to keep the thought at bay. Yes, there would be babies. And they would all live. And Bhaiya would trade some of them when they grew for other kinds. Soon the coop would be full again.

Prayers finished, her resolve to help Ammi with the housework wavered. *Well, I prayed, didn't I?* And fortified by this thought of her goodness Noor wandered out to the corridor to see what was happening in the world.

The charpai was still standing on its side, leaned against the wall, but the empty coop was not there. She couldn't remember if the coop had been there when she returned from school.

'Ammi,' she called hesitantly.

'Yes Noor, are you coming to help?'

'Ammi, did Bhaiya take the coop from the corridor?'

Ameena stepped through the doorway. There was a bundle in her hands she meant for Noor to take to the presswala. The bundle contained Talib's shirts and pants. These shirts and pants were purchased readymade and required the kind of pressing she could not give them at home. Secretly, Ameena doubted this claim of Talib's. What difference did it make whether the shirt was stitched at the downstairs tailor's or purchased at a showroom in Lajpat Nagar. It was not as if shirts purchased in Lajpat Nagar came into existence already stitched—was there a tree that grew them 'readymade?' No, they were first cotton then thread then cloth and then stitched by human hands. She had never voiced the argument to Talib, but now uncharacteristically she found herself complaining about her son to her daughter. 'Why does he think I can't press his shirt? What is "readymade" except somebody he doesn't know who stitches it? Does he imagine the tailor who stitches "readymade" is any different than our Hasan Chacha?'

'Ammi, it's not the stitching. It's the cloth. Feel how silky. They bring the cloth from foreign.'

'Do they give you the money to press it from foreign, that's what I'd like to know.'

'Ammi?'

'Yes, what were you saying?'

'Ammi, the pigeon coop is gone.'

'Go look under the stairway. I am sure the sweeper woman put it there now that it's empty.'

'But I am almost certain it was here when I came home from school.'

'Noor, you only just came home from school? It hasn't been twenty minutes even. Now go take these clothes to the presswala.' With that the clothes were thrust into Noor's hands and Ameena turned away.

Noor saw her mother enter the room in the direction of the rest of the family's clothes that awaited pressing and folding. She saw her mother stop short at the bedside. Her hand was still in the air above the clothes piled on the bed, but Ameena's eyes swung away. Her eyes caught Noor's searching eyes and glanced off the daughter she could not see. With a whimper she ran to the clothes cupboard, opened it a mere inch and slammed it shut.

'Ammi?'

Next, Ameena hurried from the room. Noor stared after her mother who was calling through the curtain at the entrance of their next door neighbour's home. 'Lata, arre Lata.' Noor heard the fear in her mother's voice and lingered not knowing what she should do. Her mother waved emphatically at her—to go. Go!

Noor turned and ran so she could be back the quicker.

It seemed to her as she raced down the stairways that she was always racing, and somehow never making it in time to the events of her life: something had happened to Haseena, she didn't know what, something that she would find out only at the taps this evening, and then there was Haseena's periods that came before this more recent something, that too had happened away from Noor, and the many times Noor looked up in class to wonder at what was happening because somehow everything happened just outside her reach, somehow there came to be a Girls vs Boys, and Ajith, there was the horrible feeling, and light, and more feelings to do with Ajith, even all that had happened without her knowing it.

She stood in the shade under the tree just outside the entrance of Prakash building. This was the press stand where Suneeta Aunty laboured all day and sometimes into the dark of the evening to press the neighbourhood's clothes. Noor would have liked to dump her load and run back upstairs. And here instead was a delay because the press stand was mobbed by children waiting to hand over their bundles. But of course, mothers would have waited for children to come from school, to give them the bundles of clothes that had been washed in the early hours so as to take full advantage of as much of the winter sunshine as would be afforded them. Even with a whole morning and afternoon of drying, the clothes in Noor's hands were clammy. The press would be employed to dry them.

'I have to give these. Suneeta Aunty, please.' Noor pushed through the crowd of children who pushed back. 'Take these clothes,' Noor pleaded at the head of the line where she was installed between two sets of elbows that dug into her from either side. Suneeta looked up from the shirt she was pressing, and indicated with her chin that Noor could leave it where many little bundles were gathered at her feet.

'What's the hurry?' Suneeta asked.

'She pushed me,' squeaked the boy with the elbows.

'So?' Noor shouted into his face. She squared her shoulders and leaned over him.

The logic she presented was insurmountable and the boy acquiesced.

'Suneeta Aunty,' she asked 'have you seen Talib Bhaiya?'

'He went this way on that fancy cycle of his, maybe five minutes ago. He said he'd come by for his clothes later. I told him no, your mother hasn't left them with me.'

'He was here five minutes ago?'

'Maybe less.'

'And he had a wooden box with him. The box he kept his pigeons in?'

Suneeta paused to move the paan in her mouth from one side to the other. Then spitting into the gutter nearby she said, 'Oh yes, *that box*.'

There was no escaping the significance she placed on the words 'that box.' Noor shrugged it off. What did it matter to her? If people wanted to call her a pigeon killer they should just do so. She turned away and fought her way past the four or five children waiting for Suneeta Aunty's attention.

'Hey there. If you don't wait to count out the clothes in front of me don't bother telling me there's something missing afterward.'

The children who were waiting to get their clothes counted snickered. For good measure a couple of them landed jabs as Noor broke free from the group. Outside the circle of the tree's shade, she shielded her eyes and looked to the left and right. Something felt wrong. Where could Talib Bhaiya have gone at this late afternoon hour? She tried to reassure herself. Talib Bhaiya might well have gone to the market to buy pigeons. Wasn't that what she had prayed for? Yes, she knew she was supposed to pray for her brother to understand her father. Or maybe it was the other way around. She wasn't sure which her mother had asked her to pray for. But yes, she had prayed for something like that, as well. And there was no limit to what one could pray for. And Bhaiya must have taken the box because he would need it to place the new pigeons in before returning home. But the box was large, almost as large as Bhaiya. And two new pigeons could be squeezed into a shoe box. Well, he made money. And he liked to spend it. Maybe he would buy thirteen pigeons in one go and needed more than a shoe box to accommodate such an extravagance.

But at this hour in the afternoon the shops in the market would be closed—the shopkeepers dozing while their stomachs woke to gigantic lunches that needed digesting. And then why did her mother go off to Bhaiya's friend's house? And why did Bhaiya need to ask for his shirts at Suneeta Aunty's? Should she see if she could run and catch him on the street—to ask him these questions, and many more? Did god really listen better to the prayers of children? Was it because as her mother had told her in the past children were without wrongdoing? And what of her—what kind of child was she? Should she turn and run toward the maidan where he played cricket, or the other way toward the main road and the flyover beyond which was the bus stop from which a bus would take you to the far corners of the city?

She shivered in the afternoon warmth. It was her mother's voice she could hear wailing from upstairs.

11

Ameena and Motherhood

Of course, her mother made no dinner that night. This business of not cooking was becoming far too common, Noor felt. There her mother sat, in bed while it was yet evening and not at all the time for bed. She sat with her head in her hands. After the initial wailing she had taken to silence. Noor willed her mother to look at her.

Ameena beckoned Noor to her side and once she was seated there Ameena played with her daughter's hair absentmindedly. But to her daughter's questions—'Ammi, where's Bhaiya?'—she gave no real answer, saying only, 'We drove him away. God forgive us for driving our own son away.'

Noor made the mistake of persistence. Ameena repaid her by pushing her daughter from her. Then she continued talking to herself: 'Our own son. Our only son.' Ameena didn't care that Lata from next door had taken the opportunity to squeeze her way into Ameena's home. She sat now at the foot of the bed. She made clucking sounds as Ameena pushed Noor from her. She beckoned to Noor with caressing motions of her hand. Ameena turned away from Lata's efforts at mothering Noor.

Noor was astonished that her mother would not try to hide her emotions from Lata Aunty. She shook loose Lata Aunty's clumsy hands that were tangled in her hair. If her mother wouldn't show Lata Aunty the door then it was up to Noor to defend the family honour. She, Noor would have nothing to do with Lata Aunty's pretences to affection. Noor sat by her mother with an obstinate look on her face. See if Ammi pushed her away, she would refuse to budge. And what's more she couldn't wait for Baba to come home. She would complain to Baba about Ammi.

Lata Aunty remained for an hour then another, abandoning

her own home. 'To console your mother,' she told Noor. Her consolation took the form of reminiscences about Talib. *As if he is dead.* Noor scowled at Lata Aunty, who would have none of it and scowled back at Noor. Noor willed her to leave. But when she finally did it was to return five minutes later with an elaborate meal that she laid out for Noor. Noor was alarmed to note her stomach growling at the sight of food. And what was this—saliva flooding her mouth?

Noor wondered if in his mother's absence, it was Ashish Bhaiya who had done the cooking. How strange to think of Ashish Bhaiya and cooking. To Noor's knowledge, if Ashish Bhaiya were to approach a stove it would only be for the same reason Talib Bhaiya might approach the stove at their home. Every bit of living in both their homes was carried out in the proximity of every other bit and there was therefore no avoiding the stove. So of course Noor had in the past seen Ashish Bhaiya playing cards with Talib Bhaiya, the cards slapped down on the counter by the stove, and Lata Aunty joining in the game in between stirring the meal on the stove.

Yes, Ashish Bhaiya's home was like Noor's—four walls, each wall serving a different purpose—one against which they leaned their beds, one against which stood the stove and cooking utensils, the bucket on the floor for rinsing vegetables and for carrying the dishes out to the communal washing area and a third wall against which stood four plastic chairs, stacked atop one another, a table for the TV, which was also the table for studying at and pressing clothes on and for leaning against when one did not feel like pulling a chair from off the stack. As for the way they conducted themselves, the only word for it was—noisily. They conducted themselves noisily what with all the living that took place in that one room—crowded with umpteen brothers and sisters and cousins who came to stay, crowded also with puppies and mynah birds and yes, the evil cat. Noor's home, by contrast, was quiet. Dignified. Noor sniffed her dignity and searched for what other differences might come to mind.

The only outward difference between their two homes was the fourth wall. In Ashish Bhaiya's home this wall was brim to the ceiling with images of their gods. In Noor's home the fourth wall was where her mother's cupboard stood. It was from the top of the door of this cupboard that Baba had strung the curtain her mother stitched for their own private dressing room. This made Noor wonder where Lata Aunty went to change her clothes. And this made Noor wonder again what it was that Lata Aunty had said to cause Noor's mother to wail and then to seal herself in silence.

Noor ate Lata Aunty's food with relish. It was hard not to. Her mother's food was of course the best, familiar not only in that each dish was executed as it always had been but also in that every dish was executed just like every other dish. Yes, she secretly agreed with Talib Bhaiya's assessment: Ammi's food was all the same from one day to the next and from one dish to the other. The food Lata Aunty brought was strange, vegetarian, but splendidly varied in taste. She decided it was impossible for Ashish Bhaiya to have cooked the meal. It was as likely for one of their many puppies or even their evil cat to have cooked this good a meal as it was for Ashish Bhaiya.

'Ah, you like that! My son is a good cook. He can tempt even a non-vegetarian like you.'

Noor scowled again. But this time Lata Aunty did not scowl back. She crooked her finger at Noor. Reluctantly Noor pulled herself up from the floor where she had been eating and went to Lata Aunty's side.

She whispered in Noor's ears:

'Your mother will be too sad to tell this to your father. You go meet him. He must be on his way. You tell him before someone else meets him with the news.'

'Tell him what, Aunty?'

'Ashish didn't want to tell me. But it's not what Ashish wants that matters. We can't just be doing what children want. No. How easy it would be to have a child if that's all there was to it. No one's going to say that I don't know how to keep my son in order. I gave his ears such a boxing, his ears are burning for sure, and that's how I know I've gotten the truth out of him. And your brother? Yes, I'm coming to that. He's run off. To Rajinder Nagar.'

Noor stood mutely not understanding what Lata Aunty's whispers meant. Certainly she knew by now that the feared for event had come about. Talib Bhaiya was gone, gone from their home. At some point he would return for the rest of his things. Then Baba would shout at him and Ammi would plead with him. And probably where other such sessions had ended with him flinging himself out the door this one would end with him flinging his things along with himself. Out the door. But Noor knew it couldn't be out of their lives.

*

Talib Bhaiya had taken her aside and promised her this. 'Noor, you don't worry your silly head about Baba and me. I make good money and Baba wants me to hand it all over to him. He wants me to account for every paisa as if I am a little boy still. Well, I can't. And I won't. I mean to keep my earnings. He thinks I will spend it all. But I mean to save.'

'For what, Bhaiya?'

And even Noor knew as she listened to him describing his plans that while he may not be a little boy, his plans as a grown boy were not very good ones. He had outlined for her the need to buy a coat and tie, a proper suit. The proper suit was only the first part of his plan.

'But why a suit, Bhaiya?'

It was to be Western style and with matching pants. That would be Rs 3,000. And why not? Why shouldn't he have such a suit? He made Rs 9,000 per month. But then he needed an additional fifteen thousand.

'Fifteen thousand?' Noor sucked in her breath.

There was a meeting he would have to pay to attend. And if he went to this meeting then he would be given a membership. There was a process, Talib said.

'Process?' Noor repeated the English word, looking for its meaning. But in the moment of its handling the word lost all its meaning. Like water gushing from a broken pipe. She tried again. 'Process?'

Talib was vague about the process. Some videos would be shown. And what would watching these videos accomplish?

'Forget the watching,' Talib commanded his sister. After the meeting he would be allowed to bring other boys in suits to the next meeting. And from their Rs 15,000 he, Talib, would get Rs 5,000. 'Imagine,' Talib had said, 'I can easily get three people from work and make back all my money and earn more starting with the fourth person I bring to a meeting.'

'Do you know four people at work with suits?'

He had scolded her and called her a silly girl for asking him such a stupid question. Why, he said, he knew all sorts of people. And besides she hadn't understood the real beauty of the plan.

'You get to wear a nice suit?'

'No, silly. When the four people bring three or four people each then I make money from each of those people's membership fee as well. Then they too will bring in people. In business they call it income-generate. All these people will income-generate for me.'

But Bhaiya couldn't tell Noor what was so special about the meeting that would make people want to attend. At least not so she was convinced. 'It's business, Noor. What do you know about business? I, on the other hand, have studied business.'

'When did you study business, Bhaiya?'

'Oh, you also think business is something to go to school and study. The best businessmen I know are our uncles. You know how much money they made selling our grandfather's land. And not a single paisa came to us. That's how businessmen do it. And if Baba wants to say they are gangsters, it's because he's committed to being poor all his life. Well, I am not. And I mean for you to not be poor, either.'

But Noor was thinking: before he goes should I ask him to show me how to ride Baba's bicycle? Then I can go to Baba and tell him that I am ready to help him with his work. He will ask me, 'What do you mean, Noor?' And I will jump up on his bicycle and show him.

But Noor had never gotten around to asking her brother. The end of the pigeons put an end to asking for anything. Talib Bhaiya hadn't spoken much to her after that day. Just cleaned and fixed his coop, fashioned a new roof for it, which unlike the plain piece of board from the past was covered with little shingles of wood. He put new brass bolts on the doors to each of the eighteen little hutches within the coop.

She had ventured conversation. 'You could paint the coop?'

'Paint is poison for pigeons.' And then with bitterness, he added, 'Oh well, they are dead in any case.'

She had wanted to flee. But she remained to take her punishment. And he kept working on the coop and she grew bored rather than ashamed. She decided the self-punishment wasn't working and returned indoors. And the next time Bhaiya and Baba fought she reminded herself of what he had told her, back in the past when he caught her crying 'Noor, I'm going to have to leave. But I will come see you and you can come see me. I'll take you in a bus to my new place. You'll want to move right in, it will be that fancy.'

She asked, 'And Ammi and Baba?'

'Oh when they see my new place…'

'And your new suit.'

'And my new suit. Of course I will come and take all of you to see my new place. We will go by bus. In fact let's leave the bus be. We will go by taxi. Someday of course we will go by personal car. My car. But first I have to buy a motorbike.'

And he had dreamed aloud. Noor was busy dreaming, as well.

Of a bicycle outside Bhaiya's new place. It would of course be a green bicycle and Bhaiya's new place would be in one of those neighbourhoods where there would be a park and a path to practice riding.

*

'Rajinder Nagar. That's where Shahrukh Khan's family lived before he became a big name. Matter of fact, he was born there. Child, you didn't know that, did you now? And you don't know this either. Rajinder Nagar is just a word he told Ashish. After all, Rajinder Nagar is not so far from the railway station. Probably somewhere really far by now, in Mumbai for all we know.' Noor refused to believe any of what Lata Aunty was spouting. But it explained Ammi's distress.

'If you ask me there's likely a girl in the picture. That brother of yours thinks he is a Shahrukh Khan type, a looker. Well,' and Lata Aunty stepped out the door and leaning beyond the railing she spat hard, 'I won't say what I think of that. But oh yes, he looks. We've all seen him with that eye of his. When he was little I told your mother keep him under control. But your mother is soft.'

Noor would have liked to pinch Lata Aunty's mouth shut. Why did Aunty let her brother spend all his time in their house if this is what she was thinking all along?

'You're thinking your brother is some hero and whatever girl he is mixed up with is a heroine? And he and this heroine will have a happy ending—filmi style. Oh no. Take my word for it there will be no happy ending.'

Noor had not been thinking any such thing.

'Your mother was so proud when he got that job. Now I told her, who knows what all goes on in such companies. Who knows, eh? It is one thing for him to go to a school full of girls. And you also they send to that same school, I don't believe in mixing boys with girls, no. I was happy to send Ashish to Government Boys School. But imagine my surprise. Now here is Talib, a grown boy, and your parents are still turning a blind eye. Maybe they are thinking he will make good money there. But is money everything? In any case Ashish makes as much as Talib and it is not in some place where girls and boys sit next to each other—and in the middle of the night.

'And who is watching over them—this is what I want to know?'

Noor wondered if she was supposed to answer this question. Probably not. Lata Aunty loved to talk. There was no doubt about that. And the disappointment of living next to Noor's family must eat at her—only the four of them, and their quarrels had always been conducted in whispers. Ammi's emphasis on never revealing what happened at home to those outside the home meant Lata Aunty couldn't possibly know anything about Talib Bhaiya's reasons for leaving home. Of this Noor was certain. Ammi shouldn't be wailing since after all it was only Lata Aunty whose talk was not to be believed in any case.

But Ameena was listening and unable to bear any more she looked up to say, 'There is a supervisor where Talib works.'

Lata Aunty's response was to screech. 'A supervisor? What good is a supervisor? Can a supervisor stop boy-girl love-shove business? No.'

Turning with some emphasis from Ameena, and bending close and dropping her voice dramatically, Lata Aunty spoke right into Noor's ears. 'You are his sister. He must have said something to you.'

Suddenly Noor was sick to her stomach. 'I should go,' she whispered, not knowing why she was whispering. 'Maybe I can still find Talib Bhaiya.'

'What? Find your brother now? He's all the way to god knows where by now. For certain he is somewhere outside Delhi by now. Gurgaon, at least, maybe even Mumbai.'

Ameena started up from the bed. 'Gurgaon? I can call my brothers. They will search for him.'

*

Ameena's parents and brothers lived in neighbouring Gurgaon. Her two sisters, married off at young ages, like she had been, were more scattered—Shabana to Pune and Anusha to Mumbai. These marriages to men living in big and little cities far from the girls' rural upbringing had been a cause of pride for their father. And he had paid handsomely for the grooms—all of them settled in trades other than farming. He had seen far into the future: the prospect of dividing his own land into four lots for four sons helped him see that land divided generation after generation would yield no more than meals of dry roti and, if fortunate, an onion or two for its owners. Their brothers-in-law were to be a connection for his sons if they were to desire a way out.

To his astonishment it was his sons who prospered and on the very land he saw as too shrunken to be fit for anything. The faraway city of Delhi sprawled out and bit into its surroundings and it was his sons who came to him and argued for their pinprick holdings to be transferred to them. 'Immediately,' they argued. They more than argued, they towered over him. He did not wish to admit it, but he was shaken by the exchange. They returned having sold the lots one by one, each one to a higher bidder than the last.

Their neighbours, old men like him, had been more than a little astonished themselves. 'Why? How? Who wants the land? For how much?' It was land that had nearly wrecked them in its refusal to yield the rice, wheat and vegetables they planted with hopeless obstinacy. What could Delhi want with their bit of parched desert? But Delhi wanted this land and it did more than take a bite, it swallowed the land, and the land yielded to Delhi as it had not to their hands. It yielded buildings paned in shining glass rising up at such speed that many a building teetered searching for balance, others perched at odd angles to the earth, but all indications were they would remain, and in time seed new crops of buildings and highways to connect them to one another and to the city—Delhi. So it was, the old man saw his sons become city men without ever leaving their land. And he, their father remained the same and different—seated on his charpai, pulling on his hookah, but now dependent on his sons and not unhappy for it.

His sons approached the neighbours, old friends of his, and offered to sell their land, as well. 'To whom? How?' The neighbours were bewildered by the whole affair. 'Do they want to farm? The men from the city?' And how was one to talk to the men from the city or understand their talk? But his sons said, 'Uncle, not to worry. We will take care of it.' But somehow when these lots sold, it was for less than his sons made selling theirs. It was a mystery how one person could make this much from worthless land and another far, far less. But then the land was worthless, wasn't it? At least this is what his sons assured him and he was easily assured. The neighbours were not.

Ameena's brothers lived in two- and three-room cement houses now. They complained these homes were not enough for them; they complained the glass-paned buildings sprouting on what had been their land, housed mansions within them. They complained the buyers had become wealthy off of them. But Ameena considered her brothers to be far from poor. Not only did their children live in two- and three-room homes, but they also went to school on the backs of motorcycles that all four brothers now drove.

The four brothers had even gone so far as to put up a cement structure, right up at the edge of the road; they called it their office. Outside the office they hung what pleased the old man, their father, best of all—a sign that read in bright blue letters 'Iqbal Ali and Sons' and below that in red letters, 'City Property Dealers.' They did little in this office besides calling for tea across the compound that separated them from their wives. There was no more land, neither theirs nor their neighbours', to sell.

Her brothers' good fortune had created distance Ameena was loath to bridge with reminders of their kinship. The last time she had visited them was two years in the past and then too it had involved Talib. She had called on her brothers then and it was they who had helped Talib get the coveted call centre job—a job her husband feared was taking their son from them. And now her son was gone. What if it wasn't the job that was to blame? What if her husband was to blame? What if his obstinate refusal to change with the times had pushed her son from home?

The woman, Lata, and her talk made no sense to Ameena. But she heard in Lata's talk some of the same ideas her husband had been declaiming. Listening to Lata, she heard what Talib had heard in his father's speech—the nonsense spoken by a person living in a small world, one at odds with a much larger one. She had trusted her husband in this matter for far too long. It was time to look elsewhere.

She thought of her brothers in their office; their practice of supervising their wives' housework through the office door had caused Mohammad Saidullah to tease Ameena that she was lucky to be married to a kabadiwala, who left home daily. Then she had agreed. But now she thought: my brothers are clever. I will call my brothers. They will know what to do.

*

Once again Ameena motioned for Noor to come to her side. She felt a tug of sympathy for the girl who stood next to Lata, held there by the woman's grip though with her face averted from Lata's whispering. Lata let go of Noor. And instantly Ameena was no longer sympathetic. The girl came to her shamefaced as she should be after gobbling her way through second helpings of food on what should have been a day of fasting. But it was no use blaming the child. She had remained the baby of the family for far too long. And kept in that place by her father. At an age when she should be learning the skills of home she spent all of her time scribbling pictures on paper. If the scribbling would result in a child who brought home good marks, even a second or third place in any subject other than Drawing, Ameena would be happy to let the child grow in her own direction. But this girl behaved like one with no direction—she simply whiled the day away—sucking on toffee her father fed her, and gazing out on the street.

And why did her husband allow one child freedom from any expectation while the other must conform to expectations from another century—that of blind obedience. Ameena shook free the anger that was building in her. She forced herself to put her arm around Noor. The child looked more than ashamed; she looked fearful, as well. Her heart constricted. *She* had willed the child to remain a baby. No, it wasn't her husband alone. She too had persisted in seeing Noor as younger than her age. Why had she waited to explain the business of being a woman to her daughter—waited till Noor heard it at school and came to her with questions? Maybe because Ameena had to forego her own childhood. And she thought to prolong Noor's. No, that was only one part of the truth. The rest of it was hard to face: with her son growing up and growing away from them she had not the strength to face the same from her daughter, as well. And now there was Noor—recently given to sulking fits. Certainly she was growing. It could not be denied.

Tenderly, Ameena whispered to Noor. 'Go to Madanpuri market, there where your father sells. I do not want him to come home for some time. I need some time. I need to go to make a phone call to your uncles. This Rajindar Nagar makes no sense. Go and stall your father in the market. Tell him something to hold him there. Tell him—tell him this—Ammi sent you out so she could fumigate the house. Tell him there was a problem with termites in our cupboard. That Ammi could not cook today, that you are to eat out and bring food home.'

*

Lata pretended to be disinterested in the whispered consultation of mother and daughter. She gathered up Noor's plate and took it to where Ameena kept her bucket. It was coincidental that this move put her closer to the consultation. But even when closer to them she heard no better and to make clear her good intentions she set the plate down with a clang and announced she was returning with food for Ameena. 'There is no use your sitting there without food in your belly. And I must return to my household. Ashish's father will be home soon. I cannot afford to linger here feeding you. Nor will my heart allow me to remain next door knowing you have not eaten since noon. I will return with food for you and for my sake you must eat.'

And with an air of triumph mixed with humility she set off to her home. The humility was as thin as her sense of triumph was thick. She was triumphant because she felt motherhood to be a battle—one in which she had won. What she had won took a moment to establish—yes, she had kept her son at home with her. She had not lost Ashish as Ameena had Talib. Ameena with all her soft airs and speech may have thought raising a boy was a business for the gentle. But Lata knew it was a business for the tough-minded, those who could tussle with men, vocally and with their hands, if necessary.

Enough of their whispering, she muttered. What good has her whispering done her?

Though she did not admit it the battle she felt she had won had less to do with her relationship to her son or husband and more to do with her relationship with her neighbour, Ameena. The battle of motherhood was not a battle for sons and daughters, but one against other mothers.

*

In the home Lata had just left, the whispering that had so frustrated Lata gave way to raised voices:

'But Ammi, Bhaiya is not in Gurgaon. Earlier Aunty said Rajinder Nagar. Now she says Gurgaon.'

'Noor, it is not because I think he is in Gurgaon. He is somewhere near here only. But I need my brothers' wisdom.'

'And not Baba's. You want me to lie to Baba. Well, I won't.'

'Then don't lie to him. Tell him his son is gone and so is his wife. I have to go make a phone call and there is no food in the house for him because his daughter ate everything in sight. Tell him whatever makes sense to you.'

12

Baba at Night

Noor lingered by the downstairs water taps. But she was late for her meeting with Haseena. There was hardly anyone else by the taps. And when the last stragglers left with their containers all that remained was a group of dogs, who having slept the day away had woken at dusk and come to the taps to lap from the puddles on the ground. Noor kicked at the air and the dogs shied away but they were only pretending to be fearful just as she was only pretending to be fierce.

She sniffed the air, and the smell of the meals being cooked and eaten in the homes of Chirag Dilli helped her to fix her sorrow on her mother's failure to cook their evening meal. The home-cooked dinners scenting the air mingled with that of food being fried in carts a little distance from the taps. Noor became aware of the jalebi man, and of the lucky children lined in front of his twin basins of hot oil and hot sugar syrup. She joined the children in watching the man transfer intricate spirals of fried dough from the oil to the syrup. At the cart next to his, men, not children, stood with their hands outstretched. Money was exchanged for plates of rajma and rice. This is where her mother thought she and Baba should eat. She rejected the idea—this was the meal of men who must not have wives at home to cook for them. How was her father to eat such a meal? All the while she pushed from her mind the memory of the too-large meal she had already consumed.

On the muddy ground next to the cart a boy hunched over a wooden board, chopping onions he heaped into a bucket. These would be sprinkled on top of the rajma and rice. Lingering there only brought tears to her eyes and she turned from the cart just as the boy looked up and flashed a smile through streaming eyes. It was Santosh, the bad boy from her class. She waved to him before remembering that Girls vs Boys meant no waving at boys. *But this is outside class*. And in a bit she consoled herself with *he waved first*. Then a bit later with *oh well, no one will know*. If he starts to say I waved to him, I will say he is lying. Who is going to believe him? No one, that's who.

She walked in the direction opposite to the one she should be taking to reach Baba. This was so she could stop by Haseena's home. Maybe, just maybe she would find Haseena taking in the evening air on the little rickety balcony overhanging her street. Haseena would be angry that Noor had not come to meet her at the taps. She needed to explain to Haseena that it was not her fault that Talib Bhaiya had left home taking his empty pigeon coop with him, that her mother had detained her in the house, and that she was being sent now to lie to her own father.

She stood on the street under Haseena's balcony but there was no sign of Haseena. She was no doubt serving the meal she had prepared for her father and little brother and sister. Noor sighed. Why was her friend always so busy? Noor needed so desperately to speak with her.

To make up for lost time she ran back past the rajma cart and jalebiwala, back past the taps and toward the end of her alley. The many balconies and verandas overhanging the narrow alley blotted the street lights so she was plunged repeatedly into ink darkness and emerged from it to be blinded by yellow light. But she ran by feel of the rough stones under her feet and knew from memory to jump over stagnant pools and to skirt the piles of rubbish thrown to the street. She also avoided those dogs still sleeping in the dry gutters running alongside the street. If the dogs only pretended to ferocity when awake, the same could not be said of a dog stepped on in its sleep.

Ahead was the centuries-old crumbling archway of stone that looked at from the other side marked the entrance to her alleyway. But from her point of view, the point of view of a grumbly and confusedly teary girl, the archway marked her exit from a one-room place called home, an exit into the lit up world of the main road. The market, laid out along the main road was extra bright with white lights that stretched further into the night than they normally would. Today being Friday the travelling market with its travelling lights had made its way to its weekly appointment with Chirag Dilli's daily market; its temporary stalls of tarpaulin stretched on bamboo poles were set up alongside the fixed structures of the daily market.

Friday market began with stall after stall of chowmein and then rubber chappals, then spices, then plastics—buckets, spoons and toys of red, green and pink—followed by a stall full of the sweetest little baby clothes knit in stiff ruffles of orange and purple and blue—she nearly stopped here to admire the clothes—and then dozens of stalls devoted to clothes for women, mountains of brassieres and panties so she felt herself seize up in embarrassment. The crowd was thickest at these stalls. She had to push with her hips and poke with her elbows to get through. The market she was headed for was beyond this one.

She came to the end of Friday market. The lit street had given way. Ahead was the dark of the kooradan and maidan. The last stall by which she stood was not really a stall, but a truck, the bed of which was piled high with gur. The heavy scent of burnt sweetness enveloping the truck was like a scratchy blanket. Thick and warm and uncomfortable, it wrapped itself around Noor. A boy, perhaps her age or just a little older, grinned at her from where he lay atop the mountain of gur. In the dark he was just the white flash of his eyes and teeth and the darker black of his silhouette.

'You want to come up here with me? It's very sweet here.'

'Listen to you talking about very sweet. You smell like an onion, you do.'

'A little bite of onion and then some gur. It's a tasty combinaton.'

'What's the matter with you? You think girls like to be talked to like this? Don't you have any sisters at home?' Echoing Lata Aunty, Noor added, 'This is not the movies, and you are not a hero.'

'Well, you're no heroine, yourself. And that makes you perfectly suited for a non-hero like me.'

Noor put her hands to her hips and turned to look at him. The darker dark of his silhouette against the night came apart to send a chunk of something flying at her. She caught it and nearly threw it back at him before she realized what it was.

'A gift for my heroine,' he called down to her.

She gnawed at the soft brown chunk of gur, peeling from it ribbons of melting sugar. And though he kept at it with some more hero-heroine dialogue, she ignored him. She needed a moment to figure out the direction to take to the kabadi market. It was a long way past the Sheikh Sarai neighbourhood ahead of her. She should really take a bus but she had left the house without money. And what if Baba were already on his way home? She might arrive at the kabadi market only to find him gone. She cursed herself for delaying on the street outside Haseena's home. Now she would have to walk all the way and keep her eyes peeled so she didn't miss her father coming home on his cycle.

'What's the matter heroine? You're not crying, are you?'

'You be quiet. I am thinking. Something a glue-sniffing baboon like you would know nothing about.'

This he found enormously funny and his laughter followed her as she ran down the road.

She ran, passing the shadowy forms of many others on foot and on their bicycles. Her father was not among them. It was the hour of power cuts and by the time she reached Khirki village the street lights were turned off and if her father had happened by she would not have known him in this dark. When she came to the kabadi market it looked nothing like what she had seen of it in daylight. The lanes were empty. Little stalls, filled with teetering stacks of newspapers twice as high as she was, rose on both sides of her. But there was no one in these stalls. She hopped over the smaller weighing scales and ran around the ones so large they were surely used to weigh trucks. She was trying hard not to imagine ghosts in the deserted streets when she finally saw shadowy forms ahead, at work lifting and bundling and weighing loads. The men who were not busy with work were squatted here and there, singly. She couldn't say why but she was afraid to approach them. She ran up then down the lanes and finally stopped when she found a group of men gathered around a chaiwala. She stood switching her weight from one foot to another till one of the men asked her, 'What's the matter, little one? Are you lost?'

'No.' She replied, 'I am looking for my father.'

Another one of the men tilted his head away from his cup and looking at her with amusement, asked, 'Is your father lost then?'

She wondered why everywhere she went people were in the mood to be funny when the business of her own life was so serious tonight. She decided the inside of her and the outside did not match. Then she wondered if that was true for everyone else, as well. And then she wondered that she was wondering this much. I think a lot was her conclusion. At which the first man said, 'Well, such a serious face. You, I know. You are Mohammad Saidullah's daughter. Yes? You will find him in the lane behind where the plastic is sorted. Turn from back where you came with the newspapers. You might find him near where the trucks are parked.'

It was a compliment, she felt, to be charged with wearing a serious face. There was pleasure in the idea that this compliment was in some way connected to the fact of her being known here as her father's daughter. Yes indeed, she was the serious daughter of her serious father. And these men knew it.

She hurried to follow the man's directions. Ahead were the trucks the man had spoken of, the trucks she had conjectured would be weighed on the larger weighing scales. These trucks were in process of being loaded not just with newspapers and tin cans, but with all manner of stuff—ropes and cloth and black serpents, which as she drew nearer segmented, then came apart to be revealed as tyres. One truck was loaded with what glowed in the dark—thousands of plastic canisters empty of everything except a yellowy light. She stood in amazement in front of it but could not understand how these ordinary canisters, very much like those she used to bring water home from the communal taps, could be so beautiful.

When she circled the truck she saw what lit them was simply a kerosene lantern. It hung from the roof of a little gunny sack shelter. The men standing underneath it were stooped, the structure was that low. The charpai on which they should have been seated if they had wanted to be comfortable, stood empty. Even as she watched, one man backed from the group. She understood he was backing from the jabbing finger of one of the other men. The other men advanced as a group. Though he backed out till he had retreated from the structure this man remained stooped. His stoop was one of apology. His hands were in front of him. They were placed, palms together in pleading. She could not hear his words that were spoken softly. But the men who backed him out from the structure and who stood tall outside of it spoke loudly.

'What are you accusing us of, Mohammad Saidullah? How can we take advantage of you? You know the trouble we are in? They are putting an incinerator in. This will burn plastic yes, and it will burn our business with it. What will be left for us to buy and sell? You can't recycle ashes, can you?

'You are a lucky man. You have a son who earns. So what if he is throwing his weight around a bit. Go home and show him what a father's hand feels like? And then you take it easy. It is your time to rest. Instead you come here to create trouble for others who have to struggle to make ends meet.

'Why do you hold your hand out to us? We should be begging from you.'

The man, who spoke, joined his palms together in imitation of Mohammad. Another man laughed harshly. He cut his laugh off abruptly and pushed Mohammad out into the street.

'So the municipal worker has asked you to pay hafta to keep your route at Panchsheel and you decide to point a finger at us? Do you see us getting rich on hafta? If we are getting rich then what are we doing here buying garbage from you?

'We have only one piece of advice for you, if you don't want to pay hafta, then make way for those who will. The man you are complaining about has a family to feed. As for paying us, that's not hafta. That's just the rising cost of doing business.'

'But I paid you,' Mohammad cried out.

The man who had complained about the plastic incinerator put his hand on Mohammad's shoulder. They looked for a moment like two friends conferring over something mundane. He sent Mohammad sprawling to the street and turned back to the shop.

From within the group of men, someone said, 'Now why did you do that, Raiz?' But Raiz was already inside the gunny sack shelter and the others followed him.

Noor could not hear the words of the man they left lying on the street. But she could hear the soft hiss of the faraway kerosene lamp. She could not hear his words, but she could feel them. He was speaking of her—something to do with her schooling and with her growing.

'My daughter,' she imagined him mumble. Why hadn't she noticed that these days, even at home, her father hardly spoke; he only mumbled like this. She wheeled from the scene and went to the other side of the truck full of glowing bottles. She crouched on the ground, trembling, a feeling of panic rising in her, certain only that her father must not see her here. She counselled this panic to subside. 'You are thirteen years old. You will learn to ride a bicycle. You will show these men.' But the panic kept coming, pushing up from inside her till it was in her mouth, a salty taste and thin trickle she spat. With the spitting she was released; she ran past the chai stall and the men outside it, through the ghost streets till she was at the entrance to the market. She waited between tilting towers of newspaper for her father to emerge. And while she waited she rehearsed the lie she would tell him.

'I just got here Baba. Ammi sent me to find you. But I didn't want to go in because it is so dark. I am so glad you came and found me. Baba, Ammi sent me to tell you that she wants us to eat outside and come home slowly. She has wiped the house down with kerosene because just today she found termites in the cupboard. She showed them to me. The termites nests. Made of mud. In our cupboard.'

13

Shouting in Two Lanes

Saturday morning, January 26, gave slow way to Saturday afternoon, January 26. And very slowly it was Saturday evening. And it was still January 26. Republic Day. A day when the tenants of Prakash Lumber building got together to watch the Republic Day parade on TV. She had spent most of the day in her home, hiding from the noisy cheer next door, praying no one would push the curtain at the doorway aside, to look in to see where Mohammad and Ameena were, and what of the children, Noor and Talib?

Noor crept out of the house and down the stairs. She paused at the top of the street. Ahead she saw the line at the taps was long. She couldn't bring herself to approach it. The line had been similarly long and tightly strung in the morning. Then her approach had resulted in the line coming momentarily apart as a buzzing sped from one end of it to the other.

Noor stood hesitating for too long at the entrance to the street. An unfolding movement under the tree nearby, and a length of sheet opened as Suneeta Aunty stretched her way out of sleep. She rose, blotting the light from the entry way. A moment later she was conducting swift trade in gossip. Her heavy iron press had been allowed to cool off when she retired for her afternoon nap. Now it waited for its evening infusion of coal and for that other trade—crushed clothes in exchange for smooth in exchange for a few coins. Children gathered to wait patiently and impatiently for Suneeta Aunty's attention to turn to their bundles. But she was immersed in the newest instalment of the ongoing saga of the second-floor Muslim household and its errant son. 'A brand new suit-coat and pant from Hasan Chacha? What are you saying? A brand new suit-coat and pant for what? For how much money?' A further jumble of words were exchanged among the excited women.

In the shifting crowd of those waiting, a child stood trembling. His mother's emissary in the battle of life, he held a once blue and white striped shirt now singed brown all over by some particularly energetic pressing Suneeta Aunty had administered it. In his anxiety to be done, he discharged into the crowd the abuse his mother had not coached him in. What burst from his mouth was not: 'Do you think we don't know the difference between a pressed shirt and a burnt one? You think we pay you to burn our clothes?' His mother's words were mislaid like the stripes on the shirt he waved energetically. He cursed fluently and bleatingly, 'Prostitute. Bitch. I will beat you till you are dead. I will kick you and shout you and fall you. You hen with a head like a cauliflower.' Children howled with laughter. Suneeta turned slowly, glanced his way and he fled, still waving the shirt, his burnt battle flag.

In turning from the boy Suneeta spied Noor and called her forward. 'You didn't bring any clothes today? Doesn't your mother want any clothes pressed?'

This was Noor's cue to mention casually and unconcernedly, 'My mother is gone to visit her family in Gurgaon.' She had rehearsed the words for those who would ask at the taps. But as in the morning so now, she was incapable of being casual. The words faltered from her, 'My mother is gone to visit her family in Gurgaon.' Suneeta nodded sagely at this admission of guilt. 'Her home, eh? And who is to bring your brother home then? Or is it that he is gone to Gurgaon, as well?' Noor nodded yes, then no, then her head shaking every which way she turned and fled in the direction the bleating boy had taken.

Suneeta Aunty's words followed her, 'Never mind. All will be well soon.' These were not words intended to soothe her. And they didn't. They contained in them the accusation that all did not seem to be well at her home. And this was the very thing Noor felt to be most important at the moment: not that all should be well at her home, but that all should seem to be well. Accordingly she had spent the previous night blocking her ears against the shouted accusations that her mother had aimed at her father. The same accusations had found their mark and travelled from there to all of the neighbours, none of whom had blocked their ears. And when her mother had left late in the night with a bag of clothes Noor had unblocked her ears long enough to shake her head against her mother's entreaty that Noor leave with her.

Noor had stayed so she could lie stiffly at one end of the bed and pretend to sleep while her father mumbled and groaned his way through wakefulness. She had woken in the morning and prepared tea and breakfast; she'd brought water from the taps; served the meal of roti and potatoes into the communal plate; seated across from her father, she'd pushed pieces of roti into the mound of potatoes, brought some to her mouth and found herself unable to swallow any of it. Her father ate without looking up at her. She swept the house and watered the plants and when the call for prayer came, she prayed. She had wanted all of the bustling and noise of sweeping and praying and chopping vegetables to push from the house the absence of her mother. She prayed for her mother to return soon.

*

She ran past the taps, her plastic canisters rapping against her legs. Arriving below Haseena's balcony, she stood panting. A boy standing in Haseena's neighbouring balcony called down, 'I told you this morning. You are the same one that came this morning, aren't you? They are gone for their village. They left late last night. Didn't you hear all the shouting here last night?'

But the shouting in Haseena's lane had not travelled to Noor's which in any case had been filled with its own shouting. Noor had run to Haseena's lane in the morning full of the need to tell her friend everything, to have Haseena who had lived without a mother for as long as forever to explain to Noor how the impossible could be done for even one day. And this same neighbour-boy had told her then what she had not wanted to believe. She had run here again hoping the boy would be gone and that in his place Haseena would come down to listen to Noor's woes.

'What good is she as a friend if she is never going to be here when I need her?' Noor spoke through clenched teeth. And really she was so frightened at this point she had to clench her teeth to keep them from chattering.

'What did you say?'

'Nothing. I didn't say anything.'

'You're at Jyotimala School, aren't you? Same as Haseena?'

'Yes.'

'You might as well tell them at school she is not coming back.'

'Why don't you tell the school yourself since you know so much.'

'Well I would, but I don't go to that school.'

He looked at her triumphantly. Then seeing no further challenge from her he leaned over the balcony railing and in an almost whisper, spoke to her conspiratorially. 'She put up a fight you know. She didn't want to go. But her father made her. He was just determined. No one knows why he was determined. But he was just determined.'

Noor didn't want to know why or of what it was Haseena's father had been determined. But the boy volunteered the information as if granting her the very biggest favour in the world.

'Well, if you must know, her father said he is determined that she shouldn't go to school anymore.'

And when Noor didn't reply, the boy went on as if she had. 'Well you might say, what's wrong with school? You listen to me and I will tell you.'

The boy took up the arms-crossed-behind-the-back, legs-apart stance Noor knew instantly: a speechmaker. At whatever school it was he attended, this boy must make all the speeches. Probably he was even sent to other schools to represent his school in speech competitions. Any minute now he would begin wagging his finger at her and addressing her as 'Honoured Madam Principal.'

But in this instance, the speechmaker boy, perhaps sensing the limitations of time and of his only audience's interest, had already waded into the thick of his speech: 'That is what our generation would say. But those of his generation, and by that I mean Haseena's father's generation, they think differently. Instead, they need to be modern in their thinking as we are.'

'Oh, it had nothing to do with school.'

Noor and the boy turned to the speaker who stood next to Noor. She jumped back a little, in surprise. It was tall Amit, Amit the pervert. So this was his neighbourhood as well as Haseena's. Noor had not known. She inched away from him.

'There's any number of other reasons Saleem Chacha needs Haseena back in their village. And no, none of them have anything to do with school. Saleem Chacha's mother died just a few months back. And his brothers have shown up at the family home. Her father needs Haseena there to make sure his brothers don't leave him out and claim all the land for themselves.

'Or,' Amit spoke with a small smile, 'her father wants her there to claim all the land in his name. Although god knows how a girl can do any such thing. Or,' and here Noor was sure his smile turned evil, 'he plans to marry Haseena off to one of her cousins and that's another way the land will stay all in the family, if you know what I mean.'

'But, but,' Noor spluttered, 'Haseena is only in Class VIII. Like me.'

'Like you?' Again that small smile.

But the speechmaker was underway. 'There is no greater loss to the development of our nation than the loss of the girl child. Be she given in marriage at too young an age or be she left without an education or be she never born, our nation suffers.'

Noor could have hurled a rock at him, one big enough to stuff his mouth shut.

She turned to Amit and spoke to him for the first time in her life. 'So she is gone?'

'Yes. There was a big to-do because she cried and ran into that boy's house. So we all came to know. She was asking people, anyone at all, to help her. But people agreed,' and here Amit shrugged his thin shoulders helplessly, 'it is for a father to decide what is best for his daughter.'

'But she is my friend and...'

'And you have your troubles. You must solve them without your friend. She has her own troubles to tend to.'

Noor backed away from Amit. If Haseena were here she would understand. Understand what? Noor couldn't say. Something. Something to do with Amit and what he was saying.

She couldn't just turn and run. No, she would first say thank you. She did.

'Thank you,' she mumbled, and turning she walked back through Haseena's lane on shaky legs.

At the mouth of the lane instead of turning left toward the public taps and then home, she turned right. Immediately, she was in the tight intersection of two lanes; the corner where she stood unfolded in front of her in a fan of shops wedged side-by-side. Counters overhung the gutter that ran along the lane to better drain the animals butchered within the shops. Old blood lay pooled black, and the walls were spattered orange and green. Four of the shops were bright with light that bounced off white tiled walls from long tubes overhead. In front of four shops carcasses hung pearly pink and blue, striped in ribs, missing their heads and hooves. But the fifth shop, Haseena's father's, was closed. The counter pulled up and secured to the opening rendered its front a blank wooden board. She knew then Haseena was gone. She cried in gulping noisy sobs that broke from her. A kitten sated on the butcher's bits and bobs rubbed itself against her legs, hungry for her touch. The business of buying and selling carried on around her.

She stood there for such a long time the kitten changed from a purring fur puddle at her feet to an irritated then a vengeful creature of claws and teeth. She kicked it gently and it walked with its tail high and curved at the tip. Newer customers replaced old ones many times over. She remembered she had dinner to make. Already she was a day behind in washing clothes. But she could make up for that tomorrow since there was no school on Sunday. Tomorrow she would do all over again what she had done today—the sweeping, the cooking, the washing. What would happen on Monday? How would Baba eat while she was at school? And who would clean and wash? And would Baba remain in bed on Monday as he had all this day?

14
Shilpa Ma'am Intervenes

Monday morning assembly was a mess. Shilpa Ma'am kept shaking her head and wondering out loud, 'I don't know what's gotten into Class VIII C.'

Because there wasn't enough space in the courtyard, classes took it in turn each week to line up along the two sets of stairs that climbed up from the courtyard. The stairs were narrow and the only way to fit a whole class in one stairway was to get students to squeeze in tighter than when they stood in the courtyard. Led by Poonam, the girls declared to Shilpa Ma'am they weren't going to squeeze into the same stairwell as the boys. 'You can put us anywhere Ma'am but we won't stand with the boys of Class VIII C.'

'But tell me, Poonam, what is this all about? These boys are like your brothers. Haven't you all grown up together since nursery class? Enough. Now get into line before Principal Ma'am comes over here to see what is happening?'

With more coaxing and cajoling she shooed the girls up the stairs. Poonam wore an air of triumph. The boys, almost to the last one, hung their heads. Only, Santosh did more than hang his head; he winked from under his hung head. Noor jerked her head to see if this wink was aimed at anyone else. Josy looked blankly at her. No, Santosh was not winking at anyone else. She flushed, remembering just a day ago they had waved to each other in the market. Shilpa Ma'am had caught the wink, as well. And Noor's discomfort.

'Santosh?'

'Yes, Ma'am.'

'Santosh, I don't know what this is all about. But I suspect you do. And Poonam, you as well. The two of you please come with me to the stage.'

There was an audible sucking in of breath. A few of the girls actually clasped their hands together as if they were ready to step forward and plead for their leader's life. But Shilpa Ma'am continued in her quiet undramatic voice, 'I want you both to lead us in the national anthem today. And by the end of the day I want all the girls and boys in Class VIII C to return to being friends.'

Noises of dissent and assent followed. A very stiff Poonam, future head of every neighbourhood association in which she would live, and a very smirky Santosh, soon to leave school and turn into a full-time onion chopper, took the stage together; the squeezed-together-to-fit-in-one-stairway students of Class VIII C managed to find the room to expand their lungs and sing.

Jana Gana Mana always made the morning tightness in Noor's stomach relent. And this morning was no exception. It must have had a similar pacifying effect on everyone else because soon after morning assembly her classmates turned and climbed the staircase two by two, boys in their line and girls in theirs, chattering so loudly with one another, Maths Sir shouted at them in Bengali to 'Be quiet. Or I will kick you lot into the next century.'

The end of Girls vs Boys meant Noor could speak to Ajith. She looked for him and she saw he was looking for her. She tried a smile and felt how unused her face had become to smiling in the last two days. He didn't smile, just nodded gravely at her. And she thought he might know already—about Talib Bhaiya, about Ammi. Or maybe about Haseena. Maybe all of it.

During writing period Shilpa Ma'am handed out the diaries. She handed Noor Haseena's diary as well as her own. She spoke quietly to Noor. 'Noor, I understand Haseena's father has withdrawn her from school. You live near each other, don't you? Will you take this to her? I want her to have this. It is not something I can just throw away. Remember what I said about your notebooks. It is a sacred space, an extension of your own mind.'

Noor should have said, 'No, Ma'am, she used to live near me.

But not anymore.' She accepted the notebook, nodding that yes, she would take it home to Haseena. She would do no such thing of course. She would take it home to read it. And really she wasn't very sure what Shilpa Ma'am meant about the notebook as a sacred place. Sacred places had to do with temples and gods and festivals, not notebooks.

At lunch period she allowed Ajith to leave the class first and a few minutes later she trailed over to his place against the wall. From the ground where he was seated, he squinted up at her. Once again she thought sadly how small and dark he was. At the same time she thought how much she wanted to grab the hand he was shading his eyes with and squeeze it.

'So how are you going to get her notebook to Haseena?'

'I don't know.'

'Well then you shouldn't have taken it. How would you like it if someone else had your notebook with them?'

'Well, I'll go over to her house after school and give it to her.'

'She won't be there. You know that.'

She shrugged. She had thought Ajith might know already. Probably many in the class did. So lying to him wasn't exactly lying, was it? Not when she knew he would catch her at it. She cleared her throat and tried again.

'I meant I would take it to her home and leave it there for when she returns. She will return, you know.'

Ajith lapsed back into one of his long silences. She didn't mind. She concentrated on thinking her thoughts and she imagined he was thinking his. Then she imagined he could probably read her thoughts. He was so smart after all. And then she imagined that wouldn't be any different than if he was reading her notebook. Then she flushed remembering that after he got through about a hundred pictures of her green bicycle and her various letters to her aunt and to the chief minister he would come to today's entry: Ajith Ajith Shivkumar. Shivkumar, Ajith. Ajith Ajith Ajith....

'Fine then. I am going to go right now to return the notebook to Shilpa Ma'am.'

She got up from the ground and made an elaborate show of dusting her skirt but when he didn't take the opportunity to tell her that she was good to return the notebook, she left. In the time between taking the notebook from her desk and heading in the direction of the staff lunch room she stopped at the bathroom and locking herself into an empty stall she opened the notebook. Skipping pages, she read in great gulps; beginning toward the end of the notebook, she swallowed as many words as she could cram into herself, now flipping forward and now backward through Haseena's diary.

When the bell rang she dried her eyes with her skirt and pushing her way against the students streaming into school, she ran outside. Ajith was just picking his things up from the ground. She thrust the notebook toward him.

'Fine. I read it. You know now. You return it to Shilpa Ma'am.'

Ajith hid his hands behind his back.

15

Gulping Haseena's Notebook

January 14, 2013

It's been five days. Mohan came running to me in the market. Other children were behind him when he came running to me. They were smiling with him. They said to me, the men are taking your Blackie. I didn't know what they meant but I immediately started running. It was like my feet knew. When I came to the street in front of my house there was a truck and a man was dragging Blackie from the staircase. He was holding a long iron stick and it was bent like a hook and it was around Blackie's neck and the man pulled the stick up in the air and Blackie could not make a sound he went up in the air and his neck broke. I saw his tongue. He was thrown to the back of the truck with other dogs. I couldn't see inside the truck. He must have lain there dying. All the children were smiling and waiting for me to say something or cry but I didn't do anything. I just went upstairs and stood by the front door. There on the ground Blackie had done his toilet all over the front of the house. They had chased him to the house. He came to the house to look for me. He thought I will save him. He did the toilet in fear. It was runny and yellow and streaks of it went from our house down the stairs where he was dragged.

My father came home later and shouted at me why I had not cleaned the mess in front of the house. But I couldn't clean it. I was sitting and thinking why is my father like this. Why cannot he see that I am crying? I kept sitting till he stood over me and shouted and Aseef started crying. Then I cleaned it. The cement was clean afterward. I cleaned even the cloth afterward. I cleaned my hands. But I cannot clean Blackie's fear.

September 21, 2012

Last week my periods began at school. I am thirteen and a half years old. If my mother was still here, what would she say to me? The senior girls who came to help me said it would be fun for me to stay home from school. They said I should ask my mother for pads. I don't want to stay home from school. I had to go home and tell my father. He took me to Chand Uncle and Aunty's house. Aunty showed me what to do.

October 10, 2012

Today Reena Ma'am called me outside class and she scolded me for sending Aseef to nursery without his lunch, I tried to tell her I always make lunch for him. I don't know what he is doing with his lunch, if he is throwing it away or giving it away. Or most likely, he is eating it on his way to school. I told Reena Ma'am to ask him if I don't make lunch for him. But she wasn't listening. She kept saying since Aseef doesn't have a mother, I am to be his little mother. I should make certain he has food and he wears his sweater now that it is winter and soon it will be raining and he will catch a cold. I started crying. I got angry at her for making me cry. Then she started to put her arm around me. This is why she was making me cry, so she could put her arm around me. I hate her. She must have thought she was being my mother. I hate her. I will write more tomorrow because Shilpa Ma'am says no more today.

October 11, 2012

What I was saying about Reena Ma'am. I told her, ask Ruku. I make lunch for her. I make lunch for me. I make lunch for my father. Why will I not make lunch for Aseef? Aseef is my little brother. Why does everyone tell me how sad it is for him to not have a mother? I also don't have a mother. Why doesn't anyone say anything about that?

October 24, 2012

I have been staying home all the time. I don't know my lessons. When Aseef was a baby, Aunty took him from me so I could go to school. But now when Aseef is sick or Ruku is sick I have to stay home. Aunty says I am old enough to take care of them and remain home since I am old enough to not need studies. Now I am back in class and I don't understand anything that is happening because I have missed so many lessons. If I get sick then I am not going to tell anyone. Aseef sometimes pretends he is sick. But last week he had chicken pox. I put oil on his skin and bandaged his hands so he wouldn't scratch. I stayed awake all night telling him stories. I felt so good that I could take care of him. Maybe it is better if I don't return to school.

September 27, 2012

Yesterday I looked at Noor writing in her notebook. She was drawing a picture. Of a cycle, of course. She is very silly. It is no use trying to talk to her about anything. She doesn't listen to anything that isn't about her.

January 3, 2012

Father asked me if I liked when I was in the village. I said yes, but there was nothing to do there. He said I was busy taking care of Dadi last time I went and that's why I had no time to make friends. He said he will take me there again and I will see there are many girls I can play with. I told father I have many friends here. But this is not really true. I only have Blackie these days. Everyone thinks it is dirty for me to touch Blackie. Poor Blackie. He isn't black anymore. He is pink from the scratching disease. But he makes me laugh when he scratches himself. He looks so foolish. When I laugh he comes to me and wags his tail and I can see from his mouth he is laughing also. But sometimes he scratches till there is blood. I know there is a medicine for Blackie. But how can I get money for it? I remember him when he was born. He was black all over with brown patches only on his face. He was so round then and his whole body shook when he wagged his tail. Round and round he shook. Even his eyes were round. Everything changes for the worse.

November 9, 2012

I am tired of Noor. A few weeks ago I went and drew a line between us. I hope Shilpa Ma'am will soon change our seats. But maybe I will have to wait till next year. But I don't want to wish next year to come soon. I think father is planning for me to go to the village next year. This time it will be forever. I will have to live there where I don't know anybody. I hope next year never comes. Even if Noor always sits next to me I don't mind as long as I can stay here.

November 12, 2013

We are still writing letters in class. Letters to ask for leave of absence. Letters to ask for meetings to take place. Also we wrote to the railway minister's office to request him to open more ladies' compartments. I am tired of these letters. Shilpa Ma'am doesn't know that I will never have a job where I can ask for a leave of absence. What use are these letters to me?

December 17, 2012

Father and his friends were talking about politics and how bad the leaders are. I told father about the letter to the railway minister. He laughed in front of his friends. But I think he was laughing with happiness. I made fried chicken for them to eat. He was happy with me. If I cook good food he will let me stay. But I cannot cook chicken every day. I can only cook what father brings from the market. When he has leftover meat he brings it. But it is always mutton. I wish sometimes we could eat mangoes. But I know if I say that he will tell me I can eat all the mangoes I want in the village. I won't say anything to him about mangoes. I will ask Chand Aunty to tell me how to cook better. After his friends left, father prayed and blessed me. I thought he is feeling good and I can talk to him about staying in school. He replied I can go to school in the village.

January 4, 2013

I told father, who will take care of Aseef and Ruku if I go to the village. He said Ruku will take care of Aseef. But Ruku is only eight years old. Father said you were also once only eight years old. I wanted to cry when he said this. I know he is sad for me. But I cannot tell him everything and he cannot tell me everything. Is it like that for everyone? Does everyone carry things in their heart they cannot tell to anyone? I don't remember mother. But I think I remember a feeling of telling her everything. Maybe father also told her everything. Sometimes I think I can try to tell Noor's mother. But it makes no sense because Noor and I are not friends anymore. What reason will I give to visit her mother? And what will I tell her mother even if I visit her? There is nothing to tell. I don't want to go to the village. I am lonely there. More lonely than when I am here. If I go away I will miss Aseef and Ruku. I will miss Blackie. I will even miss father.

January 17, 2013

I don't know what is wrong with Noor. She keeps sitting in her side of the line. She never looks here. I look at her but she never sees me. Nowadays she is sitting at lunch with Ajith. She doesn't know but people are talking about her and Ajith. Soon they won't just talk about them. Soon people will start saying bad things about them both. She is so stupid. If I was still her friend I would warn her to not talk to him. Not when he is by himself. Maybe I am jealous. She at least talks to someone. I have no one to talk to.

January 18, 2013

Poonam is always eating the best food from every one's tiffin at lunch. But she has pocket money and treats us to samosa. I know she only does that to keep everyone following her. She does everything to make people follow her. Even when she takes the best food from everyone's tiffin it is just to show she can. If someone ever says no she will know they are not following her.

Then she will punish them. Like when she told Josy to sit and not play catch with us. I hate playing catch. I hate all games. I don't know why this is. I have never liked playing. When everyone is running and playing I have to pretend it is fun. I wish they would stop running. I would rather talk. Today there was a fight in class and Poonam said none of us should talk to the boys anymore.

January 24, 2013

My periods didn't come for many many months after the first few times, at least three months. But it is back. I didn't tell Chand Aunty when they had stopped, so that she would keep giving me the pads every month. I stored them up in the trunk. This way when they send me to the village I will have as many as I need for a long time. I don't want to use cloth and wash it. It is impossible to hide the cloth. Where am I supposed to hang it to dry? Not outside. Here we just throw the pads in the back gutter. Sometimes it is scary because I have to wait till night to go out and throw. I don't want father asking me why I am opening the door at night. So far he doesn't say anything to me about anything.

January 23, 2013

Politics is all father talks about these days. He says if politicians are handled correctly then we can get what we want from them. Father votes in the village. But he told his friends he will change his voter card to make it so he can vote in the city. Maybe this means he wants to forget about the village. This is good for me if it is true. Father says he wants a voter card for the city so he can vote here and this way he can handle the politicians here correctly. So how is he going to handle politicians correctly? Already it is time for another election. I think about how difficult it is to handle people correctly. No one can handle Poonam correctly. She handles them right back. When she cried after Santosh found Bhawna's pad, I thought now she is done for. But right away she knew she had made a mistake and then she made us all follow her in the fight against the boys. Everyone is too afraid to tell Poonam they don't want to follow her. I understand. I too am too afraid to tell father I don't want to go to the village. In the beginning when I said it he used to listen. Then there was a chance for me. Now he gets angry to make me afraid to ask. But if I don't ask then how will he know what I want?

January 10, 2013

Yesterday I was walking in the market. I was happy. I didn't know I was happy. Why was I happy? I didn't know something bad was going to happen. Mohan came running to me in the market. I didn't know till then I was happy. Even when he came running I was still happy. And he was smiling. I didn't know that what he was going to tell me was going to end my happiness. I was walking with Poonam and she bought a Five Star chocolate to share. She always has money from her father-mother. I was still tasting the Five Star bar when Mohan told me. How soon happiness goes. Only when it is gone you know it was there. Why is it like that? Oh Blackie. I will write your name. Blackie.

16
Of Plastic

In the weeks following her mother's departure, there was little time for Noor to miss Haseena. Her father got on his bicycle every morning and rode away as smartly as ever. And he was able to do this because Noor washed and starched his kurta, his pyjamas and his topi. Her father stopped her only from her efforts to press his clothes, telling her he could afford to pay Suneeta Aunty to do this work. When she started to protest that she could indeed handle the press, he shouted that he was not about to pay doctor's fees for treating a burnt arm or god forbid a burnt face. She gaped at him. It was unbelievable to her that her father might shout at her. But this morning scene of tension followed by an explosion of angry words became a daily event and Noor learned to hunch her back and turn from her father.

As for his argument that he was not going to be responsible for her burning herself while pressing his clothes, she responded by muttering that she was more likely to get burnt cooking on the stove she could not seem to get used to lighting. Its hiss was only less frightening than the high-pitched and long-drawn scream of the pressure cooker letting out steam.

Most days the daily morning tension ended with her father looking mournfully at his plate of food, then shaking his head, 'I will eat it later, daughter. It looks good but I am late now.'

And so though he rode away dressed smartly in clothes she had whitened following Lata Aunty's direction—laying them flat on the roof, weighed down with small rocks and exposed to sunlight—his stomach was empty and Noor did not have the heart to eat more than one roti herself. She ate it rolled up with a lick of sugar down its centre, all the while her feet running her to school.

She was late for assembly as she had been daily since her

mother left. She stood at the entrance to the school's courtyard and as she did daily, she scanned the Class VIII line to see if Haseena was back, somehow miraculously standing in line, waving Noor toward the space saved for her, a space into which Noor would slide quickly before Bengali Sir set eyes on her.

There was no such space and there was no Haseena. Instead Bengali Sir's hand pressed down on her shoulder. Noor swung around and cowered.

'Sorry, Sir. Sorry.'

He indicated with his finger to his lips she should be quiet. The assembly was yet in progress. He indicated with a crooked finger she should follow him. Outside, they reached the compound. Without a word, he handed her the board and she hoisted it onto her head. She hid her relief from him. It was only the board, after all. She had been afraid of something worse. She wasn't sure what this worse something could be. But she had worried the school would come up with something new, something horrible to deal with a girl who was late nearly every day of the previous three weeks. Had anyone ever been late as often as she was?

Bengali Sir turned back to the assembly to catch more latecomers Noor took her first step and then a few more of the tiny circle she was required to take around the compound in front of the school. And she sat down and cried. Yes, Haseena too had been late like this. Haseena, who it was clear now been late for the same reasons Noor was now late. Because of meals that needed preparing and tiffins that needed packing. Because of clothes that were mysteriously grey after each use and that therefore needed diligent effort to whiten, clothes that were then forbidden to be pressed. Because of Baba's hungry stomach as he rode off to someplace that was not work. Where did he go all day now that he did not go to Panchsheel to collect kabadi from the homes there?

And why when her mother called and spoke to her father did Noor slink away from the house? And if, as in the beginning her father was to catch her by the arm and attempt to place the receiver in her hand, why did she, who longed to talk to her mother, respond with fists shoved into her pockets and a shake of her head in refusal? If Haseena were here, would she know to explain Noor to herself? And where was Haseena, and how did she spend her days? Was she alone in her home in the village?

Bengali Sir did not forget to release her to attend class. The five others with boards on their heads ran in, pushing past Noor who dragged herself into class and took her seat just as Shilpa Ma'am finished handing out diary notebooks for their daily ten minutes of writing.

February 15, 2013
Dear Haseena,

Noor blinked hard to push the tears back into her eyes. Bent over the page, she wrote steadily.

> I read your notebook last month. I am sorry I read it. I know it is supposed to be private. I am sorrier that I was always drawing and writing about my bicycle and never even asked you what was happening with you. I will never write or draw about wanting a green bicycle ever again. And I am really, really sorry I am always doing things that result in having to say sorry to you. You are my best friend in the whole world. Even if you are far away in your village. Even then you are my better friend than Ajith. I know you know about him. I read it in your diary. And if you must know, I no longer talk to Ajith. Ever since I read your diary I have not spoken to him. He just thinks he is so much better than anybody else. If I am ever able to get a bicycle, it doesn't have to be a green one, I will try to find your village and ride my bicycle there. I will return your notebook to you. But you are right about one thing, the reason I don't have a bicycle is because I am afraid to learn how to ride one. I mean I am not afraid to fall from the bicycle. And I don't

> even care if everyone laughs at me for riding a bicycle. So I don't know what I am afraid of but I know I am afraid. You would probably know. If you were here you would explain it all to me. I don't know how you are not afraid of anything. I was afraid of your father. That is why I never came inside your house when you asked me to. How are you able to be not afraid of him? How are you able to do the work in the house and keep your father and brother and sister happy? I want to ask you these questions because now I have to live in my house without my mother and brother. How can I manage this, Haseena?

Noor hastily shut her book as Shilpa Ma'am extended a hand for it. It seemed she had come to Noor for her book only after she had collected everyone else's.

'Good work writing so much, Noor.'

Noor mumbled her 'yes, Ma'am,' and continued the letter in her head as Shilpa Ma'am moved onto discussing plastic bags.

Sometime later Bhawna's prodding snapped her from her thoughts back to the classroom.

'Vote,' Bhawna hissed.

And Noor raised her hand to add her vote to the 'yes' side of the debate. She did not know what she had voted for and little cared. Except now they were counting the 'no' votes, of which there was apparently one: Ajith's.

'This is very interesting, Ajith. Can you explain to the class why you have voted no.'

Ajith stood up, but for once seemed to not have an answer to venture. Noor looked at him with interest. Her recent cry, the time spent writing to Haseena, and the self-absorption that had followed left her with a pleasant sense of detachment. The classroom was hazy and Ajith hazier still. Why should she care about him standing there by himself, his eyes fastened to the ceiling. She had avoided him in the last few weeks since reading Noor's notebook. But it couldn't be helped. Her eyes followed his to the floor and she saw he was drawing on the ground with the toe of his shoe—circles and more circles.

'It's all right, Ajith. You may take your seat.'

And still he continued standing. Now the class was truly interested. Noor had to give her head a shake and then she too was interested.

'Ma'am, they are building a new plastic incinerator near the maidan.'

'Yes, Ajith. It's good to know a boy in this class pays attention to what happens in his community. We must all reduce the use of plastic. And everyone who voted "yes" is indicating they are willing to take their own bag to market every day so they will not ask for their groceries to be placed in a plastic bag. If the whole city will follow this rule, how much better off we would all be. Can there be a doubt this is the best course?'

'Ma'am but the plastic incinerator is not good for us to have next to the maidan. Some people are saying it is bad for the air. And since the air goes into our lungs, that's bad too.'

'This is a good point, Ajith. But we were discussing cutting down on the use of plastic bags, weren't we? How is that related to the plastic incinerator? And certainly if we reduce the use of plastic then we can reduce the use of the incinerator, as well.'

Poonam was waving her hand wildly at this point. Shilpa Ma'am smiled at her and she jumped to her feet.

'Ma'am, we have to eliminate the use of plastic bags because cows are choking on these bags and dying. We should not use plastic bags for this reason. And if any plastic bags are used then afterward they should be burnt so they don't lie around to choke cows.'

'That's true, Poonam. Earlier, this exact point was made. Was it by Shubham? It is a good point. Cows are one more reason for us to stop using plastic bags. But Ajith, you seem to have a reason to not ban the use of plastic bags. Ajith, will you share your reason with the class?'

Having abandoned the circles on the ground, Ajith was back to looking up at the ceiling. Shilpa Ma'am turned away from him. 'Ajith, you may sit down, but if you think of a reason to support your "no" vote, please share it with the class.'

Ajith took his seat and the class heaved a sigh of relief. Shilpa Ma'am's class was often interesting in the way in which it pushed students into discussions far beyond what was in the textbook or in their daily lives. But interesting things were often quite provoking, as well. And Noor, who was studying Ajith could see something was truly bothering him. Seated, he kept his hands in his pockets. From the way his pockets pulled, she guessed the hands were clenched.

Shilpa Ma'am returned to the board and wrote 'Incinerator' off to the side of the tally of 'yes' and 'no' votes.

Thirty-eight 'yes' votes and only one 'no.' Noor thought it was a good thing the city was going to stop using plastic bags that choked cows. Certainly, the bags were everywhere. They blew about on the streets, and carried higher still they festooned the branches of trees. Filled with garbage of every kind they gathered in mountains along the naala. Why, she herself threw a bag or two filled with kitchen waste into the naala daily. And she had seen the men who waded into that pile and sorted through it for what could be salvaged. She shuddered at the thought of stepping foot in the naala, imitating the shudder her mother practised whenever she passed by the men who did this work.

She looked again in Ajith's direction. She wanted to catch his eye and smile at him. Maybe somehow indicate to him that she understood. Even though, of course, she did not understand anything. Why would he vote 'no' for something when everyone else was voting 'yes'? Why would he vote 'no' when even Shilpa Ma'am seemed to be pushing for a 'yes' vote?

Ma'am was always saying everyone should think for themselves. But it was quite clear to Noor there was a right answer to the question of banning plastic bags. She looked again at Ajith and her mind returned to what he had said about a plastic incinerator. There was something about what he said that she was certain was important to her. Something she knew and was now forgetting.

She thought again of the plastic bags in which she threw away the household waste, this time with a twinge. What would she put the garbage in after the plastic bag ban went into effect? But Ma'am was right. The bags choked cows and the naala and they lay under the earth and did not decompose the way paper did. Maybe she would take her garbage to the naala in newspaper bundles. Her father could save some of the newspapers from his rounds. Her heart sank as she acknowledged the truth that it had been weeks and more since Baba came home with kabadi loaded onto the back of his bicycle. His clothes were spectacularly grey when he returned from work and when she washed them, the contact with water released a smell, strange and metallic.

Again she looked over at Ajith and this time he turned in his seat and looked back at her. There was an odd expression on his face. As if, she thought, he wants to say something to me. Suddenly, she was nervous. She ducked her head. She looked away from him. There was a buzzing in the space between her ears, and her jaw ached. She tried to meet his eyes, and tried to make her mouth open in a smile. But he had turned back in his seat.

He looked at me, she sang to herself.

He had indeed looked at her, directly and with urgency. Until now it was she who had been interested in him, in his ideas and in his talk. It was she who had been chasing him. Her cheeks hot, she looked around and yes, Bhawna and even Josy were looking at her, smirks on their faces. She hung her head. So she was a 'boy chaser.' She looked up and Ajith held her gaze. She ducked her head again.

At lunch she walked past the girls huddled in the girls' corner of the field and past the long stretch of the field that belonged to the boys and over to Ajith's spot by the side of the building. Behind her, she was certain the girls' corner was more animated than usual. As for her, she didn't care even if the cricket game on the field came to a halt while the boys took in the spectacle of her chasing Ajith. Opening her tiffin box, she held it out to him.

'I made it myself,' she offered about the omelette sandwich. He shook his head. Of course, she realized, he must be a vegetarian. She snatched the box back and tried to remember if she had ever eaten meat in front of him.

He held his tiffin out to her and she gladly tore a piece of roti and smudging some achar into it she brought it to her mouth. He fiddled with the contents of his box, tore a piece himself and held the box toward her. Nestled under the half torn roti was his omelette. He smiled at her.

'I made it myself.'

'No, you didn't.'

'You're right. My mother made it. And your mother? She isn't back, then?'

'No,' she shook her head.

'That's too bad.'

'It's okay. I am managing. And she will be back soon.'

'Maybe.'

She pushed him then. And he moved a couple inches away from her. They sat for a moment. He got up and methodically clicked shut the four latches on his tiffin box. He placed the box under his armpit and bending, he picked up his books. Before turning to walk away he looked at her with the same expression he had worn in the classroom, the expression of someone who had something urgent to tell her. Something that could be told only to her. In the moment before he spoke she was afraid. The air expanded and contracted above her and she remembered the cheel and the omen she had puzzled over without understanding it.

Don't look away, she commanded herself. And she was glad later that she didn't.

'My father works like your father. But also not like your father. Your father's work is better. You won't see us being allowed to ride like kings from house to house on a bicycle. A bicycle like you say you want to ride. And you say you want to be a kabadiwali. That's some joke. I don't know if women will ever be allowed to do that. But my father is not allowed to. You could say even Muslims have it better than we Dalits have it.'

'The plastic incinerator,' she squeaked. 'Tell me about the plastic incinerator.'

'Have you ever been to Ghazipur? I'll take you there someday. You can come on your Muslim bicycle to see the work we do.'

'Wait,' she called after his retreating back.

He was already running. But she ran behind him and he threw over his shoulder: 'My father used to work there. In Ghazipur. There's a mountain there of everything everyone ever threw away. Even good shoes sometimes. I've gotten many good shoes from there. Well, no one wants a mountain of garbage so the government is taking it all and burning it. Shilpa Ma'am and all of you can vote to get rid of plastic bags, and the government can put in the incinerator in case anyone accidentally uses a bag and needs to burn it up afterward. But as for me I am voting for plastic bags.'

And though she knew the answer, she called after him, 'Why can't he ride a bicycle?'

The face he turned to her was still. He opened his mouth to speak and the still face crumpled. His voice was loud enough to startle the cricket players some distance away. They turned to stare.

'He can ride a bicycle and I can ride a bicycle. We even have a bicycle. He just can't ride it like your father, not from house to house, not to get kabadi. Those jobs are only for people like your father. And anyway I don't want to ride a bicycle like your father. I am going to be an engineer,' he shouted. 'And that's more than you will ever be with your bicycle.'

17

Mohammad Saidullah

When he was a boy his father explained to him that he needed to find his own way. Mohammad couldn't remember how he took the news. He might have been ten at the time. He was not sure of his age on that day, but ever after it became the day he thought of as his birthday. He began life over again on that day.

Of his first life there was little memory: some vague scenes surrounding his home far outside Patna. A tin shed, if he remembered correctly. The lanes he played in. And the man his father entrusted him to. The man with whom he left that day. Among the names and faces he could bring to mind from the period prior to that day, he knew some belonged to his brothers and sisters. But which of the faces belonged to his siblings and which to other children—cousins, perhaps friends—even this, he did not know. His life began over seated on the back of the man's bicycle. The faces were part of the scene from another life that dated from before the day he left with the man. They were there to wave goodbye to him. The man rode away, taking Mohammad with him.

Did his father come to wave him on his way? Mohammad sat straddling the bicycle rack; he twisted in his seat, turning away from the back of the man who rode him away. He tried to look over his shoulder at everything that was receding from him. He made a record of what he saw that day. When he consulted the record, there was no memory of his father shrinking into the distance. Mohammad's father might have been there. He might not have been there. From Mohammad's record-keeping he drew one conclusion, a simple one, built over another thirty-five years, the resolve that his children would starve before they would struggle to remember his face. If they were ever to straddle a bicycle and turn to look over their shoulders, if they were ever to ride away from home, he would be the one pedalling the bicycle. He swore this as often as necessary to convince himself he had the power, if need be, to alter destiny. Mostly, he swore this to himself to give meaning to his past hurt. This hurt, he told himself, was preparation for the pain he must spare his children.

He was ten when he went to live in Patna. At first he cleaned the kitchen, carried water from the well, and washed dishes. Eventually, the man who had brought Mohammad to the house in which he was employed as a cook taught the boy to cook, and thereafter avoided the kitchen himself. One evening, the householder dismissed the cook and Mohammad. Mohammad's cooking was to blame. The next morning the cook dropped him off at the market and that was the last of the man he had called chacha, or uncle.

That evening he squatted outside one eatery and another, finding his place in the line of men who sat waiting for a meal ticket. Families crowding the market with their family-joy would eat at restaurants and before leaving they would perform their charitable duty by buying tickets for so many meals to be fed to so many of the squatting beggars.

It never occurred to him to go looking for his own family. They were two years in his past. A search would have necessitated knowing more than his name, Mohammad. It would have necessitated knowing his father's name and at least some sense of the way to the village in which his family lived.

A year or more of scrapping and he was hired in one of the restaurants he squatted outside, and learned there to dress meat. He was fortunate because his entry as meat-dresser was a jump over a veteran of the shop, Lakshman, whose job it was to rid the shop of offal and other animal waste, and in addition, to clean the bathroom behind the shop. He was grateful that he was Mohammad with no other name, and not Lakshman whose name guaranteed him the job of latrine cleaner. Thus it was Mohammad learned even misfortune has its high and low mark.

He was lucky on many other counts, as he soon discovered. His new employer told Mohammad to call him chacha. But unlike the previous chacha, Rizwan Chacha never knocked Mohammad on his head, not even when he proved himself as uninterested in cooking here as he had been at his last employer's. And instead of a sheet that could only be spread on the hard kitchen floor once all the dishes were washed and packed away, here Mohammad was given a cot away from the smelly shop, at a madrassa presided over by Rizwan Chacha's friend, Mullah Saidullah. The mullah's last name became Mohammad's.

The resentful Lakshman eventually gave in to Mohammad's attempts at friendship, but not without first airing his grievance: 'Pig, you show up from nowhere and think because you are Muslim, same as the rest of the pig Muslims here, you can shove me around.'

Mohammad promptly shoved Lakshman. Lakshman shoved Mohammad to the floor. Mohammad grinned from the floor and producing bubble gum from his pocket, jumped up to wave it in front of Lakshman. Lakshman threw in a last dig, 'Who do you think you are? Is this your father's home for you to go waving bubble gum around?'

'No, it's my chacha's home,' came Mohammad's reply.

The pecking order was established, and once the bubble gum changed hands so was friendship.

When Mohammad was done with his teens, Rizwan's anxious guilt that he had done nothing for Mohammad beyond a bed at the madrassa was replaced with a more serious anxiety. The mullah at the madrassa had come to Rizwan with a complaint. Mohammad, it seemed, remained hunched up in his cot when the other residents of the madrassa, all of them younger than Mohammad, rose at dawn and dusk and marched off two-dozen strong in their sparkling white caps and kurtas to pray at the mosque. The mullah confided to Rizwan Chacha the report the pious among the two-dozen had shared with him. Muhammad's absence at prayer had been prefaced by this lofty statement to the pious: 'If I am to skip prayers to work during the day, there is no reason I cannot skip prayers to rest in the evening. Anyway, I don't see any need for prayer.'

Rizwan Chacha agreed it would not do to let matters stand as they were. Secretly he was less worried about the state of Mohammad's soul. What concerned him more was the rest of the report which described Mohammad's hunched stance on the cot when the rest of the boys returned from the mosque and, still dressed in sparkling white, took to the field to play cricket.

Confronted by the two gentlemen, Muhammad readily, if sulkily, recanted his words, 'I only said I didn't feel like praying. I didn't say anything about not needing to pray.'

The attempt to clear himself theologically with the mullah got him the ear-drubbing he was due. But the matter didn't end there for Rizwan Chacha, who consulted Lakshman. After wiping his nose and spitting to the side, Lakshman offered this: 'I don't know, but I think Mohammad is sad.'

'Why?' Rizwan muttered to himself. And the answer was clear enough. Having taken charge of the boy very nearly as if he were the son to supplement the three daughters at home—'very nearly' since after all he had not thought to take the child home with him and dress him in a school uniform and send him off to school—Rizwan was certain he had some claim to interfering in the boy's affairs. Rizwan remonstrated with himself for not noticing the boy was clearly in need of the kind of direction boys in these troubling times needed from fathers and/or chachas.

So a second confrontation was organized without the aid of the mullah. If Mohammad had been sulky before, he was downright mutinous this time around.

'I feel tired after I work from six in the morning till ten at night without having to give up the few breaks I get to troop off to the mosque at the mullah's orders.'

This should have been Rizwan's cue to grab hold of Mohammad's thin kurta-front as the mullah had in the earlier theological dispute. Though his own children did not work from 6 a.m. till 10 p.m., with breaks for meals and prayers, Rizwan was smote with the same love for the boy he felt for them; he could no more shake this boy than he would his three- four- and five-year-old daughters.

He took the trouble to diagnose the problem. If he had probed Lakshman any further, Lakshman would have saved him the trouble. 'Girls,' Lakshman would have tattled. 'Our hero has his eye on girls.'

As it was, Rizwan came close enough to the truth: 'A girl, it must be,' he concluded. Rizwan kept the conclusion to himself, although his anxiety only sharpened when this first and slightly faulty diagnosis was speedily overtaken by a second, faultier, diagnosis: 'He is lovesick for our Ameena.'

Mohammad was welcome at Rizwan's house, and often came by in the evenings to give an account of shop matters, staying to play ludo with the little girls and to eat Chachi's moderately decent cooking. On a recent visit, Rizwan had stepped out of the living room and returned to find Mohammad bent over something. Rizwan recognized the picture album which his wife kept for display on the centre table alongside the glass vase of red rosebuds beaded with plastic dew drops. The album contained a handful of pictures, all of them so formal as to be forbidding. The youngest subjects in these portraits were so unsmiling they would have looked prematurely aged even if they weren't additionally rendered in black, white and every shade of grey in between.

There was a hushed quality to the boy's stance; he sat neither turning the page nor putting the album away. Rizwan had hesitated a moment before clearing his throat to draw the boy's attention. The boy did not seem to hear him and then Rizwan saw he was staring fixedly at one of the pictures within.

Rizwan had taken the album from Mohammad and passed over the picture with the explanation: 'My cousin, Iqbal's daughter who visited some two years back. Must be a few years younger than you. Fourteen, fifteen, yes, I think that's about the age our Ameena is.' Without thinking about it, Rizwan had moved hurriedly on to other pictures and other explanations.

He had seen something in Mohammad's eyes, something that made him uncomfortable enough that Rizwan had wanted to rush past the moment. Yes, there had been something like tears in the boy's eyes. But Rizwan was no more ready now than in the past to acknowledge the truth of what he had seen that day—a boy and his loneliness.

He rushed instead to his confused but convenient conclusion: that Mohammad was the right age to look at pictures of girls and shed tears. Yes, hadn't Rizwan done the same in his day? Why else would the boy stop at that picture to shed tears if it was not a case of young love? Rizwan sighed at the thought of young love. And sighed again as he realized this was modern love, of the variety that cropped up in movies. This kind of love inevitably ended with feuding families who were reconciled only after the young lovers threw themselves off cliff tops. Oh no, Rizwan needed no such drama. The thing to do was to nip it in the bud and allow the lovers to live, first by letting them love, and in that most sane way in which he and his wife loved. That is, by first getting married, with full blessings of all families. Yes, he would prevail on cousin Iqbal to let Ameena marry Mohammad.

What Rizwan never let himself know, and perhaps it mattered little, was that Mohammad's tears were for the wealth he sensed in the scant two dozen pictures stuck to the plastic pages he had been delicately prising apart and studying. Bound together in that album was something he sensed had once been his and which was lost to him now—the ties of family. It was chance that he had stopped at Ameena's picture that day, overwhelmed by the need to call out for people he could barely picture in his mind. Sister, mother, his soul cried. He had wiped his eyes when the sound of Rizwan Chacha's cough grated against his sorrow.

'Who am I?' was the question that held him to his cot when the other boys headed off to prayer service. The only time Mohammad called his own was the time the other boys were gone from the madrassa. And he needed this time and its attendant silence because this question he asked himself, this question, it shattered him.

A letter went from Patna, Bihar, to Gurgaon, Haryana. Another letter and a round of phone calls later, Mohammad was pulled into the discussion. He would be fronted some money to go into business, to set up shop for himself, hire some boys who would cook and wash dishes, like he had been hired to cook and wash dishes. There would even be a Lakshman in his shop, like there was a Lakshman in Rizwan Chacha's shop. And best of all, he was told, his dowry would include the chance to broaden his horizon. The kebab shop in Delhi that Rizwan Chacha had long dreamt of opening with help of an investment wrested from cousin Iqbal was handily realized in the shape of this boy who was henceforth a nephew. The two men had agreed, 'a dowry that stays in the family is worth more than one that follows a girl out the door never to return.'

Throughout the negotiations for Mohammad's marriage to Ameena, Rizwan suffered from embarrassment he could not explain to himself. At times he had the sense that he was cheating someone somewhere—whether Ameena or Mohammad was impossible to tell, and possibly beside the point. Rizwan was a kind man and knew that in this difficult world, an orphan like Mohammad was unlikely to do anywhere near as well on his own. At twenty, with no family to direct him, and literate only in so far as he was able to write his name, Mohammad was a cipher. As for Ameena, she was the youngest of seven children, three of whom were girls. Where was her father going to find the money to pay for the kind of wedding a boy with a family would expect?

'Good for you, son,' Rizwan Chacha said clapping Mohammad on the shoulder. The confusion on Mohammad's face did not clear up. It embarrassed Rizwan no end, this confusion on

Mohammad's face. Rizwan's own children were too young yet and he had no experience with this sort of responsibility. He decided his inexperience was to blame for this embarrassment.

In spite of Rizwan Chacha's air of good cheer or perhaps because of it, Mohammad's confusion remained. This talk of money and a shop and cooking and washing was mixed up at times with a girl named Ameena (and who anyway was she?) and at times with a man, Iqbal, who they said was her father, in any case a man as eager to part with money as Rizwan Chacha was to see Mohammad opening up a kebab shop in Delhi. Was Mohammad willing to go to Delhi? Who wouldn't be? But he was reluctant to grasp the talk about Ameena. His questions about her found reply in talk of a picture he had once seen. Of this he was certain: he had never seen any picture of Ameena. And why was everyone so eager to hand her over to him? Was there something wrong with her that she was being unloaded on him? He itched to ask to see her picture, but was afraid of the teasing and perhaps scolding his request would undoubtedly arouse. He could only mumble and that too the worst sort of philosophy: 'Who?' he asked, and amended it to 'What?' finally concluding, 'Why is she?'

'She, who was in the album,' Chachi hid her smile behind her hand.

'And you cried when you saw how beautiful she is,' the little girls chorused.

'No, I didn't,' he protested feebly.

His bafflement only provoked mirth in the suddenly crowded room. And now he nodded along, glad to do anything that would end the teasing by various strangers who might have been Rizwan Chacha's relatives and were apparently soon to be his.

At the earliest he could, he consulted Lakshman, his gum-chewing confidante in all matters life- and love-related. Between having his mouth stuffed with congratulatory sweets and distributing sweets to his customers at work and companions in the madrassa, Mohammad thought hard about Lakshman's advice to him. Yes, indeed Lakshman had to be the smartest human being he had ever met. Between skewering chunks of meat for kebabs and slapping roti into the tandoor, Mohammad decided he would do as Lakshman had advised. He would take the money and marry the girl, this Ameena, whoever she was.

Between sulking on the cot in the evening and hanging his laundry out to dry in the night, he said goodbye to the only girl who had ever returned his beseeching looks. She, whose name he would never know but who had never failed till now to step out of her home and smile shyly at him over the laundry line, she simply stopped stepping out one day. He knew then she must have heard the news somewhere. His goodbye was mouthed into the empty night after which he excised the girl from his memory.

Chachi teased Mohammad: his soon-to-be wife though all of only fifteen had expressed a desire to see his picture. Ameena had been scolded plenty but she insisted she would not take a step forward without studying his face first. Mohammad was packed off to the photo studio where he posed in front of a technicolour seascape complete with pink palms and a scattering of purple clouds in an orange sky. Ameena was shown the picture. And she approved the match. The ache of rejection so constant in his chest he had lost consciousness of it in the years since the bicycle ride into orphanhood now revealed itself by giving way to something new. His heart made itself known to him as it soared and then sang and then plummeted and then managed all of the three and many more acrobatics. His heart belonged to Ameena. But this heart of his, it was not the heart of a kebab-stall cook.

Lakshman had been a fountain of information about Delhi. It seemed Lakshman knew everyone and everybody in Delhi. And all of them worked in the magical enterprise of turning waste into money.

'You think koora is just something we bhangis should work in, like you think I am fit only for cleaning up after you in the shop and latrine? Let me tell you something, you might be right about the koora in Patna being worthless. But the koora in Delhi, it is a treasure. Even you Muslims crawl all over it. You never know when someone is going to find a bag of gold in the Delhi koora. Happens all the time.'

What convinced Mohammad was not the image of a bag of gold buried in garbage. He wanted to get as far away from the heat of a tandoor oven and the smell of offal as anyone could get. He wanted a bicycle to ride on and the streets of Delhi to ride in.

Lakshman explained the various gradations of work available. If Mohammad Saidullah ever became so successful collecting kabadi and selling it to the godown owners that he had money to spare then Lakshman advised him, he could move into the ranks of those owners themselves. Although, Lakshman warned, a Muslim would not find easy entry. On the other hand, the life of the door to door kabadiwala, that was the best. Ride your cycle all day and go home to your wife's cooking at the end of the day.

Of course, other types of waste work was beneath Mohammad. Keep your distance from the shit, Lakshman warned. And Mohammad had the strong sense Lakshman was mocking him. 'It's work reserved,' and saying this Lakshman laughed aloud, 'for the Lakshmans of the world.'

'No,' he advised his friend, Mohammad, 'You don't want to work in the godowns sorting rubbish all day.' And lower still there were those who picked rubbish up from the shit-covered streets, from the shit-filled garbage piles around the city, and worse. The best job was the one Lakshman was setting him up with, a job that would take Mohammad to the homes of people who would sell him kabadi they had sorted themselves.

'Take the money they are giving you in dowry,' Lakshman advised, 'and pay for a route that will be exclusively yours. I have relatives in Delhi who will help get you the best such route and point you to the person to whom you will hand over the money. After that money will just roll in on your two bicycle wheels. The big people in big homes will sell you their kabadi and from your hands they will not mind taking your money. Then you sell those goods at the market and make more money. It is good work, Mohammad. When I come to visit you, you will no doubt offer me the best entertainment Delhi can afford.'

Mohammad did not hesitate to hand his dowry over to Lakshman, who he knew would get his cut for sending the money onward to Delhi. He suffered second thoughts about betraying Rizwan Chacha stoically; it could not be helped. The idea that Ameena might object to his way of life never occurred to him. This was finally his life, one which would begin now: on a bicycle, Ameena perched up there with him and eventually, he dreamt, there would be the family they would make together—a boy first, then a girl.

18
Ammi and Baba's Helper

Baba was home earlier than usual on this day. And he was talking to Ammi on his mobile phone. Noor listened hard while pretending she was interested in nothing besides the mess in the pot she was attempting to turn into a chicken curry. This was her first attempt at handling meat in two months of feeding her father vegetables and dal for dinner leavened only by the daily omelette sandwich lunch. The newspaper-wrapped pieces of raw meat in her hands had been enough to set her stomach bobbing loose from wherever it was usually anchored. Mercifully, her father had accompanied her to the butchers and seen to it that the hen was cut and skinned so she wouldn't have to do it at home. But was that thin thread of red in the gravy blood still seeping from the meat? She retched silently.

Her father's end of the conversation was the softly whispered yes and no that infrequently punctuated the silence in their room. She stirred the pot and the red pinked and disappeared into the onion and masala laced gravy. She had to admit her mess was starting to smell like food.

Her longing to speak to her mother was ragged from the torture to which she subjected it. As quickly as it rose in her, she stifled this longing. When it persisted, she poked at it and swore at it and when all else failed, she resorted to what she knew from the movies: 'You don't have a mother. She is dead for you. She only lives for Talib Bhaiya' etc. She took the kind of pleasure intoning these sentiments she would have felt picking at a wound, unwilling for it to heal.

Though she had imagined it often enough she knew Baba would not stop midway in his conversation to announce, 'Noor, it'll all be fine now, Bhaiya just wanted to teach you a lesson for not taking care of his pigeons; Ammi just wanted to teach you to do more of the housework; and now that you have learned your lesson, they are both on their way back.' But he might, she knew, turn to her with the phone and offer that 'Ammi wants to talk to you, Noor.' Of course, if Baba were to turn to her with the phone, and this because Ammi had asked to speak to her, then Noor would have no choice but to refuse to speak to Ammi. She had done this as many times as Baba had held out the phone to her in the past. Lately though, her mother had not been asking to speak to her. Noor didn't know what this meant, nor what she should do about it. Should she ask to speak to Ammi? Or perhaps she should ask instead to speak to Bhaiya.

Those early days after Bhaiya left home, Noor had watched Ammi come and go from their home. The coming was accompanied by shouting such as had never before been heard in their home.

'You took the money my father gave you to run a business of your own, handed it over to some gangsters, that's what you did. What did you expect from gangsters? That they wouldn't keep asking for more? Twenty-five years you have been paying them, more each month, more each year and finally it's come to this. You could have had your own shop, instead.'

And Baba, whispering to Ammi that the shop too would have cost more each month and more each year. Baba whispering that he knew he was a small man and he would always have to pay for his smallness, but he would not be small in front of his son.

At this Ammi broke down and pleaded with Baba to listen to Talib. And Baba whispered his reply so Noor's confusion only grew. But then Baba placed his hand on Ammi's hand and they sat in silence, their heads touching. Noor tiptoed out of the room and stood in the corridor unsure of what she was waiting for, but filled with the sense of waiting for something.

When Ammi was done with the shouting then the whispering that marked her coming home, she turned to the work of packing that accompanied her going from their home. Half of everything was packed: sheets and towels and dishes. All of Bhaiya's things were packed in one swoop. This lot disappeared when Noor was at school one afternoon. She did not ask Baba whether he had been home to talk to Bhaiya. It had to be Bhaiya who came and took his things. The rectangular and square outlines of dirt on the walls and the brighter patches of paint within them marked where Bhaiya's pictures had hung for as long back as Noor could remember—pictures of cricket players, of foreign cars and of foreign countries he said he would live in some day. She noted to herself the impossibility of those pictures coming away from the walls without ripping apart first.

Noor had collected the clothes he left behind for pressing on the day he first left and added them to his stack in the corner cupboard. Noor had washed the pants he left slung over the curtain partition behind which Noor and her mother dressed; they had been pressed by Suneeta Aunty, and only then were they added to the top of the stack in the corner cupboard. With those clothes gone, there was nothing of him in the house, not his mug with the expensive razors and the transparent red toothpaste and not the towel hung from the nail by the front door.

Ammi's clothes left more gradually but Noor knew they too were gone. Only her jewellery in the black velvet pouch remained in the back of the closet. There wasn't a day Noor did not check on the bag. One of those afternoons Ammi had come home, she had taken Noor aside and pointed the bag out to her and told her it was safer here than in Talib Bhaiya's new home where Ammi did not yet know anything about the neighbours. Noor told herself the daily peek into the closet was just her complying with Ammi's instructions to keep an eye on the bag. She tried not to admit to herself how much she had come to rely on seeing the bag there every afternoon when she returned from school and checked. She did not ask herself if Baba knew about the bag, if Ammi had asked him to keep an eye on it, as well, and if so when he checked as instructed was he, like her, checking for something else, as well.

When Noor turned mutinously from the phone Baba held out to her it was because she needed to be angry at someone. If not at Ammi then at whom was she to exercise her anger?

'Noor, my daughter,' Baba had tried to persuade her, 'your mother wants to tell you about your brother's new place.'

No, Noor told herself, it was not she who had pushed her mother away. Here she intoned the words that comforted her the most, 'Ammi only loves Bhaiya.' She repeated more of this sad comfort to herself, building to a welter of pain and pleasure, shame and pride. This was her refuge.

Loath to taste her creation and confirm it done, she turned the stove off at the point when she could not bear the silence at Baba's end of the phone and stepped outside the front door. He should be a man, she thought fiercely, and shout at Ammi instead of whispering to her. In the corridor outside her door, Lata Aunty was waiting for her.

'That's your mother on the phone, isn't it? I haven't seen her in some days now. All her coming and going, is she not done settling Talib in his new home? I understand he has moved all the way to Chattarpur area. Surely there was no need to move that far away. Luckily for your mother she has you, Noor, to take care of that poor man, your father. But she will be returning soon, won't she?'

'Ammi is taking care of Talib till he learns to manage for himself.' This was the explanation Baba had offered her with eyes dropped and a generally sideways air which was not at all the way Baba had ever talked to her in the past.

'Oh a boy who is big enough to rent himself a place can surely manage for himself.'

Lata Aunty's statement was one Noor subscribed to wholeheartedly but it wouldn't do to let her know this. Lata Aunty was not in any case looking for a reply from Noor.

'People are talking, Noor,' Lata Aunty attempted a softer tone of voice though the harshness of sentiment was nowhere softened, 'not that I see any truth in what they are saying. After all, they don't know Ameena like I do. Why I have known your family from before Talib was even born. I would certainly not believe it of Ameena that she would leave you here to care for your father if she did not have her reasons.'

Noor blinked and swallowed, and Lata Aunty leaned in closer, 'Oh, but you mustn't take it the wrong way Noor. People say so many things just for the sake of saying.'

Noor did not cry. Tears, she understood, were both 'the wrong way' which Lata Aunty was warning Noor against, and the very outcome for which Lata Aunty now eagerly scanned Noor's face.

She pushed past Lata Aunty and was back inside the room, which was darker now than when she left it. For a moment she thought her father had ended the call and left the room, somehow walking out the door and past her and Lata Aunty without their seeing him. But he was by the stove, his phone pressed between shoulder and ear, and hand busy dipping roti into her chicken curry.

'She's put so much masala; it's fiery,' Noor heard him tell her mother. He was not complaining. She could hear it in his voice: he was proud of her.

She held her hand out to Baba before she could change her mind. She brought the phone to her ear and listened to the silence. Her mother repeated her name into the phone and the sound 'Noor' floated out from somewhere in Chattarpur and travelled over the roofs of a thousand and ten-thousand and hundred-thousand homes filled with families come together from work and school and cricket fields to eat meals cooked by mothers who remained home to cook and clean and care for these happy families.

'Ammi,' Noor allowed her name for her mother to travel across this space, 'I want to come see you and Talib Bhaiya.'

19
Returning

Noor did not stop at her home after school on Friday. She walked past the water taps, then Hasan Chacha's tailor shop and the juice stall and finally the mattress maker's stack of mattresses. The black dog trailing her was nothing like Blackie and yet her fawning scampering mischief weighed Noor down. Ahead was Haseena's father presiding over his stall, one of the butcher shops clustered in a smelly but immaculate lane of butcher shops and here Noor lost the dog to a pile of offal and now she was in Haseena's lane, and now under her balcony. The speech-making boy was absent and so was Amit the pervert. But there was a familiar face peering down at her and a shy voice called her by name.

'Noor Didi, have you come to meet with Haseena?'

'No silly, I know she is back in your grandmother's village.'

'Yes, but my grandmother isn't alive anymore.'

'Still, it is her village isn't it?'

'Yes, you are right. And Haseena Didi is there. You are right about that too.'

'My neck hurts looking up at you like this. Can I come up?'

Now the head hung over the balcony rail bobbed up and down, bobbing two shiny black ponytails that spilled, one from above each ear, over the balcony rail.

'Noor Didi is here. Noor Didi is here.'

It was a pleasure for Noor to climb up the dark stairs. Though Haseena wasn't upstairs, her sister, Ruku was. And the exclamations of her delight at welcoming Noor were gratifying to listen to. And how much Ruku had grown in the last two months. Noor mouthed what she would say to Ruku, 'How much you have grown, Ruku.' Ah, but what choice did Ruku have other than to grow up now that Haseena was gone, leaving eight-year-old Ruku in charge of the household. Noor allowed herself a philosophical sigh at the thought of the difficulties Ruku must face. Poor eight-year-old Ruku.

Noor was quite pleased with how grown-up her sigh felt, and she allowed herself a rather more elaborate one. Once again, she practiced what she might say to Ruku: 'How grown up you are looking Ruku.'

She thought of how Ruku's hair had looked neat in the two ponytails. But the staircase was dirty, filthy even. On the other hand, Noor wasn't really sure if it had been otherwise in the days of Haseena's reign over the household. Come to think of it wasn't she, Noor, supposed to take a turn as her mother used to, cleaning the common stairs in their building? She had not thought to figure this out. Her own reign was not going so great either. Anyway it isn't even a reign, she told herself. For it to be a reign, I would have to be a queen. It's more like I am a servant. My mother's servant. This last bitter reflection brought her to Haseena's front door. Before she could knock, the door was flung open by Ruku.

Ruku's reign, Noor could see, was least reign-like. The single room looked like a storm had blown through it. Thin mattresses and sheets were flung about and the segregation of the cooking space from the sleeping space was further confounded by the migration of pots and pans onto items of bedding. From deep within this chaos Noor heard harsh sounds of anguish.

Noor's eyes swept over the room, first in the direction the bedding had taken then in the direction taken by the cooking pots, and settled finally where the two directions had met and collided. The object of her scrutiny found it hard to keep up his wailing, nearly gave it up, and then outraged that he should have to give up his grief for the useless though genuine emotion of shyness overtaking him, he burst into piercing shrieks.

Noor turned wide eyes and arched brows toward Ruku, who shrugged and then looked down. In the instant Ruku's eyes fell, shame flooded Noor. Ruku's intent examination of the cement floor, her bare feet, and the floor again would yield her no more than the stiff neck similar examinations had yielded Noor. Ruku's face, averted from Noor's, might as well have been a mirror in which Noor saw her own face, the one she averted when confronted by Lata Aunty's false compassion.

Stop acting like Lata Aunty, Noor scolded herself. *Do the opposite of what she would do*. Ignoring Aseef's tear-stained face, she took Ruku's hand and dragged her toward the balcony.

There was no sense in sticking to the earlier plan to tell Ruku how grown up she had become in Haseena's absence. Instead Noor looked here there and everywhere beyond the balcony, to give Ruku time to figure out what she wanted to say.

'He's stupid. He never stops crying. It doesn't matter what I do or don't do. He cries and cries. When he is not crying, he is running outside in the sun. If some dog bites him or if he gets sunstroke, it will be my fault. Abba says he will whip Aseef if he gets sick. Am I supposed to tie him down then?

'I even let him make a mess, playing house with all the sheets and dishes. He started crying only when he heard you on the stairs. Only because he wants you to think I beat him. He wants everyone to think we beat him all day long so he cries endlessly.'

'Does your father whip Aseef then?'

'No, how can Abba whip Aseef? He is only a baby of six. Our father doesn't hit us.' Ruku sounded indignant.

In every other home Noor stepped into there was a mother. If there was also a father in those homes, Noor was hardly aware of the fact. But in this one home the absence of a mother laid bare the fact of the father. And the fact of the father was simply that he was to be feared. Not Noor's father, of course. Noor's father was Baba with the beard and the hand that pulled at the beard, the kurta that pulled across his middle and his way of pulling Noor into his lap, one-handed, as if he were the strong man she had once seen in a traveling circus, hefting the pretty lady with one hand, the other hand busy with a chair, a sword or even a horse.

But in this home, without a mother to cover for the father, a mother to shoo out children when the father's temper flared and to usher in children when the father had sweets to distribute, Noor had been afraid of Haseena's father, so afraid she had never wanted to step foot in their house while he was within. Even today she had checked to see that he was in his shop before arriving here.

She should not have blurted out her fear to Ruku. It was rude to do so. This lesson in manners had been taught her by her mother. Never ask people about what goes on in their home. It was a lesson that went hand in hand with the one about never revealing the business of their home life to anyone outside the home.

Noor had often itched to ask Haseena if her father ever beat her, but in the years they were friends she had contained the question. If she had blurted out the question now it was because Haseena was not there to stop her. How had Haseena stopped her? By being Haseena, by anticipating the question, by meeting Noor's eye with the sidelong look which made Haseena suddenly more frightening than Haseena's father. But also, Noor had held the question back because the idea of an answer was unbearable whereas the question itself was always at least bearable.

'Does your father beat you?' Ruku was glaring at Noor, her shiny ponytails dancing as she jerked her head emphatically.

Noor shook her head 'no'. So now Noor knew. Haseena's father did not beat his children. And by way of apologizing to Ruku and the absent Haseena, Noor offered, 'But sometimes he shouts at us.'

Ruku gave an exasperated sigh waving Noor's words away, and this gesture copied from the older sister brought Haseena back into the room. Noor blinked to right the vision. Ruku said, 'Of course everyone's father shouts. Haseena Didi used to shout at me. Now I shout at Aseef.' She finished wistfully, 'Probably, if our mother was still with us, she would shout as well.'

Noor remembered an afternoon when she and Haseena had

fallen asleep at Noor's home. When Noor woke in the nearly dark room it was to the sound of Haseena crying, perhaps one of the only times Noor had ever seen her cry at full tilt. At the end of the crying, she told Noor, 'I know you think I am crying because my mother is dead or because my father shouts at me or because I don't have your kind of nice clothes and nice home.'

Noor had of course only vaguely been thinking that Haseena's crying might be related to her scary father or her sad home. As for the 'nice clothes' she had no more known to think of Haseena as not having nice clothes than she had known that she herself had nice clothes. In any case she was fully prepared to deny thinking any of it, and to possibly even do it in a huffy tone when Haseena hurried forward, 'Don't bother telling me that it isn't what you are thinking. It's always easier for people to think terrible horrible things are happening. And so hard to think about how there are harder things than terrible horrible things.'

'What do you mean, Haseena?'

What could be more horrible, Noor had thought than fathers who beat you, and mothers who died giving birth to little brothers.

'The most horrible thing,' Haseena sobbed, 'is the horrible thing you do yourself. '

That was about as confusing a thing as Noor had ever had to think about. She had understood then Haseena's life was complicated whereas her own was quite simple. If she had ever thought anything more about the question of why Haseena's life was complicated, it was to somewhat guiltily conclude that it had at least a little something to do with Haseena herself. If Noor were Haseena, Noor had followed her disloyal speculations to their logical conclusion, with or without a mother she would manage to live with fewer complications than did Haseena.

Noor was still thinking back to a past in which Haseena had done something she considered horrible when Ruku asked her, 'Is it true? I heard your mother has moved to another country.'

'Another country? Who said anything about my mother to you? Did that stupid boy next door talk about my mother?'

Again a sidelong look from Ruku and a subdued Noor continued, 'My mother is taking care of my brother in another part of Delhi. Why would she go to another country?'

'Oh people go to other countries all the time.'

'So who said anything about my mother going to another country?'

Ruku scrunched up her face, genuinely puzzled that she did not know the answer to this question. Then brightening, she said, 'Why, everyone knows your mother had to leave the house after your father and she had a fight about him losing his job.'

The two of them sat glumly, listening to the stop-start crying sounds Aseef made inside the house. When a few minutes later, he wandered out, the two busied themselves spreading sheets over the balcony, tying their corners to the railing and the balcony door to create the roof of a truly elaborate house. Mattresses were dragged out to become the carpeted floor of the house and actual biscuits from the actual kitchen cupboard were cooked over an imaginary fire. Aseef blew on the biscuits and holding them cautiously and with many exclamations of 'ow hot' he handed the girls their dinner.

'I will be the father,' he told Noor, 'and you be the mother. Ruku Didi can be the baby. Now we must all eat and be happy.'

20

Metro

When Noor left Haseena's house, it was late evening and she felt defeated. Ahead was the dinner yet to be cooked. Thankfully, she had purchased the carrots and peas on the way to Haseena's and now they dangled from her hand in a plastic bag. Behind her was the friend's home she had entered thinking that she could be of help.

But I was helpful, she told herself. Ruku said I made Aseef laugh; Ruku said Aseef had not laughed like that since Haseena left.

That part was good, she reassured Haseena. Reassuring Haseena of this, she felt reassured herself.

And now I have your address in the village. Don't worry, I am not coming riding on my bicycle. And anyway I still don't know how to ride a bicycle. I just wanted the address so I could send you the notebook. No, I didn't leave the notebook with Ruku. Anyone could read it there. I know, I know, I am the one who read it when I shouldn't have. You see that's how I know it will be easy for someone else to want to read it. You wouldn't want that nasty boy next door to you, what's his name, the speech-maker to read it, would you?

Noor was a little nervous hinting to Haseena her fear that it was Haseena's father who, having the most access to the notebook in that household, would be most likely to read it. That's why I'm keeping the notebook, she said to Haseena without naming the father, who though he did not beat his children must possess yet other faults otherwise why would she fear him so.

At home, Noor opened the cupboard and checked her mother's velvet jewellery bag was there. Then she lifted the newspaper lining of the shelf on which her own clothes were stacked and united the address Ruku had scribbled on a slip of paper with Haseena's notebook still chockfull of entries Noor had not read, and which Noor hastily shut after placing the address within so she would not read them. Then she felt further back on the shelf to check that the crumple of newspaper, Haseena's birthday present—the single orange and black seed—was still there.

See Haseena, Noor continued her one-sided conversation with her friend, as she launched herself at the onions, I am not some stupid who just keeps making the same mistakes. I am not reading the rest of your notebook, not even if it takes me years to get it to you. Her eyes were now streaming from the effect of the onions, but the rest of the work preparing the meal fell into place in little time. The onions were on the stove with tomatoes and ginger when she turned to the peas and began shelling them as efficiently as if she had been cooking in place of her mother for more than two months now. I cook every day, you know, she scolded the admiring Haseena. No need to look at me like it is anything big. I can make chicken curry now. Baba and I went to your father's shop last week to get the meat. Then when Ammi called to talk to Baba, because you know she has stopped asking to speak to me and I thought it was because earlier I had not taken the phone when Baba gave it to me to speak to her, then Baba told her my chicken curry was really good, and after that I thought I would go ahead and speak to her.

If I can make chicken curry—and today if you must know I am making peas and carrots and next I will make roti, but between the vegetables getting cooked and the roti I have to run down to get the water before the line gets too long—so I am saying if I can do all this and make chicken curry the other day, I can certainly talk to Ammi also. So I talked to her, and I didn't want her to think we needed anything from her after she had gone and left Baba and me the way she did. So I just told her I would come see her and Bhaiya.

You see, after she left to go keep house for Bhaiya, she came back many times to pack her things, and every time she said Bhaiya was asking me to come visit his new place. But why would I want to go? Did she say she wanted me to visit the new place? Or did only Bhaiya want me to? But since we are doing fine here, me and Baba, I thought, why wouldn't I go there.

But Haseena, we are not doing fine here.

The tears pouring down Noor's face were not a result of the onions she had cut sometime in the past. The peas and carrots were cooked. The small light given off by the kerosene flame, extinguished when she turned the stove off, had given way to near complete darkness. She needed to turn on the overhead light and gather the plastic water containers and run her tired body downstairs before it became too late. But she sat instead and cried to her absent friend.

I wish you were here, she cried softly. I think I know what you mean by the horrible things that are more horrible than even the most horrible things. I hate my mother. And that's the most horrible thing.

Today I will go see her though. I have to go alone on the metro because Baba won't come with me. I am not afraid to go alone. Baba says he will take me inside the station and put me on the metro and he has told me at which station to get off, and that Ammi or Bhaiya will be there to take me to Bhaiya's house. I am better than you would be at things like going alone on a metro. I am not afraid of the metro. I am afraid of other things.

But Haseena, I thought I was so smart knowing how to cook and clean and get water and go to school late and take the punishment from Bengali Sir, and even learning how to make chicken curry. But none of it matters, Haseena. No matter what I do, Baba still doesn't have his old job and who knows if he has any kind of job and how can I get Ammi to come back here when he doesn't have a job? And I can't tell anyone this, but sometimes I don't even want her to come back.

Lata Aunty told me Ammi is staying away to teach Baba a

lesson. And when Baba learns the lesson, she will be back. I don't know what that lesson is that he is supposed to learn. Baba was always nice to Ammi. So the lesson can't be about treating her nicely.

Once when I was little and Ammi hit me with the hairbrush, I told her that I would have Baba beat her up when he came home. Wait, I told her, I'm going to tell Baba what a horrible woman you are. I don't remember if I told Baba anything when he came home. If I did, I know Baba must have laughed at me and taken her side. He was always on her side. Even when she was not on his side. Like all those times Bhaiya fought with Baba and she took Bhaiya's side, still he was always on her side. So what lesson does Ammi need Baba to learn? Lata Aunty didn't say. I think she wanted me to ask her.

And why did Ruku say Baba doesn't have a job? Baba has a job. He works in Panchsheel getting kabadi from the people who live there.

When it was pitch dark in the room, Noor switched the light on. A vacant click from which sprung no light. Oh no, a power cut. She groped her way down the treacherous stairs, brushing past the darkened silhouettes of children coming back to their homes from the darkened streets. Downstairs the taps were still dispensing water and she groped back upstairs with her full containers. She washed the dishes by feel, and by feel kneaded and cooked rotis enough for two nights.

*

The lights had not returned when Baba came home. She took him by the hand to show him the covered dishes of food, the full water containers. This close she could smell him; he smelled as he had for the past many days. Of fire. His clothes, which she could not see in the dark, she knew would be covered in ash. What this meant was something she had dared not ask him.

'Noor,' he said, 'I will manage.'

She thought he wouldn't. She imagined he would sit here in the dark, forget to eat and forget to lie down to sleep till she returned on Sunday night.

'But thank you, daughter. I can smell how good your food is, and I will certainly eat well tonight though it will be a quiet meal without you.'

The 'thank you' made her shy, but she also thought it wasn't ever anything but quiet when the two of them sat down to eat. It wouldn't be any quieter with her gone than when she was here. Suddenly she couldn't wait to leave. Her fear of the metro vanished and she did not have to be urged to get her bag.

At the metro station she saw what till now she had only seen on television: a silver staircase, which moved of its own accord. 'Baba,' she pleaded, gesturing toward it. He restrained her, pulling her back with a head shake. 'See?' and he pointed out the stairs moved steadily up to the street where they stood and not down to the station where they needed to go. Noor had a moment of horror as she pictured herself stepping onto the stairs. What would have happened? Certainly people would have laughed, and probably she would have gone tumbling down, injured herself grievously. Grateful her father had saved her from catastrophe, she followed him down the cement steps.

She studied her father's fumbling at the ticket counter. He nearly stepped into the women's line and it was she who pushed him into the line for men. One by one, the women in line ahead of her passed into the curtained booth where Noor spied through a slit a woman in a khaki uniform wave a black device around their bodies. She was offended when the the woman declined to pass the black metal contraption over her body. The device had beeped repeatedly for the other women telling them something which Noor would have liked to know. She stood resolutely till the guard gave in and waved the device in the air around her. For her there were no beeps, and then she was on the other side where she could see her father was still in line. Then they were both at the turnstile and it seemed everyone had plastic cards to get through and Baba instructed her to make do with the plastic coin he had purchased for her from the ticket counter. She was ashamed of her plastic coin and could hardly comprehend his instructions for how she was to use it to get through this turnstile and the one at the end of her journey.

On the other side of the turnstile she turned and waved and Baba repeated himself, 'Don't lose the coin. Go downstairs to platform 2, and get on the train to Huda. You get off at Chattarpur. You can read so you just look at the sign inside the train and it will show you when it is Chattarpur. But, you must ask someone so you can be sure. Don't get on the train to Jahangirpuri. That will go the other way. You want Huda. Not Jahangirpuri.'

A woman pushed through the turnstile and grabbed her by the hand, calling over her shoulder to Baba, 'I'll take your daughter. I'm going that way myself.'

Noor went clattering down the stairs, pulled by the woman who ran ahead; at the bottom of the stairs she had barely stepped onto the platform when she was swallowed up by the arrival of the train, sleek, silver, pushing a cool gust of wind ahead of it. She was thrilled at the sight, and then she was inside the thing that thrilled her, and then she pulled away from the woman and found herself a spot hidden within a jumble of other bodies.

Haseena, she sang with happiness, I am on the metro.

Taking up the conversation from earlier, she continued, 'I can't ask Ammi to come home. The minute she comes home she will want to take over everything. And I do want her to take over everything—like cooking and cleaning and Baba. But I don't want her taking over school. Well, she can take over school too. I would start being on time to school again. But I don't want her taking over me. I don't want her telling me what to think and feel. I don't want her telling me anything about Ajith.'

Noor stopped, embarrassed and even aghast at what she was thinking. Ajith? Why was she thinking about Ajith? Ajith, who clearly hated her. Ajith, who she had told herself she would have nothing to do with. Rude Ajith. Rude. Rude. Rude.

But Noor knew her mother would not stand for her daughter running behind a boy. Someone would tell her mother, 'Your daughter spends all her time talking to a boy.' And her mother would take Noor aside and tell her, 'Noor, you are too grown up now to talk to boys.' Noor felt mutinous at the thought of her mother's understanding eyes. What can Ammi understand if she has never been in school? She will end up thinking like Lata Aunty. Noor shuddered at the memory of Lata Aunty's suspicion that their family had gone wrong because her parents had sent her to a boys and girls school; they had gone wrong because her parents allowed Talib to work at night in a place where boys and girls worked together.

Just because boys and girls studied together or worked together did that mean they would end up doing the love thing? She curled her lips in scorn at the thought of the love thing. *With Ajith of all boys*. The train juddered and she grabbed a hold of the pole in front of her. But the train's shaking was slight and she noticed no one else had reached for support as she had. It was once again a smooth ride and she looked around to see if anyone had seen her panic. Could they tell how silly she was? Could they tell from looking at her that she was thinking about Ajith? That when she thought of him her insides flamed up and the pain within was pleasant.

Please, she prayed, let him like me. Please, she prayed, make it so I don't like him.

I don't like him, she resolved. The business with the light around him was something stupid that happened just once.

But certainly, Noor was not going to allow anyone to tell her who she could or couldn't talk to. What did she have in mind then, she had to ask herself. Nothing. Nothing at all. And she knew then she meant to chase after Ajith. Yes, she was going to chase him down. But only to talk to him about bicycles. Hadn't he said he had a bicycle. And that business about his caste, did she care about that? No. So she should talk to him to show him she didn't care. And she was going to ask him to teach her how to ride. That's all. She wasn't boy-mad. She was simply bicycle-mad.

See, Haseena, if you were here I would not be friends with Ajith. It is because all the other girls are useless that I have become friends with Ajith. And she hung her head, once again embarrassed. She was embarrassed she was lying to her best friend.

21

Chattarpur

Another gentle shake, one Noor felt an old hand at withstanding, and the train broke through to light. They were above ground, the train slowed and pulled into Chattarpur. The helpful woman was on her in an instant, dragging her to the door before it slid open and through the door the instant it did. All around her people were similarly rushing out but of their own volition. She squirmed in the woman's hand and the woman let it go and rushed back into the train before the door closed.

'This is not my stop. But don't worry someone will come for you,' she smiled reassuringly. The door slid shut. Noor seethed. Then looking at the woman through the glass pane between them she shrugged elaborately. The woman continued smiling, then looking confused, shrugged as elaborately in response.

The train pulled away and she was surrounded on both sides. Here was Bhaiya and here Ammi. Her strenuous efforts at ingratitude to the woman meant she had not yet had time to worry about whether her family would show up to collect such a rude girl as she was turning into. Having foregone worry, she was not inclined to be glad to see them either.

'You're alone,' Ameena spoke sharply and looked around for her husband with an equally sharp eye.

Noor didn't stop to think of what came over her. She shrugged, if possible, as elaborately as she had at the woman on the train. Her mother looked at her not with confusion, but with pain.

Her brother put two hands under her arms and pretending to dismay, exclaimed, 'I can't lift you anymore. Why in two months you have grown to the size of a truck. No wonder Baba sent you alone. You're practically a grown up.'

A silence settled on the three of them as they contemplated the two months gone by since Noor and Talib had last seen each other. They stood unsure of themselves. The strangers that swirled around them were as filled with purpose as they were without. In no more than a moment the station settled into silence. If they waited another moment the next rush of strangers would arrive on the platform to board the next train. They did not wait.

Talib grasped Noor by the shoulder and steered. Ameena followed. They were outside and then Noor was ascending an escalator for the first time in her life. She forgot to be angry. She smiled at her brother and squeezed his hand. She sang to Haseena, 'I am on a staircase that climbs up on its own.' Shyly, she thought of Ajith. What would he have to say about this? Would he have an explanation for this as he did for so much else?

'Did Baba say anything about you wanting to visit me here?'

'No, just that I should get off at Chattarpur station and you and Ammi would be here waiting.'

'But he shouldn't have sent you alone. If he had said he couldn't bring you then I would have come to get you. Weren't you scared?'

She didn't want to say anything about the woman, but nor did she want them to blame Baba for sending her alone. She settled for, 'He put me right inside the train, right by where the driver sits. He told the driver to put me out in Chattarpur.'

Bhaiya and Ammi exchanged glances. She saw that they knew she was lying. She shrugged again.

Bhaiya's home was a disappointment. When he had spoken of finding himself a home in the past it was always in terms of the drawing room with its soft sofa on which everyone would sit to watch the TV on the wall across from the sofa, and of a separate kitchen for Ammi, and the bathroom just for the family, not one to be shared with any other household. But in every way, the one-room home they stepped into was similar to the one-room home that she had just come from. There was no sofa and no television. No separate kitchen and no separate bathroom. And horror of horrors, when she asked to use it and had the way pointed out to her along with the encouragement 'you can use it as long as you want; we share it with only one other family,' she discovered the toilet was not the kind at home. It was the kind with a seat you had to sit on. Then she saw the dirt print of soles on the seat and perched herself on it, making use of it as the previous person had.

Back in the drawing room—Talib called it that though it was the only room in the house—Noor noted the blank wall opposite the sofa. At least Baba and I have a television, she thought with satisfaction. But then she saw what was different about the new home. There was a refrigerator and a stove with two burners. The overhead light had a cover with yellow flowers drawn on it. There was a table with a white plastic lace on it. In place of a sofa, there were three chairs side by side and a rug in front of the chairs.

'You should save space and stack the chairs,' she told Talib.

He looked at her kindly. 'You mean like at home?'

She looked away. Her mother was fiddling with the stove. Here, Ammi did not sit on the ground to do her cooking. The stove itself was above ground on a counter and so she stood over it as she made tea. Noor thought how strange it was that she, meanwhile, had taken the reverse course back in Chirag Dilli. Where she had always thought it better to stand at the counter for the small bits of cutting and chopping she had done for Ammi, and where she had frowned on her Ammi squatting on the floor, now Noor did her work where it was most convenient—on the floor.

She would have liked to speak to her mother, to say something about the new arrangement of stove. But it was impossible to give up ground she had fought for. Ammi would have to make the first move. And it would have to be the right move if she wanted Noor to speak.

'Tea?' Ameena asked her daughter.

'I had some already before coming.'

Talib jumped up. 'I will take Noor outside for some proper

food. Noor, I don't let Ammi do more than make tea here. I bring food from outside for her and I eat outside, myself. Come I will take you to a restaurant. Now don't be like Ammi and refuse.'

Noor was gratified to think of Ammi refusing Talib anything. She would have liked to summon a lofty refusal herself. 'No Bhaiya, you know I made dinner tonight, chicken curry with plenty of masala, and I am still full. We eat chicken curry all the time now; we are almost tired of it, that's how much of it we have eaten. What I am saying is Baba doesn't get tired, but I do.'

What would Talib say to that? But Noor didn't have a chance to find out because just then, woken by Talib's offer of restaurant food, Noor's stomach growled loud enough to bring all eyes to her.

'I am hungry,' she mumbled. And it was true that while she had cooked and set food aside for Baba, she herself had not remembered to eat. It was also true that her prickly behaviour was fast becoming unbearable to her. It was as if every outward prickle she grew had a corresponding prickle that grew inside her; she wanted to tear off her skin, but didn't know how. No, she wouldn't unprickle herself, not so to spare Ammi, cost her what it may in prickliness inside. But if she could go off with Talib Bhaiya, then she could be herself again.

Talib fed her in a South Indian restaurant. He said, you will like it and she agreed, glad to finally be agreeable, though the food was strange and she was not at all sure she liked it. They ate quickly in a brightly lit room with smooth walls and panes of glass darkened by the night outside. She was conscious of every bite in her mouth and was glad when Talib declared the meal done and pulled out his wallet to pay the waiter who brought him the bill, a scrap of paper on a plate with sugar and fennel seeds for her. The paper said Rs 180 and Talib pulled out two hundred rupee notes from his wallet. She stopped playing with the sugar in the plate to watch him. He handed the money to the waiter who had been hovering over them. The waiter departed and Talib hurriedly called him back to hand him another twenty rupees.

'Bhaiya,' Noor hissed, 'he is supposed to give you twenty rupees.'

Talib laughed. 'I don't usually give such a good tip but this is a good day in our lives. My little sister has come to visit.'

She felt warm all over, laughed aloud. They got up from the table. There was a stumble in her step. He steadied her, took her outside, bought her an ice cream from a Cream Bell cart and sat her down on a low stone parapet in front of his home. She licked her cone and watched the traffic go by, headlights burning the night.

'Baba says I am not his son. Why does he say this? Because I refuse to give him money. It seems Baba thinks our relationship is a bill for which he wants to collect payment from me.'

Noor licked her ice cream cautiously. Would it continue to taste as good now as it did a moment ago? The ice cream was cold and sweet, but its quality of goodness or badness was no longer accessible to her. She kept licking it, though it accumulated in her mouth and she could not swallow any of it. Finally she leaned to the side and spat into the street.

'This is a bad ice cream,' she said.

'Ammi says you are angry at her. But you are too old now Noor to throw a fit like you used to when you were a child and didn't get your way.'

'Yes, I know. I am just old enough to be made to clean and cook and run and run but not old enough to speak or ask questions.'

'Ask me then what you want to know.'

'Why is Ammi living here with you and not with us?'

'I can't answer that question, Noor. That is a question you have to ask Ammi.'

'See,' she wailed. 'See, I am just supposed to do what I am told and never ask anything. I am not even supposed to exist. If I didn't exist then Ammi would be so happy. She could stop coming to Chirag Dilli to see if I am okay. She could take all the things from Chirag Dilli and bring it here. Why leave half the things when it is only Baba there? She could stop leaving her jewellery bag there and just permanently stay here.'

Talib ignored her outburst. Taking the ice cream she was waving around from her, he began eating it. There was silence as he finished the cone off. There were more questions in her mind than she could sort. She blurted one out:

'What is the bill Baba is collecting from you? Is it something for his hafta?'

Now it was Talib's turn to look surprised. 'What do you know about hafta?'

'I know,' she replied though she knew nothing.

'Baba says a father feeds and brings up his son so his son owes his father. I didn't ask to be here anymore than you did. I am here because Baba willed it. Did he bring me here to pay his bills? Yes, he needs money. Lots of it. For the last three years since I left school and started working I have been doing as he says and giving him my salary from which he pays all his bribes. But each year the police want more, the municipal workers want more, even his contractor at the kabadi market wants him to pay all over again for his route and for protection. It seems his contractor got greedy and offered Baba's route to another man. And maybe that's not so bad since each year he does his work, rides his cycle, each year Baba is a little older, gathers a little less kabadi, and makes a little less money. Each year I pay a lot more of the bills. And after I pay, I still have to come when he tells me to come, go when he tells me to go, sit when he tells me to sit and stand when he tells me to stand.'

'Bhaiya, we are his children; isn't that what we are supposed to do?'

'No, if I pay his bills then I am my own man. I will come and go when I want, sit and stand when I want. And by god, I will live where I want.'

'If Baba needs money to pay the police and everyone else to keep his job, it is so that he can get more money to pay for us to live in our house and to eat food, and for me to go to school.'

'Of course Noor, Baba wants to work to pay for us to have a good life. But I don't need him to pay anything for me. All I am saying to him is the kabadi work is over. Or at least there is less and less of it now. If his contractor is taking money from another man it's because soon even the contractor is going to get cut off from whatever kabadi there is on Baba's route. A company is going to take over the colony's waste soon. The new man will get a lot less out of the hafta he paid the contractor than Baba has gotten over the years.'

'Baba doesn't go to Panchsheel anymore. I don't know where he goes.'

'Listen, I earn enough to pay for us. I don't want to do that forever. Someday I might want to marry and have children too.' Talib paused to smile at Noor's expression of dismay. 'Don't worry, someday is far away. But meanwhile, Baba should look for some other work. What am I supposed to say to my friends about where I live? None of them have a father who works in kabadi.'

'Your place is not any nicer now.'

'No, that's because I am still paying the rent at Chirag Dilli and the rent here. But at least I will no longer pay for Baba to bribe the people who let him work in a job that doesn't pay his bills.'

'And your new suit—did it work out for you, Bhaiya? Did you get other people to join?'

Talib looked darkly off into space. Then shaking himself, he muttered, 'Baba forbade it. I lost yet another opportunity in life because of him. How can he talk to me about collecting a bill from me, Noor? Does a father talk like that?'

Noor sat silently. She understood no more now than before what was tearing her family apart.

They went inside. Ammi had laid out sheets on the dhurrie. Something tightened in Noor when Talib took his mug with its toothbrush and fancy toothpaste from the window sill and headed to the bathroom. Noor was finally alone with her mother. She spread a sheet on the dhurrie, lay down quickly and pulled another sheet over her head. Her mother scolded her gently, 'Noor there are not enough sheets. I swept the dhurrie. You can sleep on the dhurrie and use the sheet for a cover or you can sleep on the sheet.'

Noor whipped the sheet from over her and folded it huffily and set it aside. Yanking out the one underneath her she lay on the dhurrie and again covered herself. Much later the lights were turned off. She lay still till all was silent save her mother's and brother's quiet breathing. Inching closer to her mother she slept with her face pressed to her mother's back.

22
Ameena Chooses

Late into the night Ameena lay without moving. She knew a single movement of acknowledgement would send Noor fleeing. She slept fitfully. In the morning, she hid herself in the preparations for breakfast. She made Noor's favourite dishes: egg and potato bhujia, paratha and tea. She had the menu for the rest of the day planned, as well. She would feed Noor her favourite sweet, rasmalai, mid-morning. For lunch she wanted to make rice with mutton curry and for dinner chole kulche although there was the problem of finding kulche in the market downstairs. Perhaps they would have it and perhaps they wouldn't. She had not had to shop for kulche till now. It was not a favourite with Talib.

The market downstairs was as yet unfamiliar. She often found herself asking Talib to do the shopping, whereas at home she had done all of it herself. Talib, of course, resented any reminder of the provisional nature of their lives together. But there was no helping the fact that she felt strange in this neighbourhood where no one knew her. Did they look at her and question in their minds who she was and what she was doing here? Did they know looking at her that she had a husband and a daughter elsewhere? How did they judge her decision to be here without them? These questions sharpened her loneliness and she wanted more than anything else to talk to someone. But she knew no one aside from her son. And he was only sporadically present in the day and was entirely absent five nights a week.

Now Noor was here, and if Ameena did not bustle about she feared she would give in to her desperation and turn to the child for conversation and counsel. This, she did not want to do. Her own childhood had been so brief. The first traumas came too soon, a sister who departed to her married life in another family when Ameena was eight and another sister when she was nine. That same year she was withdrawn from school to take her turn in the kitchen. In place of her sisters and playmates, she found a stranger, her mother. Without choosing it, they became friends. Their friendship was as much a comfort to the woman as it was to the girl; but it was the girl alone who found the friendship burdensome. Her mother had sighed over her troubles with her in-laws, had complained about her husband, the child's father's stinginess, had filled the child with a horror over what it was to be a woman.

When Ameena was shown the picture of Mohammad Saidullah, she had just turned fifteen. She had not, as Mohammad thought, asked to see the picture to determine if he was good-looking. She had asked to see it to convince herself that this next life was one of her choosing. She found life as Mohammad Saidullah's wife was a good one but in one respect very like her life had been in her parents' home: here too she did none of the choosing. He chose to quarrel with her father; he chose to spend her dowry on setting up in the kabadi trade; he chose where they lived; and he chose the number of children she would bear, arguing her into a second pregnancy seven years after the first. 'I want a daughter,' he had pleaded.

'How will you know it will be a daughter,' she argued, but even god saw it fit to let Mohammad Saidullah have what he wanted.

That he chose to love her—and to do so shyly—mitigated to a degree the claustrophobia of her life. His shyness in particular won her for it assumed no right to love or be loved in return. The couple made their peace early in their marriage and with an economy of fuss. There was no formal announcement to usher in an era of happiness. But Ameena marked for herself the advent of this era: it began on the day Talib was born. It began with a choice she exercised in her heart, to love him above all. It hurt her to reflect on Noor's birth that this earlier choice precluded her beloved daughter. But so be it. Loss, Ameena now understood, was the meaning of choosing.

*

On this morning, she congratulated herself that she had spared Noor what her mother had not spared her. She resolved to continue sparing Noor. She would not cry her loneliness to her daughter; she would not ask for her understanding. She would accept Noor's hostility if need be.

'Does Baba eat well?' Ameena asked Noor.

'No more for me,' was Noor's reply as she put her hand over her plate in refusal of Ameena's offer of more food.

Ameena repeated her question patiently and this time Noor knit her brows and said, 'He eats sometimes, and sometimes he doesn't.'

'Baba says you have learned to cook many things. Is this true? He says you cook very well. Are you enjoying it?'

Noor finished what was on her plate and took it to the wash bucket without answering her mother. There was no water by the bucket. The bucket itself was full of dirty dishes. She looked around for where the water might be kept stored.

'There is no water right now. I will go get it.'

Noor watched her mother move around the kitchen, gathering containers, wrapping her scarf over her head. When her mother was nearly to the door, Noor blurted out, 'You don't have to do it. I will get the water. You just have to tell me where to go.'

'Come with me, Noor. I need my daughter's help to bring back all these containers. You know when you were little that's how it was—we went together to fetch water. What a help you were to me, and I noted it always. You carried a whole jug on your head when you were only six. Everybody in Chirag Dilli said of you that you were a helpful daughter. Later, it became your job to get all the water. At times I might have forgotten to tell you I noticed your help, but I noticed it.'

Ameena looked sideways at Noor and saw that again there was no reply forthcoming. She went directly to what she wanted to say.

'Talib says you want to ask me something. Is that right?'

An instant's surprise gave way to nervousness and then finally Noor was angry. She put the plastic canisters down on the road. A picture of herself running from there flashed to her head. In the end she simply stood with her head down to avoid her mother's eyes.

'I know what you want to ask me. You want to know why I am here and not in our home with you and Baba. And you are right, it is not true that Talib needs me here. The truth is I need to be here. This is not going to be easy for you to understand.'

Now Noor spoke, 'There is nothing difficult to understand here. You always care about Talib. But before, you at least also cared about Baba. These days you don't care about anything else, not even about Baba.'

She stopped herself from saying 'You don't care about me.' She would not have her mother know how she felt. In any case she did not, she resolved, feel anything. She stood mutinously then with the same elaborate shrug which had overnight become second nature to her, she picked up the canisters and strode ahead. She had no idea which direction to walk to get to the communal taps in this neighbourhood. But she assured herself she didn't care where she might end up.

Now her mother hastened her step and was at Noor's side, steering her without seeming to. The silence between them stretched over the time it took them to stand in a line of a hundred other women and girls and wait their turn to approach the taps. The sound of the water filling their containers was a signal to break their silence. Noor said, 'I don't go as often to get water as I used to. At home, I mean. I don't like going to the taps. And I don't feel like going to the downstairs bathroom for my bath.'

Ameena stumbled through the options, unsure of what to advise Noor: 'Are you afraid to bathe without me? Avoid the side with the men and go when you see the most women. But it is dark by then, isn't it? Or you can go earlier, don't wait till it is dark. Tell Haseena you have to cut short playtime and take your bath before dark.'

Back inside their room Noor spoke as if the silent walk home had not broken their conversation, 'Anyway, I don't play anymore.' She began crying. At first noisily. Ameena drew close so Noor was by her side, but she dared not touch her daughter. Only when the noisy sobs gathered momentum and turned to a feverish keening did Ameena take her daughter's clenched hands in her own. She forcibly opened the two hands, smoothing the fists into palms, stroking them over and over, whispering, 'Enough Noor, enough. You weep over what you don't understand. You must trust me more.'

Noor leaned into her mother, then jerked back. 'You're the one. You don't understand,' she shrieked.

And that is how Ameena found out Haseena was gone.

'But Baba didn't tell me anything about Haseena being gone.'

'Why would Baba know that?'

Ameena's heart constricted painfully. It took her a moment to sort out that she was afraid for her daughter. Why hadn't she been afraid till now? Had she reserved all of her fear for Talib? 'You must,' she said, speaking slowly and emphatically, 'tell your father everything. While I am gone, you tell Baba. Everything.'

Noor stared at Ameena in astonishment. 'Why are you angry at me? I haven't done anything wrong for you to be angry at me.'

The conversation was over before it had gotten underway.

The rest of the day dragged on in the same silence in which they had spent the morning. Noor spoke only to offer that she and Baba did not watch the television at home and if Ammi wanted she could take the television, as well. Ameena asked Noor about the approach of the year-end exams and Noor responded curtly, 'I will do fine.' She opened her school bag, took out the textbooks she had brought with her, turned the pages desultorily till she fell asleep with the books scattered around her. Talib stayed out, coming in for a meal while Noor slept. Noor woke to eat, pretended to study, slept some more and woke to eat. By then Talib was gone to work.

'Why does Bhaiya have to work tonight?'

'He asked for Friday off so he could spend it with you and they put him on the Saturday work schedule. He wanted to spend the day with you.'

Noor ignored her mother when she made preparations to collect the evening water. Ameena did not insist on Noor accompanying her.

But when she returned with the water, she called Noor to her side. Noor pretended to be engrossed in her studies and Ameena spoke in a voice that did not brook resistance, 'Your studies can wait. You are leaving tomorrow and I have to speak to you.'

Noor dragged herself to her mother's side. 'Say what you want to say quickly. I have to study. Maths and Hindi exams are on Monday.'

'Good, I am glad you are studying. I want to know what you would think of living here.'

'Living here?'

'Yes, in this house. Talib is prepared to pay for your school fees. Maybe he's already told you that he has been paying your fees for some time now.'

'No, he didn't say anything about that.'

'Never mind. It is not necessary for you to know these things. You are a child. Before when I thought about the move it didn't seem like the right idea; I thought your friend Haseena is there and your school...but now. Would you not like to be here with Talib? It is difficult at times. I don't like being here alone at night. But I have gotten used to it. Talib speaks of you often. He worries about his little sister and he says he would like to pay for you to go to a better school.'

Noor spoke in a flat voice. 'You might think it's nothing to leave Baba. But I won't leave him. Never. I don't care about better schools. Or eating in restaurants like you do.'

'Noor, is that what you think? Though you are a child I will explain something to you. Your brother is a loving boy but in time he will truly leave us. Imagine, he will marry, he will have a child, maybe a little Noor for whose schooling he will need to keep his money. Now while he is still here, you must take the help he gives you.'

'I won't, and you can't make me. I won't leave Baba alone.'

Ameena withdrew into silence. *I have done wrong leaving her responsible for her father. But what else could I have done*? She bit her lip and considered offering more explanations. But what was there to explain. The son earned and the father didn't. The son no longer wanted to live under the father's roof and the father would not come here to live under the son's roof. Ameena had left her daughter behind and chased after the son, for the love of him, yes. But also to hold onto the income they needed from him. How was she to explain this to a thirteen-year-old girl who sometimes functioned as if she was nine and at other times as if she was sixteen? She could offer Noor no explanation, just reassurance the girl would not or could not accept.

'Noor,' she said as gently as she could to the back her daughter had turned toward her, 'you won't be leaving him alone.'

They slept as they had the night before. Sunday morning, Talib came in soon after breakfast and announced that he, and not Ameena, would accompany Noor to Chirag Dilli. Ameena had thought the ride back together would give her one more opportunity to try to break the silence between her and Noor, but she conceded that it was more important for Talib to break the silence with his father. She kissed and hugged the stiff face and body Noor held out to her.

The women's compartment had been relatively empty on her ride to Talib's home but riding back with Talib in the general compartment, Noor saw the metro, like the bus, was sweaty and horrible work. She shrank away from the man who pressed his leg against her. When that didn't work, she thrust her knee out with a jerk and he retreated. At Haus Khas metro station, Talib abandoned whatever unspoken intentions he may have held to accompany her home and once there to meet his father. He sprang for the cost of an auto, insisted on describing it as a treat. Noor did not tell him this ride, alone in the auto, terrified her as the ride on the metro to his home had not. She tried to comfort herself with thoughts of home. What she pictured was the dark room she had left, the silhouette of her father, other silhouettes—the bucket, no doubt full of dishes, the bed and the tin trunk that hunkered under it, the cupboard in the corner. And inside the cupboard was her mother's jewellery bag. So then, her mother would return for this bag but not to remove it from there as Noor had feared, but to herself remain. Behind the jewellery bag, in the back of the cupboard was the little seed, Haseena's birthday present. Noor cursed the seed under her breath. The seed was as dead as Haseena's grandmother. Because there was no such thing as destiny and girls having to take stupid seeds with them from one house to the next. Noor was no longer afraid. Instead, she nursed the anger she had built over the previous two days.

Haseena, she spoke to her vanished friend, I did not tell them about Baba's clothes. How they smell of ashes, how they are covered in ashes, how even after I wash them they remain grey. Let Talib and Ammi come here if they want to know anything about Baba and me. I am never going there again.

23

Cheaters All Save One

Noor prayed for divine intervention in the Ajith matter. It was not to be. God, as usual, was least interested in her. Besides, the list of things she had prayed for included the request for easy examinations. And so far she had not been disappointed in this matter. And if god were only in the mood to dispense one blessing at a time, then she was not going to complain about the one she was receiving.

The two weeks of final exams got underway. Everyone in class agreed the exam questions posed to them were of the kind that allowed for easy cheating. Noor had prepared a cheat sheet for her Maths exam based on the previous year's examination questions. Astonishingly, the same questions were repeated without even the effort of re-ordering them. In Science class, a diagram of the cell their teacher had drawn during the previous week of revisions was only faintly erased from the blackboard. And indeed the first question on the examination paper asked for a detailed diagram of the cell with all parts correctly labelled. Those who were seated in the back of the class, cursed these seats which were normally the best ones for cheating. But Noor found that craning to see the blackboard yielded access to the student in front of her, whose own craning brought her the information she needed. Correct labelling proved not to be impossible for even those furthest from the blackboard.

In Hindi class, Ma'am simply remained in her seat after handing out the examination papers. At first the students kept their heads down and attempted the questions with the aid only of whatever cheat sheets they had brought with them. But to the class's astonishment, a few minutes into the exam, Ma'am pulled out a novel and propped it up in front of her face. When the whispering and passing around of cheat sheets reached a crescendo of volume and activity, when students were indeed running from one end of the classroom to another to debate over conflicting answers, when finally a line formed at Ajith's desk, Ma'am coughed from behind the novel.

Her classmates scrambled to return to their seats. Noor had of course remained in her seat all along.

'Class, it seems like we must tell the sweeper we have a mice problem in the school building. Do you hear the sound of mice scuttling around? I only wish they wouldn't scuttle so noisily as to bring Principal Ma'am here.'

'No Ma'am, we don't hear any mice,' chorused Noor's classmates. All except Poonam, who swung in her seat and glared all around.

How two-faced, Noor thought, of Poonam. She is just upset that Ajith is best in Hindi. Ajith. She repeated his name to herself—Ajith—bringing forth the usual flood of pleasure-pain. Of late, this was a favourite and deliberate practice.

At the top of her examination clipboard she had written 'God is Love.' This was supposed to ensure good luck in the examinations. Other students though swore by 'God is Truth.' Noor thought Love was far more important to god and therefore to success in an examination than Truth. In any case, even those who wrote God is Truth cheated and that was the kind of falsehood Noor simply did not practice.

She practiced love during examination season, chiefly by scraping together coins for distribution to beggars on the walk to school. She favoured those whose suffering was of an order such that her charity might yield proportionate blessings. Among them was an old man with stumps for hands and feet. He was pulled along on a cart by his screechy wife. Noor liked the old man and during examination season she made it a point to place her coins directly in his bandaged stumps. There were those who said the bandages hid functioning hands and feet and that he should get out of his cart and work instead of making his poor old wife pull him along. But Noor knew from her contact with those hands they were indeed balls of flesh minus fingers.

Flexing her own fingers Noor wrote the letter A, then J. She stopped. This wouldn't do. She would not become one of those girls who wrote boys' names all over the last pages of their notebooks. And here now she had nearly done so on her examination clipboard, nearly desecrated 'God is Love' by adding Ajith to the equation. If she kept at this she would not only fail her examinations, repeat sixth standard and eventually become the screechy old woman who had made fun of her this morning when she put her coins in the man's stumps, 'Ho, it's examination season, is it? What do you think old man, is this girl going to pass? Now how will she pass, old man, if she doesn't know yet how worthless a one-rupee coin and another one rupee is. Girl, even added up the number is only two. Ho girl, you better learn your higher numbers.'

She looked over at Ajith and yes, he immediately looked back. This too had been going on all week, despite his head-down-over-his-books studiousness during lunch period when she contrived to wander by.

But the week was drawing to a close and in another week, exams would be over and school would close. She had to make him look at her. Without her looking desperate, of course. If he had taken note of her wandering near the old lunch spot, he had not scorned her for it. When she met his eyes in class, as she had just now done, there wasn't the triumph she expected to find, the triumph that would perfectly correspond to her feelings of defeat. But neither could she read what was present in his eyes. It did not seem likely to her that when he looked at her, he might see the glow of light around her that she saw around him. Her cheeks glowed with heat at the possibility of such a thing happening. She looked at her dirty fingernails, her unpolished shoes. *So what? His shoes and fingernails are no better.* Carefully she got out her pen, clicked to red ink and boxed in the letters A and J and then filled the boxes in; the letters disappeared behind red ink.

The interesting thing about cheating was how little time it took to answer questions that did not have to be puzzled over or scratched out. Time hung on her hands. There's nothing better to do, she thought, as she carefully created three new boxes next to the A and J boxes. In these she wrote the letters I, T and H. She coloured them in so the letters disappeared. Now there were five coloured boxes hiding her delicious secret. The bell rang for lunch. Ignoring a group of girls who hissed as she walked by, she continued on her way, trailing Ajith down the dark hallway, shooing pigeons angrily as she went.

He hunkered down at his spot, opened his lunch box, then a book and buried his face in it.

'Why don't you ever look up when I come by?'

'You never stop.'

'Well, I'm stopping now.'

'And I'm looking up.'

'Why are you studying since everyone is just cheating on all the exams and the teachers are letting us?'

'I can't go to college by cheating.'

She promptly sat down next to Ajith. Of course. Of course. His answer was so right. Is this why she liked him so much? Because he always knew something she knew as well, something she was not aware of knowing till he made it known to her by his knowing it. She wanted to tell him, but her tongue was tied in every way. She managed to say, 'I am glad you are going to be an engineer on a ship someday.'

And he nodded shyly. She could see how shy he was, dropping his eyes, raising them again. She wondered again if he saw a light around her. She dismissed the idea. *Impossible.* She was only herself. No one would ever see a light around her. 'They're wrong to let us cheat, aren't they?'

He waved at the field. 'Look at the chalk lines. PT Sir and Lab Assistant Sir were out there this morning drawing a tennis court even though we have no tennis racquets and nobody here plays tennis. They have lines for football, as well, although what we play is cricket. If someone would get a football as well as drawing these lines then maybe we could play before the lines disappear. School inspection! Suddenly they are dressing up our school, and dressing us up with fine marks on our exams. Is this what we meant that day when Shilpa Ma'am asked us what was good about our lives and we answered "School"? That we can cheat, is that what is good? Is this why everyone in class is always talking about how great our school is, how much we love our school, our teachers, our Principal? Because they let us cheat? Because they want us to cheat?'

Noor dismissed this talk with a wave. She knew as did everyone the reason teachers were permitting the rampant cheating. 'It's not just our teachers and Principal Ma'am. I told my father about the cheating. I tell him everything, you know. He said I should just do my best and that it's not the teachers fault they are allowing us to cheat. They have to do it so the school can pass the inspection and keep our school certificate. Baba says without the certificate our education is worthless and then what about all the children who will come after us who also need to get an education? If our school was not here then where would they go for their education?'

'If we didn't do all this maybe those kids in the future would get a better education.'

A slow slyness crept over her. 'Even someone like you who doesn't cheat needs the school to keep its certificate. So are you going to be the one to stop the school form doing it?'

'Why should I alone act to stop what everyone wants? But you know if they could actually give us a football field, then I would show everyone here. You know I don't play cricket at school not only so I can study—and I know everyone makes fun of me for studying—but also because I am a better football player than a cricket player. The boys in the maidan never let boys like me join in the cricket games in the evening. So we have our own football team by the kooradan. And I am the team captain.'

Noor waited impatiently for him to finish his boasting. Her eyes glowed and she was excited to tell him something that he, for once, did not know. 'You think the teachers are fooling the inspectors. Baba says no one is fooling anyone. Real football fields are not drawn with a little white flour that blows away in the wind or melts in the rain. The inspectors know there is no football field here. They know we are cheating and don't have the correct answers for our examination questions. They are forcing our teachers to draw these lines because they don't want a real school here, not one where we can actually play and study. That's what Baba says. Baba says we are supposed to pretend we are studying so they can pretend they have given us a school.'

Ajith listened carefully and nodded. 'Yes,' he smiled, 'Your Baba is right. I didn't think of the inspectors pretending to be fooled. They want to be fooled so they can continue fooling us.'

'But the way you study,' she said, a note of admiration in her voice, 'you will become that ship engineer and that will fool everyone, won't it?'

'You're a funny girl,' he said warmly.

She laughed nervously and was embarrassed by her laugh, but she saw he was smiling just as nervously.

'What about your drawings? Will you do computer drawings like Shilpa Ma'am suggested that day in class? What did you draw for your Drawing Class exam?'

She spoke airily, 'Oh I drew a bicycle. I am sure you will be first this year. I could not draw the gears because I need to practice by looking at it. All day Baba has the bicycle with him and in the evening it is parked under the staircase where I can't see it in the dark.'

'Well, you are a funny girl then, and that's a silly reason to not know how to draw gears. Why, you can look at the gears of bicycles all over the street. And if you want you can see my bicycle. I don't mind showing you.'

After that the two of them sat silently together, nothing agreed to between them, and everything somehow clear in a way it had never been till then.

'I should go,' she said.

He did not disagree. She did not think she needed to ask him when and where they would meet. But after she had walked away, he called after her, and this is how the whole school came to know that Ajith was now chasing that Noor, who god knows had been chasing him since forever.

'Noor, I will wait for you in front of the school gate on Saturday morning. Will you come?'

She nodded briefly, and hurried away under the gaze of girls too surprised to hiss, and boys who were not so surprised that they failed to hoot.

24

Baba Again

Mohammad Saidullah greeted his daughter with a cry of delight. 'Done? Another year of learning and how much smarter is my daughter?' As if weighing the accumulated knowledge in her, Mohammad lifted her a few inches off the ground, panting to show how difficult a task this was. She frowned.

'Baba today is the last day of *this* week's exams. There's one more week to go.'

He responded with his own frown. 'Could be the brains or it could be fat? Well, whatever it is, you have grown.' He pinched her arm to indicate the fat. And stood by her side to measure her growth.

She slid out from under the hand he held above her head. 'I know I have grown. No one is asking you to pick me up. Is it my fault I have grown?'

'Noor, you are offended, whereas I am only showing you how very happy I am that I have a daughter who doesn't stop growing. Soon you will be taller than I am, then taller than your brother, perhaps we will have to get a bigger house to accommodate our giantess.'

'Stop making fun of me right now.'

But Noor was swept by sadness and her tone of mock anger did little to conceal it.

'Ah, are you noticing only now that you and I are shoulder to shoulder, equal with each other?'

This time she didn't stop him and Mohammad Saidullah lined up next to her, pumping his chest out and flexing his chest. She shrank next to him, no longer sad, but ashamed instead that she was indeed as tall as her father.

'No hunching. Your brother and I measured and measured, day

by day as he came up to me and eventually passed me. And such pride he took in it. He thought he was defeating me. But tell me something, was I fighting him? And why shouldn't you take the same pride? Why daughter, if need be I will buy you a taller house. Mind you I will buy it, not just rent it.'

'Baba, you didn't go to work today?'

'Lucky you, you won't be washing soot off my kurta.'

This acknowledgment of the work she did to clean kurtas whose dirt she did not understand, which dirt was only now being given a name by her father—soot—made her shy, then nervous. Yes, she realized it was soot she had been struggling with for three months. Why was Baba bringing into the light what had been in the dark till now?

Cautiously she asked, 'Is it a holiday from work today?'

'Holiday? Ha! Soon we will take holidays as and when we please. That's when I will have made the money to buy my extra tall daughter a gigantic house.'

His laughter was of a man in pain and she hurried to put her school bag down.

'Baba, go out. Let me change my school uniform and I will make tea.'

From the other side of the curtain in the doorway, he continued to speak, now with a dark exuberance and now with something more calm. She realized that it had been a long time since she had heard his voice carry such a distance as it did now. She was anxious lest Suneeta Aunty or Lata Aunty hear him. She hurried into her new salwar kameez, the one her mother had gotten someone in Talib Bhaiya's new neighbourhood to stitch for her. She found it had gone from being too new and too loose to faded and tight in a matter of weeks. She was growing, and she wasn't sure she liked it.

'Baba,' she said, handing him his tea, 'you still haven't told me if you have a holiday.'

She wanted instead to ask him what work he did and where? If it paid well, and if so was it enough to persuade everything to return to the order in which her family was once held. How much should Baba earn for her greedy mother to return, how much so her selfish brother would not have to be asked for money? Did Baba know that she, Noor, knew—about haftas, and the police, about municipal workers and about Baba's contractor in the market who pushed him down on the ground. Her mind whirled with the strangeness of thinking about rent and school fees and the cost of a salwar kameez stitched in a strange market by someone other than Hasan Chacha.

'Daughter, it is not a holiday we had today. We cancelled work to hold a meeting. I was chosen to speak at the meeting. This was a great honour. I wish you had been there to see how many people were at the meeting. If you could have heard all that was said.'

'And if Ammi had been there too.'

'Yes, your mother might have enjoyed it. There were women there, as well as men.'

'What did you speak about Baba? Was it a speech you made?' Her body moved unconsciously into the speech-making boy's stance, legs apart and hands clasped behind her back.

Her father deflected the question. 'When your brother started to approach my height, it was maybe around the same age you are now. Yes, he must have been almost fourteen, as well. I could talk to him then. Later, not so much.'

Noor dropped her eyes. Why was she ashamed, and of what?

'It must have been hard for you these last few months when your mother has gone to help your brother settle in his new house. It is not something I expected. That your brother would leave like this. I did not leave my father, you see. I was sent away. I did not want to go. So it is hard for me to understand that Talib went willingly. Your mother understands it. Perhaps because she had a choice when it was her time to leave home. Or perhaps she understands it some other way that I don't—because she is a mother. There are a lot of things I don't understand. But one thing I do understand is you too will leave some day.'

'Baba, I will never leave home. I'm not going to get married and all that.'

'Fine, then,' he laughed, 'we shall not get you married. Not even when the offers come pouring in from the Princes of Arabia. What will you do then? Become one of those modern ladies and go to office with a suitcase in your hands? Oh, that will be something for your father to see.'

'Let it be, Baba. I am too old to be teased.'

'Yes, you are indeed. Listen then to what I have to say Noor, who is too old. I was already working for some three or four years when I was your age. It is now some thirty-five years I have been working and my hair is grey. Your brother is right, I am tired and I cannot keep up. When they take a man's job and make it twice as hard, when they double the length of his workday, when a man's pay is reduced to half as much as it used to be…indeed a younger me would not keep up with what is required of me now. Well, let it be, I say. I shall live life as it comes to me. But if there is a chance to resist, why, I will resist.

'Yesterday kabadi was something I went door to door and collected. Today, the people I collected from give it to someone else. My contractor who has eaten my money for years, he tells me he cannot protect me. That the work is given to a company and the other man is an employee of the company.'

'Can't you also work for this company?'

Mohammad Saidullah frowned at his daughter's interruption. Then registering the ragged strain in her voice, he softened his voice, which had been steadily rising in volume and harshness.

'No, Noor, the company is far away. I don't know how they hire, nor even who they hire.'

'Then go to your old customers, Baba. Tell them you will give them a better rate. Remember how your customers in the pink house, Gupta Uncle and Aunty asked you to bring me to see them, and they gave me a box of Diwali sweets. They will give you their kabadi if you explain to them.'

'No, Noor. The whole colony has hired the private company to collect their kabadi. The Guptas will do what the rest of the colony does. The kabadi will be taken to an incinerator and the company will make money by burning it.'

'You get money by burning kabadi?'

'Yes, the incinerator turns the plastic and cardboard into electricity. Have you studied about electricity at school?'

'Yes, yes Baba. But also we learned about the incinerator, that it is a bad thing. Actually the teacher didn't know about it. But there is a boy in class who knows a lot of things. He told us smoke that comes out from the incinerator is poisonous for poor people. I mean it's poisonous for everyone. They want to put an incinerator even near here. In our maidan, where Talib Bhaiya used to play cricket, that same maidan. They won't put the incinerator where the rich people live. Because the rich people always say it is poisonous for them. As if it is not poisonous for us.'

'Well, you are learning a lot at school. So who is this boy who knows more than the teachers?'

'Oh nobody. He is just a show off. And sometimes he says stupid things too.'

'Stupid things, is it? Like what?'

'Oh once he voted "no" when the rest of us voted "yes" for banning plastic bags.'

Mohammad Saidullah laughed uproariously. 'If my daughter votes to ban plastic bags then what work will she leave her father who collects plastic bags for a living?'

Noor hung her head. 'Yes, I know. I mean I didn't think about that when we were voting. I was thinking about something else. Then suddenly we all voted. And only when Ajith voted "no" did I even know what we were voting for.'

'So his name is Ajith, this smart boy of yours. It is a good name for someone who goes his own direction. It has a meaning for the Hindus. Something like unconquerable.

'But tell me, daughter, we were speaking about what you will do instead of marrying when you grow up. Give this old man some warning about your modern ideas so I can get ready. Talib certainly took me by surprise. This time I must be ready even if it is to see my daughter carrying a suitcase and going off to an office.'

Mohammad was smiling as he spoke of Talib. His recent harshness appeared to have given way, perhaps in the act of imagining his daughter grown up.

'Oh no, Baba. It is nothing like that. Tell me what my name means. It means light, doesn't it?'

'Yes daughter, you know that it does.'

She hurried on, unable to sort and rank the questions that had been preoccupying her in any order of importance. Would she be allowed to ask all of them? How long before her father retreated into his customary silence or flared up instead, as he sometimes did?

'Baba, what work are you doing now? Was your meeting at the place you work?'

'Noor, I work at the dump near the incinerator. What kabadi doesn't get burnt in the incinerator is still available for someone like me to pick through the ashes and find. But it does mean that my daughter, Ms Light herself, has to wash some very sooty clothes.'

'Baba, when I grow up, I am going to be a kabadiwali. I am going to be the first kabadiwali in Delhi. I will make it so everyone in the colony will give their kabadi to me instead of to the incinerator.'

'Noor, you will do no such thing.'

'Yes, Baba. I will. I will. All I need to know is how to ride a bicycle. In fact I am already learning, from a friend. Yes.'

'Let me tell you something, daughter. Do you know that you are not just Noor, but actually Nooren. This means you are not just the light of one eye, but of two eyes. Now whose two eyes? Some people might say light belongs to everyone. But I say, not this light. This light belongs only to us. I say you are our light—

the light of your mother's eyes and the light of mine. We didn't raise you to turn you into someone who gathers other people's garbage, their rubbish. Do you think we want our light to turn into a kabadiwala?'

'Baba, I am not anyone's light. I am just me. Noor. And I just want to be like you. I even said so in class. I said it to the teacher and everyone else. I am going to grow up and be like my father.'

'Daughter, you honour me. But clearly, your mother and I have done a poor job of raising you if you have not understood that we want more for you than we have for ourselves. If you must become like your brother even to the point of turning from me, I would prefer that to you being like me.

'The meeting we had today is to fight for our work. But I don't fight for this work so you can do it. I fight for it because the work is mine. The private companies have come to do this work because there is money to be made doing it. Who made this work what it is today? We kabadiwalas did. If there is money to be made then we should make it. But if I get my work back it is so you can do better than I did.'

'Baba, Talib Bhaiya says you should leave this work and do something else. He says he has been helping you keep this job for the last two years but that he will not keep paying for you to do it. Baba, it's not just because Bhaiya wants to save money. He is worried you are getting old. And it is not good for your health.'

'Ah, so my son has talked to my daughter about this. Never mind. He is your brother after all, just as he is my son. He must have told you I am fighting because I am stubborn and because I am proud. If I am stubborn, it is for both of you; if I am proud, it is of both of you. I raised both of you by doing this work. It is work that belongs to me and no one can take it from me. For now I will even crawl in the ash heap but later it will be another matter.'

'Yes, Baba.'

'And you will not be a kabadiwala. What an idea!'

'Baba, if someone wants to be a kabadiwala, not me, but someone else, can they become one?'

A little puzzled, Mohammad Saidullah shook his head. 'Well, Noor. No one can decide anything by themselves. I cannot simply become a kabadiwala. It is not up to me alone. First I have to have a contractor who agrees to buy from me, he also takes money from me to help me get a route, and then the police and the municipal worker, they also have their hand out, then finally the customers must sell to me. And now they don't want to.'

'Does it have something to do with us being Muslims?'

'Well, some of us are Muslims. And we have good work buying and selling kabadi. But many more Hindus buy and sell kabadi than Muslims.'

'But only some Hindus can become kabadiwalas?'

'I see what you are asking me. Hindus from certain castes can do this work. Mind you it is not work some high-up type wants to do. But yes, the Hindus who do my work have some caste. Not a lot, but some. Those who have no caste do the lesser work. You see them going through the naala, looking through the kooradan. It is why your mother objects to my work, because it is so close to their work. But she is wrong. It is not so close. That is how the work is organized, so that my work is not so close to their work.

'And daughter, women do not do this work. And my daughter certainly won't.'

'But I want to show everyone I am proud of you. The kids in class, they made fun of you being a kabadiwala.'

'They did, did they?'

'Yes, they tried to imitate your call, and not even properly, "kabadiwalaaaa" and then they laughed, and then Shilpa Ma'am told me to learn to draw on a computer.'

'Nooren, I cannot answer the children in your class and I cannot answer your teacher. But I can tell you one thing, and it is this—it is not your job to be proud of me. It is my job to be proud of you.'

Noor repeated Baba's words to herself: not her job to be proud of him, but his to be proud of her. Something lifted from her and something else settled; the exchange of one weight for another left her unsteady. She saw her father ride away, soot covered, and she stood with a briefcase in her hand, momentarily lost. Then the weight settled or she accepted it, she didn't much know which.

'Can I still learn to ride a bicycle?'

'Why not? Tell your friend to teach you well. There is nothing more joyful than riding down the street on an early morning before the cars take over the road and begin blowing their smoke on me. Who says you have to be a kabadiwala to ride a bicycle?'

'No one. No one.' Noor shouted her joy.

Lata Aunty promptly stuck her head in the door. Seeing father and daughter laughing, she frowned. 'What is all the noise, then? You must have come first in class to be making such noise.'

For once Noor did not feel herself bridle in response to Lata Aunty's snideness. 'Results are not out yet, Aunty. It's still week one of our exams.'

Lata Aunty shifted her weight from one foot to the next and Noor couldn't help feeling sorry for her.

'Probably, I will be first from the bottom of the class, Aunty.'

'Humph, and you speak so easily of it. How is that something to be proud of? Your poor mother. She must surely be worrying about how you have done? Bhaijaan,' she turned from Noor to address Mohammad Saidullah, 'as soon as their summer holidays are underway, you must send this girl of yours to my house to learn some proper cooking.'

'Sister, she is the light of this home, how can we send the light anywhere else? In any case her mother has finished settling our son and she will be returning shortly. In fact, in just one more week when Noor's school closes. I dare say she will teach Noor something of what remains for her to learn.'

25

Saturday and Saturday or More Than One Chance

Her first meeting with Ajith, scheduled for a Saturday at the close of the first week of exams, had proven a non-meeting. On that day, drawing closer to the figure at the school gate she had found someone else there, not Ajith. It was too late to turn away by the time Noor saw that it was Jaffrey Sir.

'Oh, it's Noor. How wonderful. And you must live close by. '

'Yes, Sir. Please, Sir, I have to meet another student for exam revision.'

'Very good. I approve of such studiousness. Now if you will just help me for a moment.' And with that he thrust an armful of his maps toward her. Her arms responded by instinctively making the load their own. In an instant she was weighed under rolls, many of them loose and likely to unfurl if the load was not balanced just so. She arched her back to lift her arms higher, to curve them further, and to bring them closer to her chest. Higher now, the maps obscured her vision.

'We have no storage, you see. It must be something to teach in a school where materials can be kept permanently. But in any case I do not experience any hardship, not as long as there are children, as studious as yourself'—and here she could not see if he was looking in her direction but she heard his voice beaming at her—'I hope, Noor, you love Geography, which is really, you know, a study not of lands and people and our atmosphere and so on, but is actually a study of our imagination. To see the lands, to see the people, we must first be able to imagine they exist. Ibn Batuta, you must know, had that sort of imagination.'

Jaffrey Sir brought his face closer to hers, 'Next week in the Geography exam, we will have a question on Ibn Batuta. You might tell your classmates that. All right?'

'Yes, Sir.'

'Soon students as eager as yourself will be arriving here. What do you think, shall we get this lock open and let them in?' His thin arms and shoulders worked at the iron lock and with some exertion slid the bolt from its place and unchained the gate. The maps had to be placed on the ground when the gate did not budge for Jaffrey Sir. Noor and he leaned with all their might and pushed with outstretched arms. The gate dragged across the bumpy earth. All of his thinness shambled in a little dance of delight once the gate stood open.

'Sir, I didn't know you taught on Saturday.'

'Actually, Noor, I don't strictly speaking teach Geography on Saturday. But since I am already here to open the school and allow the computer class to meet in the lab, I bring along my maps. When they see these maps even some very dull imaginations are woken to imagine what else there might be beyond this very little place in the universe we call home.'

'Yes, Sir.'

Over Jaffrey Sir's shoulder, Noor saw Ajith, a speck in the distance slowly emerge astride his bicycle. Her heart beat painfully as he halted, still some distance away.

'Do you think about the world out there, Noor? You must do so because you see, at your age you have the maximum facility to imagine what has never been imagined. At my age I can merely re-imagine those things I stored up in my imagination during my youth.'

Noor shifted impatiently from one foot to the next. She could only imagine Ajith would be gone when she returned from depositing Jaffrey Sir's maps within.

Indeed her imagination, powerfully accurate though it was in its prediction of doom, fell short in realizing the details and full extent of that doom. Not only had she to carry the maps within but she also had to help Sir hang them, and then to fetch cloth and water and wipe the previous day's test question and answers from the chalkboard so Sir could put up his own questions and answers in their place.

When she stepped out the school's front door, she nearly shouted out in her happiness. Ajith was standing at the gate, one hand steadying his bicycle and the other gesticulating wildly. She saw just in time that he was signalling a warning to her and she saw the reason for his doing so. She slunk away to the side of the building as Principal Ma'am boomed from between them:

'Wonderful, Ajith. Then I shall go inside and you will allow in only those who have come with their Jyotimala Adult Class passes. Now why are you waving your arm about like that? That is completely unnecessary to the task at hand.'

Noor waited some moments after Principal Ma'am's departure. Ajith indicated when she might emerge from her hiding place behind a bush and she did so cautiously. In an instant, she had crossed the field in front of the school. In another instant she was at his side. With an apologetic glance over her shoulder, she slid past him and then she was out the gate. Ajith's whispered shout followed her, 'Don't you like the bicycle?' Her back to him, she hurried away, nodding emphatically so he might see her nod across the distance that was rapidly growing between them.

Yes, she nodded, she liked his bicycle that was darker than the dark green of the bicycle she drew in her notebook and dreamt in her dreams. Yes, she nodded, I see you, and that glow around you is still there.

Abandoning caution, he called after her, 'Where should I meet you?'

She would not reply. She could not reply. I am a coward, she scolded herself, and quickening her steps, she pushed through the crowd of computer class students that was flowing in the direction of the school gate. With a last look of sorrow at the thin figure standing sentry at the gate, she ran home.

Monday at school, he repeatedly turned in his seat at the front of the room to meet her eyes at the back. Girls nudged each other.

She and he were the scandal of the classroom. She saw notes exchange hands. She had more to lose than the note-writers if these notes about her and Ajith were to fall into teachers' hands.

At lunch, she stormed past the girls at the edge of the cricket field, and past the boys who stopped their game to watch her. She would tell Ajith he was a rotten human being, a cowardly dog and an imbecilic monkey if he thought she was some stupid girl looking to meet him on a Saturday, ever again.

He was at his usual spot, notebook open and lunch box closed. Seeing her, he hurried to open the box. She halted in front of him; concentrating on the heat within, she glared at him. He met her eyes from under his flop of hair. She opened her mouth to let out the pent up grief in her chest. 'You,' she began but the words she had planned were overtaken by the words that had been living in her since Saturday.

'At the kooradan,' she panted, 'next Saturday. And don't forget your bicycle.'

All week thereafter, she avoided him in the hope the classroom whispers would die out and the notes cease being written if she were to keep to herself. At lunchtime she ate with whichever group of girls she chanced upon. Meeting their scorn with appropriate docility she rendered herself boring. But it was all unnecessary, after all. The school was soon abuzz with a real scandal. Some boys from a senior class had been caught posting pictures on some senior girls' Facebook profile pages.

Gratefully, Noor joined the others in giving Poonam the lead. 'Is it bad to post pictures?' she asked.

'It is those kind of pictures,' Poonam said, making a mysterious gesture with her hands that some of the girls seemed to understand. They are only pretending to understand, Noor thought furiously, But she made certain to nod along, all the while careful to hide behind as mild an expression as she could pretend to.

Noor herself did not have access to whatever this thing was called 'facebook'. The old phone which Baba had given Talib Bhaiya when he was still in school no longer worked. On the bus ride back from the mobile store the day they had gone as a family to purchase that phone, Bhaiya had held the phone out of the bus window and screamed into the evening air, 'Everyone, see my new phone', so that Noor had been simultaneously embarrassed by and pleased for her brother's happiness. He had worn out the keypad of that old phone with his addiction to 'facebook', worn it out before she could inherit it. And now he would not let her breathe near his new 'smart' phone. She had tried persuading him to show her. 'It's not dumb like the old one, is it?' she'd said. He had scowled fiercely. 'My phone is my life. Don't ever touch it or you will pay.' And she had known better than to touch it.

Some other children could borrow their brother's or sister's phones and not only did they have this thing called facebook, more exciting was the way in which some children claimed they could even watch movies on their phone. It would be so much fun, she thought wistfully, to carry a phone everywhere and watch serials whenever she felt like it. But she had not lined up as so many of her classmates had in the past when some one or other child had come to school with a sibling's phone. What would she have done anyway in the line other than reveal how little she knew about what they were doing?

That entire last week of exams was dominated for Class VIII C by discussion of who among them had Facebook accounts and who didn't. All the boys seemed to have these accounts. And funny names too for their accounts, like 'Malik Swag' and 'Rap Star Singh'. Noor wondered if Ajith had an account and decided if he did then it would probably just be his name. Predictably Poonam was the only girl who had an account. But then she was the only one who had her own mobile phone and what use was a Facebook account without a mobile phone. 'I won't let any of the boys here friend me. All idiots. The only boys I am friends with are my cousins.'

Some of the girls stirred, their shoulders gently touching in acknowledgement of something Noor wasn't privy to. For once, her own crisis meant Noor was awake and paying attention. There was an audible snicker and Noor caught Shailaja and Josy exchange not-so secret smiles. Poonam knit her brows and said rather loudly, 'Anyone who wants to see my account can meet me after school.' When no one jumped at the chance, she spoke in a still louder voice, 'We can even look at the boys' because they are all such idiots they keep open accounts.' Perhaps, Noor thought, once again somewhat distractedly, Poonam will not be a head girl after all.

*

Yet another Saturday. This time, she moved quickly and with her head down. She did not want anyone recognizing her. She prayed there would be no football game underway at the kooradan. If Ajith's friends were there, would he say hello to her in front of them? She need not have feared.

That mid-May day, the blazing noonday sun, marked the high point of summer by torching the city of Delhi. All those who could, sheltered within walls. A lone cheel circling overhead saw only stray dogs sprawled about the kooradan. Those sleeping dogs, and a few minutes later two children tracing the cheel's flight on the ground below. One, a thin girl in a favourite long green dress, too tight now on her nearly fourteen-year-old body was astride a dark green bicycle behind which ran an even thinner boy, possibly shorter than she was. Their joyful sounds of scolding and exclamation, of revelation, rose and escaped the thick miasma emanating from the squat cement building they circled. The cheel joined its shadow to their dark forms below. Time passed.

The boy's exasperation—'You will never learn like this. Why are you being so careful? Why don't you save yourself from not falling off by just not riding at all?'

'What a stupid thing to say,' the girl cried. Her tears of exasperation sliding over the shine of her smile. 'The other way to not fall is to learn to ride. And I am doing just that.'

But she could be seen straightening her shoulders, gearing up to let go her fear. She pedalled harder when he shouted to her to pedal harder.

'Don't let go,' she cried. 'I already did,' he replied and she fell.

He wiped her tears. She shied from his hand the next time she fell. He was grim and kept his hand behind his back the third time she fell. She looked at him in apology but did not reach for his hand the fourth time she fell. But nor did she disallow the arms when they again steadied the bicycle, one hand on the handle bar and the other on the carry rack behind her. The hand on the handlebar let go first. She sucked in her breath and she was underway again.

'Pedal hard, Noor, pedal hard.' And the other hand was removed with a shout, 'Now.'

And she pedalled hard, the bicycle lighter without his hand there, the bicycle all her own to ride, wobblier at first, then smoother, then describing the curve of the earth beneath her, almost airborne now, she rode on her own.

He ran alongside her for as long as he could keep up. But she circled the cement structure of the kooradan, taking each circle faster and faster. Noor held her eyes wide open against the hot wind. *I am riding. Haseena, I am riding. Baba, look at me, I am riding. Bhaiya, Ammi, Look at me. I am riding.*

'Noor,' Ajith called to her, 'you are riding.'

She was dimly aware of the bicycle, its metal protesting the drag over tussocks of earth. She was riding the bicycle and something else, as well, something that had waited in her, waited for her to move like this, at this speed and by her strength.

'If I keep going, I will go right out of Chirag Dilli,' she shouted. 'Ajith, I am going to ride right out of here, out of Chirag Dilli. I'm going to go see the rest of Delhi.'

'No, you won't. Not as long as you keep circling the kooradan.'

She was riding a green bicycle, its wheels spinning and below her was the spinning earth. She was spinning with the spinning earth. This was what had waited in her all her life, this need to enter the world. In fear she called out to her friend.

'How do I stop?' she shouted. And he told her how, but she did not stop.

26
Goodbye

Ajith flopped to the ground, his chest heaving and insides burning. He hung his head between his knees and finding no relief let himself fall back to the earth. His overspread smile lay open to the sky; his eyes closed to the sun's white light continued to see its fiery centre, an orange orb that pulsed inside his lids. 'Stop,' he murmured to the girl on the green bicycle, who he believed would never stop. And neither did he want her to stop. The foolish smile on his face begged the sun to keep burning like this, to keep alive the endless afternoon.

Much later, he hauled himself up and with his usual sobriety persuaded her that she had to stop so they could see about teaching her to ride on the street. It became clear she really did not know how to stop and he had to chase her again, lunging for the bicycle, landing it and them on the ground.

There was some grumbling then: 'You didn't have to do that,' and 'What did you expect me to do then,' and 'You could have just told me how, after all that's how I learned to ride,' and 'Oh now you think you learned by just hearing some words I told you; maybe I can write a book full of words to explain to girls how to ride all by themselves' and 'I didn't say it was all by myself, and if you want me to say thank you then okay, here it is, Thank You, okay?' And so on in that most enjoyable delirium of never wanting to stop smiling not even when the pleasure of it mixed with the pain of eyes repeatedly meeting and dropping. Legs tangled in the fallen bicycle, they waited for the afternoon to never end, which inevitably it did.

'My father needs the bicycle back. I told him I was teaching a classmate and he said I could use it till it was time for him to move his goods to his contractor's place.'

Noor sifted carefully though this information. Was this an

opening and should she take it? She had ridden here this morning with two different aches in her chest. The first, the ache of anticipation was now fulfilled. The second, the ache of sorrow waiting to be distributed, tightened in her throat, wouldn't allow itself to be distributed. Suddenly, it was no longer the afternoon she learned to ride a bicycle, the afternoon she learned to stop wondering if Ajith saw the same glow around her that she saw around him; it was instead the afternoon she did not know how to say goodbye.

'You could,' Ajith said with forced casualness, 'just come with me to return the bicycle.'

And because she did not know how to tell him what she had come to tell him, she said instead that yes, she would go with him. She would meet his father, return the bicycle and yes, she agreed, if his father released Ajith from helping with the work, they would even see about finding a place to get a cold drink.

'I want a Mirinda or a Fanta,' she said, hoping he could hear goodbye in the words for these sugary drinks. She inflected the words with her sorrow but in truth her concern with how to speak 'goodbye' to him left her with less and less of her sorrow and more and more of the awkwardness of her situation. The old Noor, who did not know how to ride a bicycle wanted to blame Ajith for this awkwardness. She could hear that Noor summing up the situation with her usual disavowal of involvement in her own life: I didn't force him to like me; that was his choice to do so. The old Noor continued with a rather pronounced whine: It's my parents' decision, not mine, to send me to Talib Bhaiya's.

The earth that had always spun beneath her, never revealing itself to Noor the way it did to others—to gentle Haseena, even to silly fearful Poonam, to enthusiastic Jaffrey Sir and to Ajith, reticent and fierce and now looking at her with such warmth—this earth was now known to her. It was a place where she could and should act. She had ridden a bicycle today, felt the bicycle's wheel spinning with the spinning earth. This was the day to admit to herself that she could leave her old home and begin a new life with her brother in his new home.

'My brother says he will buy me a bicycle for my next birthday.'

'Is he coming back home to Chirag Dilli?'

'No, it won't be like that.'

Ajith did not hear what she was trying to say and they were already at his father's storehouse. Noor was not afraid as they lifted the gunny sack covering of the tarpaulin shelter. She remembered Ajith's less than funny joke about his father beating him. And she remembered Ruku's indignant, 'Our father does not beat us.' *Why had she been afraid in the past of other children's fathers? Did she think only she could have a father who loved her?*

Entering the dim dark of the shoebox-sized interior she found herself in a space that was cooler than the exterior but one simultaneously fetid and sweet. A moment later she registered sour and then sharp. It would be wrong to hold her nose. But she couldn't help the hand that reached up to her nose, so she had the hand take a swipe across her nose. Just a tickle, the swipe announced to the room, a tickle that needed settling. Again, she was conscious of her loyalty to Mohammad Saidullah. I am so glad, she told herself, that it is Baba who is my father. And then feeling a little babyish, she added, after all, he is the best father in the world.

The man inside stirred in his sleep and grumbled to Ajith that he had taken too long to come. Ajith prompted her, and she greeted his father. The man came fully awake then and hurrying to put on a shirt and to clear a space for her, he made her sit.

'Ajith, you have brought a friend with you. He has never brought a classmate before,' the man spoke apologetically. 'And you are the one then he wanted to teach to ride a bicycle? A girl?'

'Yes, Uncle,' she replied, feeling silly at admitting to being a girl.

The interior of the shelter was filled with boxes and bags of goods, sorted and waiting to be hauled away. There was, in fact, no space to sit, at least not without bumping knees with Ajith's father. She squatted on her heels and drew her knees to her chest.

But now Ajith's father continued his apology: these were goods of which he did not have enough to take to his contractor, not just yet. There were goods that took time to collect but were worth more than what he had piled up outside. Here was a pile of empty sauce packets, here a pile of ballpoint pens, here razors and wooden toys. The sacks they saw outside, bulging twice as large as the man in front of them, these sacks held goods sorted and of a quantity sufficient to be hauled to the contractor where they would be sold.

'This week I have rubber chappals I have taken a month to gather.'

Noor was able to give words then a picture to the sweet and sour smells from earlier; she was smelling rubber and sweat and ketchup and something else, she wasn't sure what.

'I will make money this week, but there would have been more if Ajith had come these past two weeks to help with removing the cardboard from the foil on these party plates. But I let my boy stay home and study for his exams and tried to do all the work myself. As you can see it's not as easy for my fingers as it is for his. And so this pile of plates is almost all of it waiting for him to come back to work so we can clear a little room in here for those who would visit us. You shaitan,' he cuffed Ajith's ear, 'now exams are over; don't think you can use that as a reason to not come around.'

'Go,' he told Ajith, 'I will manage this afternoon without you. But don't head to the football field this evening. I want you here so I can go home tonight.'

Ajith's father remained with the goods all week so they wouldn't be stolen, sleeping at home only those nights when the goods had been hauled away to the contractor or when Ajith took his place in the makeshift shelter.

Ajith nodded to his father. If Noor thought the nod stiff, she couldn't tell whether it was because of her presence or if this was how it always was between father and son. Baba would have hugged me and kissed me, Noor reflected. Then came the thought of this man, who smelled of the party plates from which he had peeled not only their thin foil coating but also old dried food, kissing and touching Ajith, then the thought of Ajith's work, peeling and sorting the same plates. She stirred restlessly, wanting to leave.

'Sit properly, Ajith's little friend. Nothing here is going to hurt you. Bring your friend something to drink, Ajith.'

'Oh no, Uncle,' she began, but Ajith had her hand in his and was hauling her up, 'We are leaving to get a drink.' It happened so quickly that she barely registered Ajith's father take her other hand and open it to deposit something he had been struggling for some time to extract from his kurta pocket.

Outside she opened her hand and saw she held two toffees, leaking from their shiny paper. Ajith frowned but did not indicate what she should do with these toffees. She had no pockets herself and finally she peeled them both, popped one in her mouth and handed the other one to him.

'You don't have to eat that,' he said, but put his toffee in his mouth. They walked along sucking on their toffees, their thirst growing fiercer, their thoughts travelling separate tracks.

Ajith left Noor on the cement platform under a peepul tree. The market was still all around them; shopkeepers were asleep behind downed shutters. Noor imagined Ajith would have no luck finding them something to drink. She wished she had asked for water at Ajith's father's shack.

Again, Noor thought fiercely of her father's goodness. Would he ever ask her to come away from her studies, to remain alone with goods that needed sorting before they were sold to the contractor? But on the heels of this came the fear of what waited ahead for her. Hadn't Ammi said it was difficult to sleep alone when Bhaiya worked in the evenings? But Baba had said he would send Noor only when Bhaiya's schedule changed to the afternoons. And it was Bhaiya who had sworn her to secrecy. He would not, he said, then he corrected himself, he could not, change his schedule. It was not because the night shift was more lucrative that he wanted to keep it. It was because working at night freed him to carry on with his daytime effort at 'business,' which would in the end pay better.

'Business, Bhaiya? You are doing business? But you are paid a lot already.'

'How small you think, Noor. You think our uncles thought small when they sold grandfather's land? No, they did not limit themselves to what was theirs. They turned around and sold land that belonged to everyone in that part of the village. Then they helped evacuate all those others.

'I am not saying I want to become gangsters like them. But there are opportunities for those who go looking for them.'

'Our uncles are gangsters?'

'Well, what else would you call men who have a sign that says "Property Dealers" but whose only property dealings consists of standing around and flexing their muscles when someone refuses to sell their property. No, Noor there are no more people around fool enough to agree to let them sell land. Just buyers who need land cleared of people and at a price convenient to the buyer.'

Bhaiya had laughed and promised Noor that he would arrange for her to sleep at the next door neighbour's home on the nights he worked.

But it wasn't the promise of a bicycle or of a school with real computers in it that had convinced Noor. It was the fact that if she moved to her brother's home then her mother would return to Baba. It was the fact that she was tired of taking care of Baba. It was the fact that Baba and Ammi once free of her could leave their one-room home in Chirag Dilli, move closer to the incinerator where Baba sorted through ashes for what could still be salvaged as kabadi. It was that the world was spinning and she was spinning with it: and now that she knew this she needed to go out into this spinning world. To her joy and her sorrow her life was changing and she was changing with it.

Ajith returned after a while with a giant green coconut in his hand.

'Have you ever seen a bigger one? I had to wake the man, he was asleep right on top of his cart. I made him wipe this one before I let him cut the top. When we are done, we can take it back and I told him I will wake him again if need be to cut it in half. He promised me there is good flesh inside.'

Noor nodded. And Ajith hastened the apology he had prepared. 'I tried for Mirinda but no one is open.' He waved around the market and Noor simply nodded again. 'I am sorry I had only enough money for two cold drinks. The coconut is thirty rupees if it's only juice we want and thirty-five for this one with the flesh. You like the flesh, don't you? I had forty rupees for the Mirindas. So now I have five rupees left and we can get something with that, as well.'

'I have money,' she said. She rushed forward. 'My brother makes a lot of money these days and gave me some for pocket money. Twenty rupees.'

'If you don't want coconut juice, just say so. I will wake a shopkeeper and you can buy your Mirinda. Or was it Fanta, you wanted?'

He stirred the straw inside the giant coconut in his hand, lowered his mouth to the straw and with great concentration took a noisy sip of the juice within.

'I didn't mean I wanted a different drink.'

Ajith handed her the coconut. She did not want to ask if he had another straw. She took a hasty wipe at it with her hem and took a thirsty sip, and another. And another.

'You stay alone at night when your father stays at your home?'

'It doesn't bother me. Being alone, is good. The only thing is, there is no proper light and I have to take my books and go sit under the street lamp.'

'Doesn't the smell bother you?'

'Does it bother you?'

'My father used to shake me off when he came home from work because he said he needed a bath first. But it never bothered me. But being alone at night, that would bother me.'

'When I was little, yes, it bothered me. All of it. The smell and the being alone. But not anymore. I don't have to do this forever.'

'I am not going to be a kabadiwali. That was a silly idea, I had. You were right.'

'You couldn't help it.'

'No, I couldn't.'

'What will you be then?'

'My father thinks I will go to an office. But I am not sure yet. And you? You are going to be an engineer on a ship?'

'Yes, on a ship. Because that will be the main way of transporting things around the world and I will go around the world on the ship.'

'And will your wife and children go on the ship with you?'

'Who said anything about a wife or children? Only girls think about things like that.'

'I wasn't thinking about anything like that. I was just being polite. I was just trying to say my brother wants me to come stay in his home. It will be good for me to do that because right now Baba is not making enough money and my brother is making some. Next year I will go to a different school near where Talib Bhaiya lives. Soon as Baba and Ammi decide it is time, we are all going to leave Chirag Dilli.'

'Then you won't be at our school when it reopens after summer?'

'No.'

'You didn't tell anyone at school yesterday. It was our last day and you didn't say goodbye.'

'You were the only person I had to tell. And I knew I would see you today.'

They sat there in silence long enough for the flies to transfer themselves from the empty coconut shell to their faces.

'Shoo,' Noor whispered to a fly and waved a hand that Ajith knocked against with his own 'Shoo.' He would have liked to lean a little closer, to tell her he had indeed thought about those things which he just denied thinking about but his 'Shoo' was as close as he ever got to doing so. He returned his hand to the cement between them. But she had learned to ride a bike on this day. It was easy for her to reach over and cover his hand with hers.

27

Always Already Gone

July 7. Her birthday was a week away. She walked home from her new school to a home that was not yet home. She still referred to it as Talib Bhaiya's house though he was little present in it. She knew she ought not to complain about this or about anything else to do with the new arrangement. But the wishful Noor of old lived in her yet, and indeed periodically inserted herself in the scene.

And so it was the old Noor who struggled with the front door's bolt and ripped her new school uniform blouse as she dove in to answer the phone. It was her mother on the phone, calling to talk to Noor about her birthday.

'Is there anything remaining for us to give you now that your brother has given you so many new things—new clothes, new books, a new school.' Quick came Noor's reply, 'On my birthday morning, I want to wake up at home between the two of you.'

'That's all? Of course, Noor. We will find a way to squeeze you in here.'

Noor registered her mother's surprised pleasure even as she was swept by the realization that what she had asked for was not in her mother's means to give and that what her mother was pleased to give her was not in fact what Noor desired. If Ameena was thinking of home as the place built from bamboo and stray bricks over a floor of earth, Noor was thinking of their old home two floors above Prakash Lumber, and the neatly stacked tins of sugar, flour and tea arrayed on shelves Talib and Mohamad Saidullah had built long before she could remember; Noor was thinking of the curtain that lifted in the morning breeze and of the trunk under the bed in which she folded and stored the night's sheets. The trunk existed in the new house where it rusted on the damp earthen floor under boxes and tins, buckets and a plastic chair on its side. Inside the trunk, under those bedsheets was her green anarkali, ripped under the armpits, the hem shredded when it had caught between the brake pad and the wheel that long ago day when Noor first learned to ride a bicycle.

'Will you make Baba come to Bhaiya's house? We can all watch TV and sleep on the floor and the next day it will be my birthday morning, and you can make Bhaiya's favourite sooji ka halwa and my favourite poori.'

Ameena nodded at this revision to the picture of the gift her daughter wanted from her. She understood her daughter, who was more of a piece with her than was her beloved Talib. She, like Noor, had experience of making minute adjustments to dreams, adjustments she was determined must have their separate reward, at least for her daughter: she would not be disappointed in her daughter for wanting what could not be had. She would not hold it against her daughter that for a mistaken moment they had both believed the mother could grant the daughter's wish.

'If that's what you want for your birthday, then I will try to talk to him. But will your father come to Talib's home? He is as upset at your brother living apart as he ever was. Still, I will try. Your idea is a good one. He will not deny you, not entirely, not on your birthday, Nooren.'

This was Ameena's first use of 'Nooren,' the name Mohammad Saidullah now nearly always used in place of the old 'Noor.'

It had not been Ameena's desire to scold Noor but her daughter saw 'Nooren' as chastisement for the special love her father bore Noor. And then the long tall name her father preferred to call his long tall daughter by reminded Noor she was too old to wish foolishly as a child would for things of the past. And so she was scolded twice in her mind. Which scolding entrenched her in her childish self, a self that was insistent in its loyalty to her father.

'Oh no, of course Baba mustn't come all the way here for the whole night. What was I thinking to ask for such a gift? It will be too long a journey for him to return to work from Bhaiya's house. I will come there to the two of you but Bhaiya…' she trailed off.

'Your brother won't come.' Ameena spoke flatly.

They might have ended the call on this note of disappointment—the mother at her failure to convince her daughter of her love and the daughter at her failure to stifle her habit of empty hope—but neither of them wanted that.

'Only another week for your birthday, I should look in the trunk to see if your green anarkali from last year can be repaired.'

'Only another week,' Noor sang. 'And I don't want another anarkali. I want something Western.'

And Ameena laughingly acceded, 'I won't try to squeeze you into that old anarkali. Something Western, you say.'

And so it was decided through a process of minute adjustments that Noor would spend her birthday with her parents in their new home, that her mother would not cook sooji ka halwa with poori, which was after all far from being either Noor's or her father's favourite; there would instead be aloo with poori, but later Ammi would make sooji ka halwa and later still Baba would wind up work and they would take the metro, all three of them to Bhaiya's house. On her birthday Noor would bring her father to her brother. On her birthday the four of them would be family for a day, not as they once were, but as they seemed now to have become. This was the plan for Noor's birthday.

*

But now there was still a week remaining till her birthday and Noor hurried to put the phone away. It was only then she struggled out of her school bag, and pulled from it Haseena's letter. She tossed the bag itself onto the week's worth of clothes piled on one side of the double bed that was for her exclusive use, so why not use it as she wished, turned the TV on, adjusted the volume to a roar, and made herself an afternoon snack to accompany the letter.

'I can eat anything I want, there is no one to say "yes" or "no" to anything I do,' she had written in her letter to Haseena. She had meant it to sound like a boast and she repeated it to herself now, but could not muster the requisite sense of triumph to give credence to the idea the bread and sugar sandwich in her hand was indeed her first choice.

Haseena's letter to Noor made reply to this boast:

'I could say the same here about how I manage for food. But the truth is I cook only when my aunt comes to see me. The rest of the time I eat dry roti and I drink tea till I can hear it slosh inside me when I move. Yes, I could cook halwa and ladoo and kheer for every meal but without Ruku and Aseef and Abba to cook for I cannot bring myself to cook anything.'

Noor would have liked to have been unhappy with this letter which had begun by scolding her, not for reading Haseena's notebook, but for spending all that money mailing it to Haseena.

'You should have held onto the notebook. You saw you had made a mistake reading some of it so I am sure you would not have read the rest. Anyway the important thing is you shouldn't have spent the money. Especially since I am returning, maybe in time for your birthday. My father needs me in Delhi to help him with the packing up and then we will come back here, all of us, to our village. My father is so pleased with me. And Noor, truly, I am pleased with what I have done. The last time Abba sent me here I was too young, and I could not help my grandmother when she needed me. But this time, if I had not stayed here how else could Abba have secured our home from those who would have taken it? I had to be the one to go to the tehsildar's office and to give Abba's papers to the officer there. I had to do it again and again because they made me wait outside the office for many days. But I did not give up and went every day and the officer had to finally agree it was our land to keep.

'The school here is not as nice as Jyotimala School. There is no one like Shilpa Ma'am here. In fact, in the girls' school we have only one teacher, and he is very strict. That's right, school is separate-separate for boys and girls. The boys go in the afternoon all the way to the next village, which is where their school is. I have never seen it. We girls go in the morning, but in our own village. We girls even have a cricket team at school and we play not only during lunch but before and after school, as well. In the afternoon, our school returns to being a factory. Some women and many of the girls from school work there to make beautiful notebooks. You might think the notebooks are for us, but actually I don't know who they are for. They get taken away to be sold somewhere else.

'When Ruku and Aseef arrive, I will have to figure out how to make arrangement for Aseef to go to school. It is a long walk for a small boy. Perhaps I will have to miss school and walk him for the first few days. Anyway, I am boring you with all these details. But I mention them because I am so filled with joy working out the details of how I will manage when my brother and sister come here.

'And I am filled with joy that I will see you in a few weeks. Maybe even on your birthday. And don't worry about the notebook.'

Noor bristled at Haseena's acceptance of Noor's sins, bristled at Haseena's serene confidence that Noor could have held onto the notebook and not read any further. Noor thought about how hard it was to not keep reading it during the time she had it with her. She said aloud what she would write if it wasn't too late for a reply to reach Haseena who would have to be on her way in just a few more days if she meant to be here for Noor's birthday: 'Miss Goody-Goody.'

But Noor could not remain angry at Haseena. She spoke into the empty room, 'Haseena, I will wait for you at the taps on my birthday. I know you will be there.'

*

Noor turned fourteen. On that day she found out how very wrong and yet right Jaffrey Sir had been about the power of imagination. Very little, in fact, of what she had imagined about her birthday came to be. True, she woke between her father and mother. But it could not truly be called waking since she had slept very little in that space too tight for her longer-taller body, on that ground too hard for the body used to the comfortable bed that had travelled with her from her old home to Talib Bhaiya's house, a bed that would have swallowed up this shack her parents now called home.

She woke on her fourteenth birthday morning impatient for the sound of squirrels to join the sound of crows, impatient for her father's snores to give way to the fuss of her mother's morning adjustments to clothing that had twisted around her in the night. Long before any of what she anticipated could come about, Noor heard a familiar musical honk from the road running a few metres from where they slept. For a moment, she imagined herself back in their Chirag Dilli home. And as when that honk had sounded in the past, so now her brother stepped through the short curtain her mother had hung over the shack's doorway. The curtain, lifted, did not show her a corridor lined with bathroom-goers waiting to sound their birthday greetings. Outside it was yet dark but a street lamp illuminated the silhouette of dwellings built as low to the earth as her father's own. Talib put his finger to his lips.

'Yes, it is waiting for you at home. Yes, it is green.'

She let out a shout of happiness, and too late her father woke to the sound of her disloyalty.

Talib's bland explanation to them: 'I got the company van to drive me here instead of home.' Her father muttered about being woken early by a son's grandstanding, and her mother did not remember, and Noor did not remind her, that it was to be poori aloo and not poori halwa on this morning. They ate after Noor fetched water. Noor cursed herself for that happy shout which hung over the unwrapping of her parents' present to her: a length of fabric her mother promised could be turned into whatever she pleased. Talib, who was restless throughout, announced his departure immediately afterward. His father said, 'Go then, go,' and looked at Noor. Noor's voice too took on the quality of an announcement: she would remain here the day and make her way to her brother's home alone in the evening.

She hated herself for the power of her wishing, wishing which had brought the bicycle into existence. This is what Jaffrey Sir had meant when he said, if you can imagine it then you will see it—those faraway countries on his map, countries he said would disappear if people didn't imagine them. But he had not explained that once imagined into existence these countries would prove to be so frightening.

Was Jaffrey Sir right and was it true that by wishing as hard as she had she had conjured the bicycle of her dreams, the green bicycle waiting for her at Talib Bhaiya's house? How frightening it was to realize this. How had she failed to imagine her dream would be realized by the wrong person—her brother, and not her father?

How had she failed to see her mother's longed-for return home would result in her own banishment from home? And that her brother's restlessness in her father's too-small house would also be her restlessness? And was her restlessness only the result of confinement in too small a house? Was it not also the result of confinement in her loyalty to him?

But her father had released her from this loyalty. He had said she was not to learn to ride a bicycle just so she could become a kabadiwala, like him. But if her father could release his daughter from the expectation of loyalty, why couldn't he do the same for his son?

She had imagined just such an outcome when she had imagined her birthday would bring everyone together. She had imagined her father would reassure her brother and her mother would feed them all. It was not to be. Here they were all together, and here her brother was walking out the door, and their father was pretending to busy himself so he would not have to see his son leave. She was confused. Could one imagine a green bicycle, one that had never even existed, into existence, but then not be able to imagine a family that had once existed back into existence? Was she wrong to want what her father could not give her, and what had her imagination cost her?

If Haseena were here, she thought. But Haseena wouldn't understand this question. Haseena wanted what her father wanted: a life in their village.

'Baba,' she asked him the afternoon of her birthday, 'have you ever had a friend who was a Hindu, like Bhaiya was friends with Lata Aunty's son?'

Her father told her the story of Lakshman. 'But no,' her father said, Lakshman was not like Talib's friend, Ashish.

'Because, he was always chewing gum and punching you?'

Her mother gave her a significant look. And her father simply answered her silly question.

'No, because he was considered so low that he was given the worst work in our shop. But that was not how I considered him.'

'So are you still friends with him?'

'No, a man cannot just wish himself a friend. Lakshman lives in Patna. Or at least I think that's where he still lives. Perhaps he has a wife and children like I do. It would be too difficult, such a friendship. But we were good friends then.'

'In my old school, our Geography teacher, Jaffrey Sir, said that we have to be able to imagine things. Like I had to imagine riding a bicycle. He said if you can't imagine it, even an entire country can just disappear from the map.'

Her mother looked up from the lunch preparations, 'Noor, remember when Shabbi Mausi wanted to teach you to ride Baba's bicycle some years back?'

'No, she didn't. Shabbi Mausi never taught me.'

'Yes, you pestered her and pestered her to teach you.'

'No, it's not true. I never learned, Shabbi Mausi never taught me.'

'No, because the moment she put you on the bicycle, some children walking by called you a kabadiwala and you cried so hard, she had to give up.'

'I don't know what you are talking about. That might have been Bhaiya when he was little.'

Baba tried to help, 'Maybe she didn't have a very big imagination then, our Nooren. She was not so long and tall then, was she?'

'Don't tease me, Baba.'

Her mother took a hand covered in flour, and gently turned Noor's face toward her, 'Baba is right. There is a difference between wishing for something and being able to imagine it. Baba and I more than just wish when we think about you and Talib. We can allow you to live far from us, that is how much we will do for you. You too had to do more than wish to get on that cycle. If only your anarkali didn't have to show all the evidence of your imagination, but it's there, the evidence, if you want to see it. You fell, didn't you?'

Noor flushed with the heat of remembering that day, remembering falling.

She kissed her mother shyly, 'I love the material. You can make me an anarkali again. It is still the fashion. But don't throw the old one away.'

*

Noor imagined herself waiting at the taps. She would go there this afternoon. And if Jaffrey Sir was right, then Haseena would be there. She imagined Haseena clapping her hands to Noor's eyes, and imagined herself spinning around to catch Haseena's two hands in her own; she imagined the two of them jumping, hands on each other's shoulders. She imagined looking over Haseena's shoulder. No, of course she was not looking for him. But yes, he was there: the small form of Ajith as she had once seen him, a speck in the distance beyond Jaffrey Sir's shoulders that failed Saturday. Then too the sun had splintered itself on a green bicycle's silver spokes, and danced a thousand lights about him.

'That day didn't mean anything,' she advised herself. 'If he had wanted to, he would have found me by now.'

If she was trying by the force of her words to erase Ajith, she succeeded only in imparting wistfulness to the familiar hurt of remembering him. Why did she continue expecting him at every turn? She busied herself in hiding from this question as she had on other afternoons.

Something had remained incomplete in her at the end of that Saturday she had spent with Ajith. What remained incomplete was what had always been incomplete in her, and would perhaps always remain incomplete in her. But that day sitting next to him on the cement wall, her hand over his, then his hand turning under hers, so now his palm met hers, and their fingers found a way to wind themselves together, and over minutes they had grown not easy but at least less frightened of the sensations coursing through them, on that day she had been made aware of her incompleteness and the accompanying pleasure of straining toward completeness.

Most afternoons, when she returned from the new school where she was only beginning to sort out faces, to see the possibility of new friendships, when she struggled with the heavy bolt of the door to a home that was as empty after she entered it as before, she missed him. She missed him with the dimmest sense of how he had never really been there, of how he was always already gone. And then she ran out the room and down the road outside her new home and baked her head in the after-school, afternoon heat in which the entire city was held. On those afternoons, the Lata Aunties in her new neighbourhood said of her, there goes that girl ruining a perfectly good complexion. You see what happens to a girl who has no mother to guide her. You see what happens to a girl who is allowed to live with no responsibilities and without a care, she becomes careless of everything.

*

'Did you know Baba, before I learned how to ride a bicycle I did not know any other girls who rode? But I see them all the time now. They ride bicycles like Shabbi Mausi and I ride bicycles.'

'Well, yes. There are women who ride bicycles. A street sweeper. I have seen her ride by in the early hours with her long broom which she carries in one hand, balancing it by her side. She rides the cycle one-handed. How about that for what you will do next, Nooren? How about you, Nooren's mother, shall we teach you to ride a bicycle, as well?'

Her mother made some reply but Noor was not paying attention. Noor was sorting out something so important she had to step outside to get away from the sound of her parents' laughter.

She found herself walking in no particular direction. But wasn't the plan for her to go to the communal tap at the old neighbourhood, to wait there for Haseena? For a confused moment, she convinced herself she might be on her way to catch the metro to her brother's home in Chattarpur. Perhaps that would be the right thing to do. To get to Talib Bhaiya's house, to tear out from there on her new cycle, to tear all the way back to Chirag Dilli, to ride past the taps where, she can see it clearly now, it is not Haseena who is waiting for her.

Because yes, Noor's feet have walked her from her father's doorway all the way to the old neighbourhood tap. And her eyes can see that it is not Ajith, who is somehow accidentally here for her to catch a glimpse of from over the absent Haseena's shoulders. It is Ruku, who is here, Ruku, who is jumping up and down, Ruku, who is waving something at her.

'Haseena Didi sent you such a fancy birthday card. You don't mind that I opened it, do you? I thought there might be a letter for us in the envelope, as well. But it's only for you. Abba has asked Didi to wait a little longer before coming here. Didi will not come for another month, but when she does we are all going home to our village.

'Together again. Together again.' Ruku's delight is more than infectious. It is prescriptive.

*

But now where is Noor to go? Now when she knows that she is not going to Chattarpur station and from there to her brother's house, she is not going to collect her birthday present from Bhaiya and she is not going to ride a new bicycle back to Chirag Dilli.

Now, when she is instead trying to make peace with the provisional nature of 'together again'.

*

She had left her father's doorway, the short cloth her mother had hung there stirred in the breeze she left in her wake; she found herself walking in no particular direction. She walked hurriedly to the end of the lane, its collection of homes as low as she was; she walked past the communal bathroom in this, her father's new neighbourhood, then the communal tap, then the temple, then the market—its shutters down, blind to the fear growing on a young girl's face; she walked past the man asleep on the cart piled with green coconuts.

She walked to her old neighbourhood, to the water tap where there was no Haseena. She took the card from Ruku, took the prescription 'together again' to task, examined its provisional nature, and now she is turning around to walk back to the market and back past the coconut seller, waking on his cart.

She is walking down a lane of homes similar to her father's new home. There are no stairways here, no overhanging balconies; there is no speech-making boy to alert her to this neighbourhood's happenings. The afternoon is soft in this one lane. Her hurry ends here among these temporary shelters, piled around which are plastic-coated bags many times as wide across as a man who once gave her two stale toffees. She stumbles among these bags each of which are filled with the discards of that other Delhi beyond here. She comes to the right pile of bags.

She rests her hand lightly on the seat of the green bicycle parked against a stack of worn tyres.

'Ajith,' she calls inside the open doorway.

It is a long wait and she fills it with all the difficulties ahead for them.

And it is once again her hand that is reaching for his and his turning under hers so their palms meet; the earth is spinning and she is spinning with it.

Acknowledgements

Kaveri Gill's work, *Of Poverty and Plastic.*

Sangam House Residency.

Readers: Michael Creighton, Kunal Ray, Parvati Sharma, Kabir Arora of Hasiru Dala and Sreyanshi.

My agents and editors: Jessica Woollard, Mita Kapur, Renuka Chatterjee and Ravi Singh.